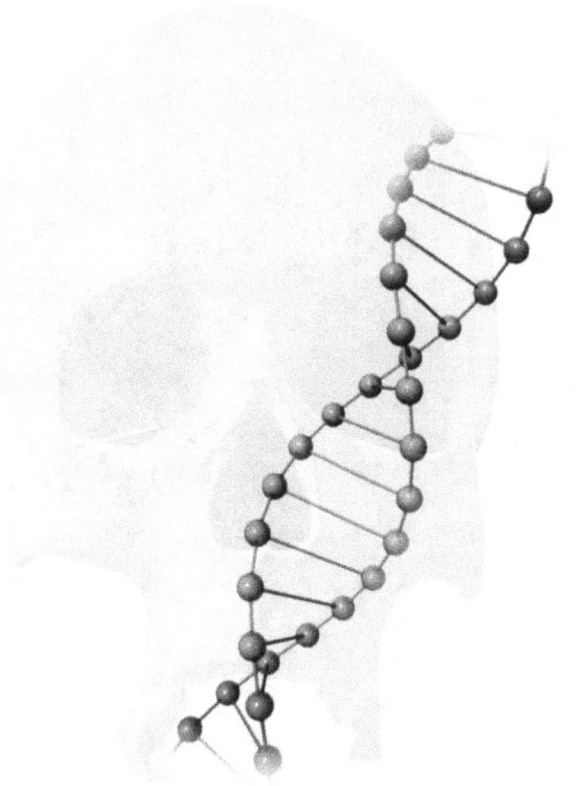

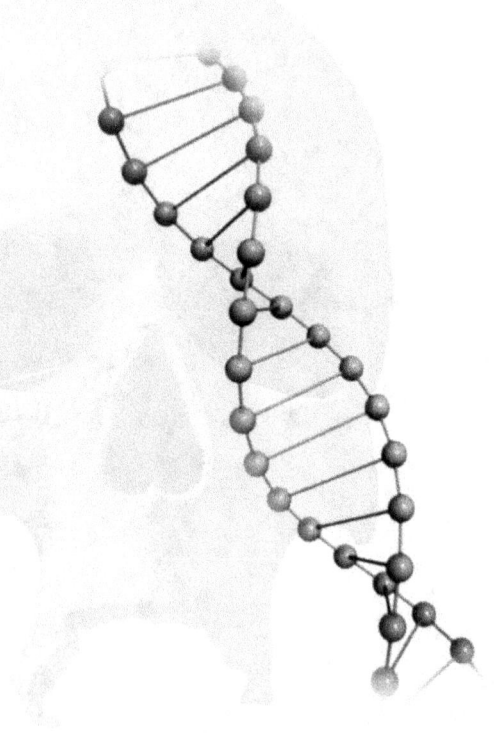

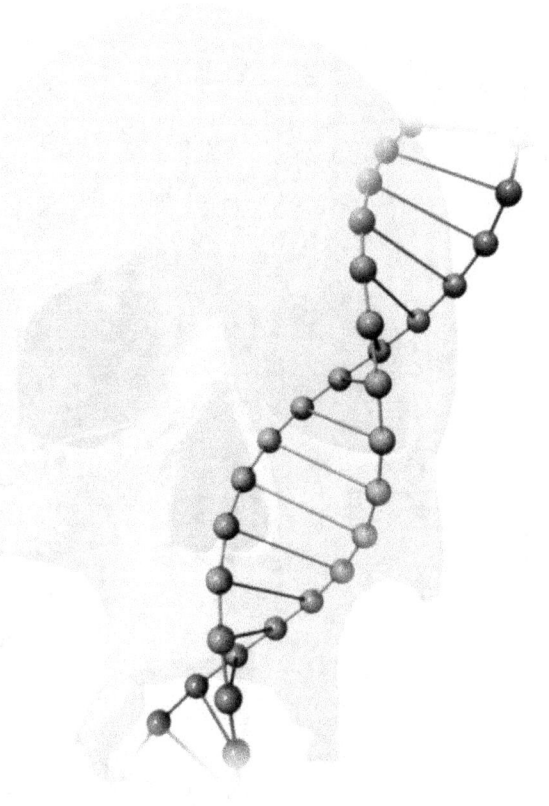

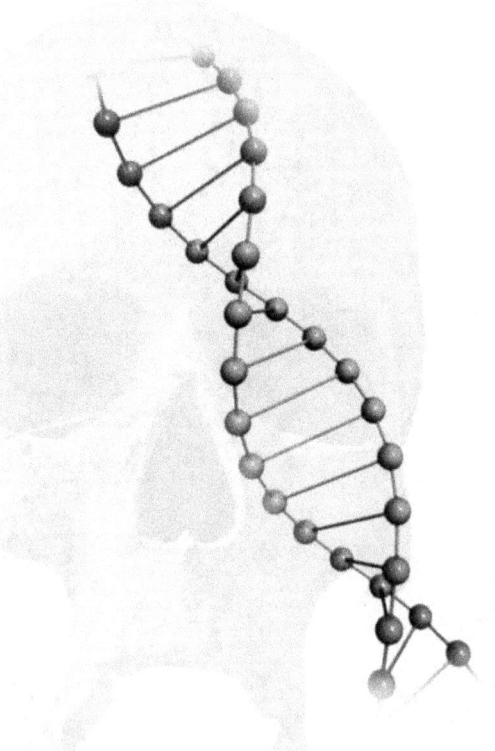

The
Orion
Enigma

By Stephen B. Botha

Dedicated to my wife, who encouraged me to the end,

my mother, for instilling in me a love of books,

and the friends whose opinions made a difference.

Table of Contents

PROLOGUE

Monday Afternoon, March 1996. Sea Shack
Campgrounds West of Paternoster, South Africa.

The stiff wind that was blowing out to sea stood the marching wave crests upright all the way across the bay before they crashed headfirst into the rocks on the shore like battling bighorn rams. Whipped sea foam drifted in the wind to pile up against the rocks on the shore across the small bay, the white foam in stark contrast to the deep blue of the Atlantic.

Sea Shack was a quaint campground clinging to a narrow, rocky beach on the edge of the shore. It was located half-way between Paternoster and Titties Baai on the Atlantic coast north of Cape Town. Made up of a small collection of a dozen or so Spartan twelve-by-twelve rental huts and a community kitchen, it was a popular vacation spot for families. The small, circular maze built for visiting children was about thirty feet across and was outlined with lines of rocks in the dirt. A child's small, plastic dump truck lay on its side in the sand of the maze, beach buckets and sand castle molds spilling out of the truck bed.

White clouds drifting across the azure sky should have completed the idyllic picture, but the figures in full bio-hazard suits working over a line of human bodies laid out in the sand introduced a jarring note to the scene. Hemorrhagic fever, possibly another African Ebola outbreak, had left its indelible mark on each body. Oversized blue bottle flies buzzed in clouds over the bodies, attracted to a macabre feast of dried blood and body fluids which had leaked from eyes, ears, noses and mouths.

One by one the men collected tissue samples from each of the bodies, locking the samples away in bright orange bio-hazard cases made of a toughened plastic capable of surviving the onslaught of a ten-pound sledge hammer. Then each body was thoroughly doused with insecticide to ensure nothing that might come in contact with the bodies, not even an insect, would leave the scene carrying the disease off site. Then, working in pairs with one at the head and the other at the feet, the men in the bio suits carried the bodies to the center of the camp and tossed them one-by-one onto the growing pile between the quaint huts and azure seas, thirty-two in all.

In the background, more Bio-suits were carefully stacking creosote-soaked beams like tepees vertically over each hut, building huge stacks over each of the huts.

As the last body was added to the pile, the men started dousing everything in the camp thoroughly with a thick, flammable, viscous liquid. Small incendiary explosives, little more than sparkling fireworks on timers, were set and tossed into every structure and into the pile of soaked bodies.

Their awful job done, and their shoulders slumped under the horrors they had seen, the men walked out of the camp to a level four bio-decontamination a half mile away. Not until they had been thoroughly decontaminated were they allowed passage through the barricade manned by heavily armed South African soldiers wearing rebreathe gas masks. A weather-beaten lieutenant in charge of the barricade detail, his face leathered by the African sun and wind, checked off each team member's name against a clipboard before allowing them to climb one-by-one into the jet helicopters emblazoned with markers for the World Health Organization. As the doors shut, the rotors started to up whip the dust as they slowly lifted off. At just twenty feet above the ground their noses dipped forward and the helicopters pushed east into the wind, making for the level four bio-safety labs in Pretoria.

As the last chopper disappeared, the lieutenant turned to watch the smoke spread across the bay, tears dripping unnoticed from his chin.

Wednesday Evening, March 1996. Emerging and Dangerous Pathogens Laboratory Network (EDPLN), Pretoria, South Africa.

Compressed, HEPA-filtered air hissed through the supply lines coiling down from the ceiling and into the two orange biohazard level four suits. The sound was disproportionately loud in the quiet lab. This level four World Health Organization (WHO) lab in South Africa was tasked with locating, identifying and containing the spread of new, deadly bacteria and virus emerging throughout Southern Africa. The starkly white, smooth surfaces of the lab simplified decontamination. Every piece of equipment was completely sealed and waterproof so that, if necessary, the entire lab could be hosed down with a full spectrum chemical decontaminant.

A heavy sheet of bullet-proof glass provided a view of the lab from the monitoring station just outside. A team of five highly trained technicians watched the two researchers work, listening to the quiet discussion between them and responding to requests for related data.

The security lock on the outer door beeped and the door opened. Dr. Gavin Mansfield, Chairman of the Board for BioMediCom and chief advisor to the CDC, walked in to join the group.

Standing a little over six feet tall, Gavin Mansfield was a well built, handsome man with striking features that never failed to turn heads. He was dressed in his usual tailored navy pin stripe suit, light blue button-down shirt and red and navy striped tie, and the large gold signet ring and cuff links gleamed in the ample light from the windows.

The technicians ignored him, intently focused on their monitors, as he went to stand in front of the glass. The silence

11

was almost complete. Only the hiss of compressed air, the hum of electronics, and the occasional tapping on a key board filled the void.

"Who is the geneticist today?" Mansfield asked as he half-turned toward the room.

The lead technician paused typing for a moment. "Dr. Andy Hampton from Baltimore. He flew in last night."

"What's he working on?"

"He just finished the gene sequencing about an hour ago. He's reviewing the electron microscope images now."

"I know Andy. He's the best we've got. Who's in there with him?"

"Dr. Hannah Smit. She identified Ebola in the recent Liberia outbreak and heads up the EDPLN facility here."

"Good, I've heard of her." Turning back to the window looking into the lab, Mansfield switched on the intercom to talk to the lab team. "Dr. Hampton, what do we know so far?"

The shorter figure behind the glass turned to face Mansfield, the harsh lights reflecting off the face shield of his suit as he answered. "For one thing, every sample is different."

"That's not possible."

"I thought so too," Hampton replied, "which is why I asked Dr. Smit to consult. We reran the tests three times and in every case the sample from each body is unique."

"What do you mean?"

"Well, the basic structure is the same for all of them, but there is a slightly different dominant strain for each sample."

"So we don't know yet what the original virus was?" Mansfield asked.

"Right, but the variances between the viruses are all located in the same exact location on their gene strings."

"Odd."

I thought so, but the really odd part is this... the variances appear to be human."

"This virus came from a human?"

"No, not exactly. But there's a small string of human genes lined up along one edge of the virus, and that string is unique to the sample taken from each body."

"Do we know anything about these specific genes?"

Hampton paused for a moment before answering. "No, none of them code for protein, so we don't know much about them yet."

Dr. Smit joined the conversation. "There's something else. Every one of these viral strains have a high survive ratio. They tolerate the same temperature extremes we do, they're unharmed if they dry out, and they even survive our disinfectants. Not only that, this thing is highly contagious across all media."

"Even airborne?"

"Yes, especially airborne. Even worse, it can contaminate right through your skin."

"What do you mean?"

"If it gets on your hand, it will get through your skin in less than 5 minutes and you're done. No need to touch your mouth or nose."

"Then how the hell do we stop it?"

"That's the good news," Smit added.

"What possible good news can there be out of that?"

"They're completely harmless now."

"What do you mean? Are they dead?"

"No-no. They're still just as viable and just as contagious, but they seem to be completely harmless now."

"That makes absolutely no sense."

"No kidding," Hampton said.

"What else?"

"There are as many variations as there were bodies, but each body was infected by every variation."

"No surprise there."

"True, but a single, different strain dominates each sample. My guess is that the dominant strain in each body was the one that killed that person."

"So only the mutation specific to the victim killed them?"

"Right. It looks like a spin-off of the lysogenic cycle."

"Meaning?"

"Lysogenic meaning once you're infected the bug will sit dormant in your cells waiting for a trigger. Variation meaning only one of the version in each body was triggered."

"So how are they triggered?"

"That's the million-dollar question," Hampton said." I personally suspect the trigger is somehow related to the individual person."

How?"

"No idea yet. We need a lot more time testing this thing."

"Have you at least tested the theory?"

"Well, yes and no," answered Smit. "Obviously we can't test it on humans, so we used primates. We infected one strain per chimp in isolation and nothing happened to the chimp. No fever, nothing. We ran bloodwork and confirmed the infection, and still nothing. But when we took them out of isolation they cross-contaminated each other in less than forty-five minutes without direct contact with each other. Within one hour every chimp was infected with every strain"

"And still no symptoms," added Hampton. "Not just that, no new strains either."

"How long do we think it takes from infection to mortality?"

"If you manage to trigger one of them, less than an hour," said Smit. "That's it."

"That's all?!" Mansfield exclaimed, stunned.

"Yes," Smit said. "It kills faster than a mamba bite, and we don't even know where to begin on getting a treatment."

Hampton thought for a moment. "Is it possible the human genes in the dominant virus came from the human it killed?"

"What do you mean?" Hampton asked.

"I'm not sure, but what if the infection occurs in two stages?"

"That would imply that the ground zero strain had no human genetic material, morphed by picking up a segment of the host DNA, and the new strain was the killing infection," Smit said thoughtfully.

"I suppose it's possible," Hampton said, "but it would be a first. But why do you think that could be the case?"

"The primates. None of them got sick," Hampton pointed out.

"If that's true," Smit added, "maybe this thing has to first code specifically to someone before it can kill that specific someone."

"Hmm," Hampton said, "So strains already coded would be harmless?"

"I think so," Smit said. "Although I'd bet money if it finds someone with a set of genes close enough to match the way they were coded, it could kill them as well. A twin, for example.

15

Not that I plan on testing the theory personally. I've seen what the hemorrhagics do."

"Alright," Mansfield said quietly. "Let's get these samples locked up in the vaults at the CDC. Meanwhile this thing is obviously in the hemorrhagic family, so get the press guys to announce a tiny, fully contained and very isolated outbreak of Ebola. That should at least get the press off our backs, anyway."

Hampton looked up from the screen. "What happens if the un-coded strain pops up again? We never did find the source."

"We pray," Smit said. "We pray it pops up in a tiny population again."

"Or that every virus organism codes very quickly to just a few people," Mansfield added. "Theoretically that will make it harmless for everyone."

"And if not? Hampton asked.

"Everyone in that city will be dead in hours," Smit said.

"Well," Mansfield said, turning to leave, "let's get this locked up."

"Hold on," Hampton said. "Do you want to meet Orion before you go?"

"Orion?"

Hampton put the image from the electron microscope back up on the monitors. The screen glowed with a 3-D image, slowly rotating the virus around its axis until Hampton paused the image.

"Meet Orion the Hunter."

The still image burned into the screen, the shape obscured by the color of fluids it floated in. With a couple of taps on the keyboard Hampton colorized. Slowly a shape reminiscent of the Orion, a star constellation seen from both northern and southern hemispheres, materialized on the screen, slowly rotating on its axis over an imaginary equator.

"Why two colors?" asked Mansfield.

"The blue," Smit said, "is what would be the original, un-coded virus. The red line spliced across the face of Orion's bow is the line of human genes. That line of red is the only difference between all the samples."

Chapter One

Senator Landon Williams paced back and forth behind the dark mahogany desk of his richly decorated office. The walls of his office were lined with book cases and display cabinets in dark woods, complemented with navy, burgundy and hunter green upholstery and the classic fox hunting wall hangings typical of men of Williams' generation. The room was dated, but it suited Williams. The wall paper was gold with subtle burgundy-and-green vertical pin-striping. Littering every available surface was a rich collection of mementoes and decorations. A series of autographed presidential photos gave ample evidence of his decades of service in Washington, and every picture and wall hanging was framed using either burgundy or green matte to match the wall paper.

He was a lean, distinguished statesman with a generous shock of silver hair and despite being in his mid-sixties, his clean-shaven face was relatively unlined. The stress and struggle of productively maneuvering through the political swamp of Washington had only left laugh lines in his face. He was a man who had clearly learned to be more amused than frustrated by the machinations of politics, and his many political successes were a testimony to his brilliance and statesmanship.

Usually his desk was entirely clear except for what he needed for the day. At that moment the only thing on his desk was a thin leather folder containing a few sheets of paper and an article clipped from the Wall Street Journal.

He stopped pacing to flip open the folder and spread the pages across his desk. He leaned forward with his palms flat on the desk as he scanned the pages. As usual, the sleeves of his tailored pale blue shirt were rolled partially up his forearms. He picked up the newspaper article and tugged distractedly on his conservative tie. He loosened the tie as he read through the article. Once he had finished, he dropped the article back on the desk with the others and unbuttoned his top shirt button.

Across the room the door clicked quietly open and Amy Morgan walked in. Her conservative shoes were silent in the thick carpeting. She carried a cup of Starbucks coffee in one hand and a note pad held to her body with the other. Her dark, straight hair was pulled back severely into a ponytail, making her face seem more austere than it really was. Her navy skirt was knee length and matched the jacket she wore over a burgundy and green blouse. Morgan's outfit looked like she had made every effort to match Williams' outdated taste in wall paper.

As personal aide to Williams for the last six years, she was well acquainted with his habits and idiosyncrasies and she could not remember ever seeing him without his tie neatly in place.

She put the coffee down on William's desk. "Mocha latte, just how you like it. You called for me?"

"Yes, I did." Distracted, Williams paused to collect the papers into the folder again. "I need you to do something a little unusual for me."

"Of course."

Morgan was ambitious. She had a habit of grasping almost desperately at every opportunity to present herself as going above and beyond, even to the detriment of her personal life, so she did not hesitate. She knew Williams had been approached to run for President in the next general elections and she was almost desperately eager to ride his coat tails into a cabinet position at any cost.

"Did you ever get that safe I recommended?" asked Williams.

"Yes, I did. They installed it two months ago."

"Good. I need you to take this folder home with you tonight and store it in your safe until I ask for it."

"What is it?" she asked curiously, taking the folder from his outstretched hand.

"I don't know for sure yet, but the implications... ".

Williams paused as he sat down in his leather chair, drumming his fingers distractedly on the arm rest. "If this means what I think it does, things are going to get really ugly."

"Is there anything I can do?"

"Just keep that folder in your safe for now."

"Yes sir."

She paused to glance down at her notes for the day.

"Session starts at ten this morning, and Senator Whitfield asked if you would be attending the Ways and Means Committee meeting this afternoon. It starts at four."

"Whitfield asked in person?"

"Yes. Something about the BioMediCom vote."

Williams frowned, puzzled.

"I wonder why he's so interested all of a sudden. He knows I won't support the BioMediCom proposal, but he's never cared before."

He paused, thinking.

"Okay, shoot him a note saying I plan to be there. And tell Andy I want him to join me in early session today. I may need a runner."

"He'll like that. I've never seen an intern so eager to be stuck in those endless meetings."

"I know." Williams turned to gaze out the window, already lost in thought. Morgan started for the door and her movement brought Williams back into the moment.

"Thanks for the coffee, but I keep telling you there's no need to go to that much effort."

She turned back to him at the door, pleased he had noticed.

"I know, but I was there anyway. I was going to tell Andy to meet you in the Rotunda before session starts. Is that okay?"

"No, have him meet me in front of the main elevators on the east side of the Senate wing. I know he likes to wander around the place first."

"I'll let him know," Morgan said.

Williams turned back to the window, immediately lost in thought again as the door clicked quietly behind Morgan.

08h45, Surveillance Room, Phoenix Headquarters, Washington, D.C.

The dimly lit room was filled with cubicles glowing with banks of computer screens. Lengthy A.I. algorithms buried deep in the heavily secured servers below ground used complex selection criteria to churn through millions of video and audio surveillance segments. Each segment was assigned a risk code. Some codes tagged the segment for manual review, routing the clip to one of the dark shadows working almost silently in the cubicles. They barely moved as they reviewed one clip after another. While most of the footage was confirmed as unimportant, some segments were saved to specific files of interest.

Occasionally a fragment would demand immediate attention and the shadow would reroute the footage up the chain. A supervisor would review and, if necessary, mark the segment as a Code Black.

Segments marked as Code Black, reserved exclusively for immediate threats to national security, were immediately assigned to highly-trained operatives scattered around the world. These teams were required to "assess and eliminate the threat with immediate effect".

The program was hugely effective at preventing attacks on Americans, even though some completed missions would never have been authorized if the true nature of Phoenix had been disclosed to the Congressional Oversite Committee. Lack of Congressional oversite also meant Phoenix resources were occasionally diverted away from national security to support the personal agenda of the station Director.

A former field agent himself, Gage La Salle was Phoenix's Director of Operations and regularly took advantage of these gaps in oversight. In his late forties and standing just over six feet tall, La Salle was a lean, swarthy man. He kept an electric razor in his desk which he habitually used during the lunch hour to manage his ever-lurking five o' clock shadow. His hands were carefully manicured, and he wore his hair in a carefully tousled style to look more youthful than he really was.

A faded scar started a little above the bridge of his nose. It ran diagonally across his forehead and into his hairline where it made the hair around it blaze white. The scar was a constant reminder of a knife fight that had almost ended very badly. The memory still made him wake up in a sweat sitting bolt upright a few times a year.

Always dressed impeccably, his tailored suit did little to conceal his muscular frame and latent strength, and he fancied himself a bit of a James Bond. Sometimes he even introduced himself with the same cadence... La Salle, Gage La Salle.

Every morning he would lock himself in his office, sit at his desk with the bank of windows behind him, and read the summary reports from the night shift. His office was sparsely furnished, with one wall from floor to ceiling covered in filing cabinets. As Director, La Salle oversaw and authorized all changes to the surveillance search algorithm, and during his two years as Director he had added several personal selection criteria. Hits to these criteria routed directly to his own office.

The door to Senator Williams' office across town had barely clicked shut behind Amy Morgan before the surveillance footage from his office triggered one of La Salle's secret search criteria. As La Salle studied the night summary, his computer beeped a warning and flashed a pop-up window onto the screen.

The standard flash format was a white pop-up window with a green border outline. It listed the date, time and location the footage was captured, along with a list of the trigger words used by the algorithm to flag the footage. Typically, the beep just copied La Salle on the standard alerts escalated to supervisors.

Out of habit La Salle glanced up at the pop-up before dropping his eyes back down to the report he was holding. It took a moment before it dawned on him that the flash border was red, a customization the algorithm used when routing hits directly to his attention alone.

Dropping the paper report back onto his desk, he leaned forward to read the names Williams and Whitfield in the trigger list on the flash. Thoughtfully he clicked on the link to the footage, put on his earphones, and watched the video on his screen.

As he watched he automatically picked up the beautiful, bone-handled letter opener he kept on his desk. Very discrete, it took a keen eye to realize the blade was surgical steel, the tip shaped to a needle point and the edge honed razor-sharp. Unconsciously La Salle balanced the blade across one finger.

As the footage ended, he put the knife down and reached for his secure phone. He tapped in a quick-dial number, waited a moment, and added a security code that randomized the encryption protocol used for the call. A moment later there was a click as the line was answered.

"Whitfield." The tinny sound over the ear piece speaker did nothing to mask the arrogance in the voice.

"La Salle. We just got a surveillance video hit on Williams."

"No surprise. I expect his aide mentioned my call to his office."

"There's more."

"Go on."

"He asked Morgan to hide a folder for him."

"What do we know about it?"

"Nothing. The cameras in his office didn't get a good angle on any of the pages, but he was worried about it. He said the implications were ugly."

"Get that folder."

"Collateral damage?"

"I don't care as long as it looks like a typical crime. Just get it. And one more thing."

"Yes?"

"Let's just say that I expect news channels will be carrying a report this afternoon before four o' clock that Senator Williams died of complications from a virus he contracted on one of his recent trips overseas."

"Yes sir," La Salle said, smiling. "I will make sure there is a reason for the news report."

The phone line clicked as Whitfield disconnected.

La Salle rewound the footage until the hidden cameras had a clear image of Morgan. He paused the footage where Morgan took the folder from Williams, grabbed a screenshot of Morgan and the folder, and dropped it into a standard document template used to send escalated directives to field operatives. He added Morgan's name, where she worked, and instructions for the assigned operatives to get the folder at any cost. He pulled up a list of available local field teams, selected one, and hit the send button.

Next, he accessed a password-protected Excel spreadsheet and keyed in the password to open the file. Sorting the list of names in the first column alphabetically, he scrolled down through the file to the listing for Senator Williams. He copied the reference number beside Williams' name, double-clicked an icon on his desktop entitled "FEED", and then pasted it into the data input window it opened.

Standing, La Salle walked over to the door of his office to check that it was locked before crossing the room to the wall of filing cabinets. Opening one of the drawers, he reached through to a hidden key pad in the back of the drawer and keyed in a code. The entire bank of cabinets to his right slid silently away from him before opening into a small, white room.

Lined with opaque glass and completely smooth, the room was a state-of-the-art decontamination room that led to a level-four Bio-Safety lab on the other side. A small safe was built flush into the wall and on either side of it was a touchscreen key pad, one for the safe and the other to open the door into the lab next door.

After suiting up in full protective gear, La Salle tapped a code into the door keypad and the door to the next room opened. He walked inside, and the door sealed shut behind him with a hiss of hydraulic air. La Salle raised his arms and was sprayed completely down by a decontaminating mist. High velocity fans blasted warm air over him to dry the mist off, and finally a third door opened to allow him access to his personal, very small, fully equipped Bio-safety Level Four lab.

A small monitor was located behind glass in the back upper corner of the lab. On the screen was the same code La Salle had copied and pasted into the "FEED" window from the Senator Williams data line in his Excel file on his desk.

Built into one wall were two multi-drawer coolers. The cooler to the left was smaller. Beside it was a small touch-screen keypad. On the screen were two concentric rings made up of small red circles. Beside the second, much larger cooler was a simple numeric keypad.

On the opposite wall was a small lab work bench complete with a small incinerator and fluid agitator.

Humming contentedly to himself, La Salle walked up to the smaller cooler and selected seven of the red dots on the touch screen. The dots changed color to green in the shape of a pattern. After a moment one of the drawers opened and a stainless-steel tray slid out. The tray contained lines of stainless steel tubes about the size of a cigar topped with either a red or green rubber seal.

Selecting one of the red-capped tubes, he touched the pad again and the tray with the rest of the vials slid back into the cooler. Then he moved over to the lab bench, carefully cradling the vial in both hands, and set the vial in the agitation mixer. Crossing the room again he walked up to the numeric pad beside the larger cooler. La Salle glanced up at the monitor and keyed the reference number associated with Senator Williams into the key pad. One of the drawers slid open. The drawer was filled with hundreds of small syringes set vertically in rows and lined up neatly side by side. One of the syringes automatically raised up out of the rest. La Salle picked it up and carefully compared the number on the label to the number on the monitor in the corner of the room.

Satisfied, he carried the syringe back to the work bench, uncapped the syringe and injected the clear fluid through the red rubber seal, adding it to the vial. Then he pressed a red button once to start the mixer on a timed, gentle agitation cycle.

While the mixer vibrated quietly on the bench, La Salle reached into an overhead cabinet. After a moment he selected an atomizer designed to look like an aerosol can. Then he chose what looked like an original label for Lysol Disinfectant from a selection in a separate drawer. After carefully attaching the label, he unscrewed the base of the aerosol. Built into the concave bottom was a small nipple used for adding pressurized gas to the can.

The mixer stopped vibrating. La Salle pulled out the vial, uncapped it, and poured the contents into the aerosol can before screwing the bottom firmly back on. Collecting the used syringe and the vial he had just emptied, he opened the incinerator door and consigned both to the flames. Finally, he used a ball-foot air chuck on a coiled hose to force pressurized air into the atomizer.

Satisfied that the lab was cleaned up and the can ready for use, La Salle worked his way back through the decontamination room and emerged back in his office.

"Where were you when they tried to get rid of Castro?" he asked himself, grinning as he glanced down at the Lysol can in his hand.

09h45, US Capitol Building, Washington, D.C.

The east entrance to the wing of the Capitol Building was dedicated to the Senate. It was a hive of activity as various Senators were dropped off outside and filed through the doors and into the lobby. Dark paneling and muted lighting gave the space a feel of rich elegance, and the polished floors reflected the lights and echoed the firm footfalls of hurrying people along the hallways.

The foyer funneled the crowds past a bank of six elevators, three on either side, and then down a hallway which extended all the way through the wing. In the center of the building it crossed the main hallway which extended from the north wall of the Senate wing, through the great rotunda in all its stately elegance, to the south wall of the wing dedicated to the House.

A single flight of stairs just past and to the right of the elevators provided access to the Senate Chamber for the more athletically oriented foot traffic.

A janitor, his clean white coveralls in stark contrast to the dark suits all around him, pushed his bright yellow handcart completely unnoticed through the throng of people moving through the building. He stopped in front of the elevators and pulled a can of Lysol Disinfectant and a rag out of the cart. Pushing the cart against the wall out of the way he started to methodically work his way through one elevator after another, wiping down the brushed nickel doors, the handrails, and the bank of buttons on the inside. After wiping each space, he carefully sprayed a little of the Lysol over the rails and buttons before moving to the next elevator.

"Why they have housekeeping clean elevators when we're trying to use them beats me," grumbled Senator Albright, one of the portlier Senators waiting for the janitor to finish in the last elevator. "Government scheduling at its finest."

The janitor smiled politely as held the door open for the group to enter, the small blaze of white hair above one eye in contrast to his dark skin and hair. Then he collected his cart and walked away.

As the doors started to close, Albright noticed Senator Williams walking briskly into the foyer, his intern in close tow.

"Hey Landon!" Albright called out, holding the door open. "You going to take the easy way for once?"

"And ride in that painfully slow, old death trap up just one floor with you? Not a chance!"

"No fair!" Albright grinned as he released the door. "This elevator is older than you are!"

C'mon Andy," Williams said loud enough for Albright to hear as the elevator doors glided closed. "We'll take our time up the stairs and wait for him at the top!"

Chuckling, Williams and his intern turned up the stairs, not bothering with the hand rail. Williams did not believe in handrails. After surviving one heart attack several years before he had turned into something of a germ-a-phobic health nut, much to the amusement of his friends who remembered his penchant for rich foods and a more sedentary lifestyle. Hand rails, as he often explained, were for lazy people, and just thinking about the rich Petri dish of germs and microbes infesting them creeped him out.

Turning right from the stairs on the second floor they waited at the elevators for Albright. Surprisingly light on his feet despite his impressive bulk, Albright's jowls wobbled as he walked out the elevator, laughing to see Williams conspicuously propping up the wall waiting for him. After a quick hand shake they walked into the Senate Chamber through the east side entrance, Albright's hand on Williams shoulder. Inside the door they chatted for a moment before separating to find their seats, Albright sneezing as he walked across to the other side.

Chapter Two

14h30, Washington, D.C.

Fuming, her hands clenching the wheel of her fully-equipped pale blue BMW convertible in futile frustration, Amy Morgan inched her way along IH 395. The wreck on the 14th Street Bridge across the Potomac River had all but shut down West-bound traffic, aggravating her already habitually short temper. Even though her ambition motivated her to present a model of calm efficiency at work, her true personality was considerably more volatile, and she was prone to losing her temper at the slightest excuse. Quick to anger and with a long history of harboring resentment, even for imagined slights, anybody who knew her outside the office avoided her because of the inevitable drama and conflict in her wake.

Not a sentimental person, the early holiday traffic and cheerful smiles around her just aggravated her, and the fact that she had been unable to pawn her daughter off on the neighbors that afternoon infuriated her even more. Jessie was sixteen so a babysitter should not have been necessary, but she was under court orders to be supervised at all times.

Several months earlier Jessie had hacked into the NSA and redirected a surveillance satellite just so that she could take high-resolution photos of Kaufman Lake, high in the Rockies north of Yellowstone National Park. The NSA had spent months scrambling to figure out how a sixteen-year-old had managed to hijack one of their secure systems and had finally agreed not to pursue charges in exchange for her cooperation.

The only caveat was that, for a probationary period of one year she was not allowed access to a computer unless it was under strict supervision. Of course, as the judge pointed out, that meant she had to have adult supervision at all times.

31

Jessie had already shown them how she penetrated the NSA firewalls, much to their embarrassment, but she had categorically refused to explain why she wanted high-resolution mapping photos of Yellowstone when they were already easily available online.

Morgan was so wrapped up in her selfish ambition that her first reaction to the hacking revolved entirely around the possible impact Jessie's actions may have had on her own career. Her selfish ambition had blinded her completely. She had no understanding of just how brilliant her daughter was.

Sixteen years earlier Morgan had chosen to get pregnant in a calculated effort to trap a Special Ops officer into marrying her before he went back into action. She had expected that being his wife would be excellent leverage for her career and she had been right. And given the nature of his job and the ongoing conflicts on the world stage, she had also hoped he would soon be KIA, getting her out of the marriage and giving her another career boost.

His inconsiderate survival and the day by day reality of marriage increasingly cramped her selfish style, so when he started showing signs of PTSD she manipulated the story to her advantage. Marketing herself as the survivor of domestic abuse, she quickly divorced him and used the story to get another career boost.

But having a child was also much more inconvenient than she had anticipated, and now she resented even the air Jessie breathed. Her feelings toward Jessie had evolved into a destructive blend of cold indifference liberally interspersed with raging insults and anger. The relationship had become even more tempestuous since Jessie had found a fearless voice of her own, aggressively standing her ground where in the past she would have retreated from the angry insults.

Morgan cursed bitterly under her breath at the slow traffic, angry because she had to interrupt her afternoon to pick Jessie up from school. She had decided to leave the office early and work from her apartment, so she had tossed her attaché case with the folder Williams had asked her to keep in her safe on the back seat.

Her phone rang, the retro ring tone playing over the sound system of her car. She had set up her desk phone at work to forward any calls to her cell phone and, since she did not recognize the number that flashed up on the Caller ID, she took a deep breath, forced a smile, and pressed the button on the steering wheel to answer the call.

"Good afternoon, this is Amy Morgan, Private Aide to Senator Williams. How can I help?"

"Hello, Amy."

The baritone sound of her ex-husbands voice instantly grated on her nerves and wiped the forced smile off her face. When Morgan had served Matt Talbot with divorce papers, the domestic abuse narrative she had so carefully cultivated had also meant that she had to get a restraining order against him to support her story. The papers had been served the day before Jessie's sixth birthday.

Using her lies that his military background and marginal PTSD had made him a threat to his family, she had deliberately kept him from any contact with his daughter out of sheer spite. Talbot had unsuccessfully fought the legal system for six years, but the combination of PTSD and depression at not being able to see Jessie had started him down a steep slope into alcoholism. Morgan had not heard from him in four years.

"What do you want, Matt?"

"The judge ruled in my favor. I get to see Jessie again."

Curbing her first impulse to lash out and refuse, Morgan immediately saw a way to play this to her advantage. She could dump Jessie off on Talbot and still play the martyr card at work. The idea that she could immediately get rid of Jessie and still play it off to her advantage at work appealed to both her vanity and ambition.

"Fine. I'm sick of her anyway. She's nothing but trouble."

"Is that why you ignored the court date?"

"No, but the last six times you tried to take me to court you showed up so drunk that the judge didn't would have denied your appeal even if I didn't show up. I really didn't think last time would be any different."

"Well I got cleaned up. I've been clean for two years. Doing pretty well, actually."

"Well, you can take her today for all I care. I just want to get rid of her."

"What does she know about me?"

"I told her you were dead, so she would shut up asking about you."

"You are some piece of work," Talbot said, an edge of anger creeping into his voice. He paused, taking a deep breath as he made sure his voice did not trigger Morgan's anger. "She's going to need some time to digest all this, you know that, right?"

"Whatever. Did you move back to Washington?"

"No, I just flew in."

"Where are you staying?"

"The Hilton in Chrystal City a few blocks west of the airport. I figured it would be close to your apartment."

"How do you know where I live? Have you been stalking me?"

"Of course not. I just have a few buddies in town that check in occasionally."

"Do you know about her hacking the NSA?"

"Yes. Very impressive. Why did she do it?"

34

"She won't say and I don't care, but you deserve her. Where do you want to pick her up?"

"There's a steak place called Ted's Montana Grill on Crystal Drive a few blocks south of your apartment. Will that work?"

"Fine, you're paying. I'll bring her there at six. She's all yours and good riddance."

Smiling, Morgan hung up on Talbot and gunned the BMW into a gap in the traffic, impatient to get rid of the girl.

17h30, Outside Ted's Montana Grill, Chrystal City, VA

The light mid-December wind was well below freezing and bitingly cold. The weak winter sun had tried all day to break through clouds heavy with the promise of snow and had finally given up, setting nearly an hour earlier. Light flurries of snow floated in the cold air, melting instantly and turning the busy streets into topsy-turvy mirrors. Talbot turned left onto Chrystal Drive, his confident stride quick and purposeful. Hiking boots, jeans and a heavy black parka kept the cold at bay while tires on passing cars hissed and splashed irritably through the potholes filled with melted snow.

Glancing in, Talbot could see the hungry patrons of the Italian restaurant on the corner laughing and eating in the warmth behind the glass. Pausing to check for exiting traffic, he crossed the driveway that led to the underground parking on his left and arrived outside Ted's. Early, he stood outside the restaurant door and glanced briefly around, getting his bearings.

Directly across from Ted's was a crosswalk to the Chrystal City Courtyard, a mini-park serving as a green space in the grounds in front of a large office building complex. Parking options on the street were essentially non-existent, but the driveway around the Courtyard provided plenty of parking, especially after the mass exodus of suits from the attached office building after five o' clock. Well lit, the paved pathways provided pedestrians with quick access to a wide selection of casual dining across the street.

After years of active duty around the world, much of it engaged in classified missions, Talbot was surprised at how nervous he was to see his daughter for the first time in ten years. In his mid-forties his well-built frame stood a little over six feet tall. His face was dark from long exposure to the sun and wind. He wore his full head of light brown hair swept back and a little longer. He preferred not to shave, but kept his stubble trimmed close.

He had a strong, well-defined jawline, hawkish nose, and dark eyes set deep under stern eyebrows. Faint lines wrinkled the high cheek bones at the corners of his eyes, the squint lines another mark of sun and wind endured around the world. When he was relaxed his face generally settled into a grim and unfriendly expression, but those few who knew him well also knew that his rare smile was warm and genuine.

As he stood outside the restaurant door his hand unconsciously strayed to his breast pocket and touched a wrinkled, faded photo. That photo had been with him now for the last ten years.

Feeling on edge he paced back and forth outside the restaurant. After a few minutes Talbot glanced down the dimly lit driveway beside the restaurant and into the underground parking lot. A family of four were huddled together out of the wind and snow, just inside the entrance and as far out of the lights as possible.

The woman and two young children were bundled up in tattered blankets and over-sized jackets from Goodwill, but the man wore only threadbare jeans and a worn-out army shirt. His shoulders were hunched against the bitter cold as he carefully shared the contents of a small brown fast-food bag between the others.

He was painfully thin, a scraggly beard doing nothing to hide the sunken cheeks and glittering eyes. Talbot watched discreetly as the man wrapped his arms around the children and smiled encouragement at them while they wolfed down the meagre scraps of food.

With sudden decision, Talbot glanced at his watch, turned away, walked down the sidewalk past the ice cream shop, and pushed through the spring doors of the busy Chick-fil-A a half block north. Without looking at the menu he ordered four chicken sandwich meals with their signature waffle-cut fries. Then he added four hot chocolates before hurrying back.

The family was still there, huddled together as inconspicuously as they could out of the wind, the man and woman trying to keep the children warm. One of the children went into a fit of coughing and the man exchanged a worried look with the woman. Gently he touched her cheek before he stood up and started to walk away. His hands dug through his pockets to pull out a small handful of coins, just enough to buy cough syrup. As he turned the corner he bumped into Talbot coming the other direction.

"Sorry," he murmured, stepping to one side to let Talbot pass.

"Hey Bud. How you doing?"

"Okay," the man said, trying to get around Talbot.

"Hold on a minute. You from around here?"

"No sir. Drove up two nights ago to start a new job. They said they pay cash every day, but it doesn't start until Thursday."

"Thursday?"

"Yeah... first of the month."

"Oh yeah, right. Saw your shirt... you serve?"

"Yeah" the man replied. "Corporal, 101st Airborne."

"Captain in the Rangers," Talbot said. "That your family around the corner?"

"Yes sir," the man answered, automatically standing taller and squaring his shoulders.

"Looks like ya'll are in a hole right now," Talbot said. "I saw you sharing that Happy Meal. Did you eat?"

The man studied Talbot coolly for a moment before answering.

"No sir."

"I was in a bind like that for two years, so I know what you're going through. I got lucky. One of the guys from my unit found me and helped me out. I figure it's my turn. There's enough food in these bags for all of you."

Surprised, the man took the bags, his face worked to stop tears from welling up in his eyes. Before he could say anything, Talbot slipped off his parka and handed it to the man as well. Then he pulled his billfold out of his jeans, extracted five twenty-dollar bills and his hotel key, and handed them over as well.

"Room 423 at the Hilton around the corner. Make sure you slip in through the side door until you get cleaned up or they may try to throw you out. Help yourself to whatever you need from my kit bag. Once you all get cleaned up, call the desk and have them deliver some cots for the kids. The room and all room service is already paid up for the next five nights. Get warm, get clean, get some rest, and get some meds for your kid."

"What's the catch?" the man asked, suspicious.

"No catch. You need it and I can afford it."

"Yes sir! And how can I pay you back when I get settled?"

"Just do the same for the next guy."

The man looked at Talbot for a moment, then nodded and turned away. He hurried into the parking lot to collect his family as the cold pushed Talbot, now minus his jacket, shivering through the doors of the restaurant.

He was still early, but they showed him to a table for three at the window looking out across the street and into the park. Talbot ordered coffee. Keeping an eye on the street for Jessie and Morgan, he pulled a worn photo from his pocket. It was torn down the middle and a little red-head girl with a pixie nose and dark eyes stared back out at him, her smile missing a tooth. Talbot gently stroked her cheek before tucking the picture back into his pocket.

The coffee arrived and after adding a single packet of sugar, Talbot turned back to the window. He had a habit of trying to keep a running total in his head of the number of each major car brand that went past. Six Ford's, three Chevy's... a passing Tesla interrupted the mind game. Before he could start again he recognized Morgan's pale blue BMW in the south-bound lane, waiting for a break in the on-coming traffic before turning left into the circular driveway around the park.

A black Tahoe blocked Talbot's view momentarily as it quickly pulled in behind her. The Tahoe stopped to wait for Morgan as she maneuvered into a parking space a short distance up the park driveway and away from the road.

Leaving his cup of coffee steaming on the table to keep his place, Talbot stood up and walked out the restaurant door, burying his hands into his jeans pockets in the bitter cold as he waited for Jessie and Morgan to cross the street.

17h45, Morgan's BMW, Chrystal City, VA

Her good mood of earlier no longer even a memory, Morgan drummed her fingers impatiently on the wheel of the BMW as she watched Jessie. She was laughing happily as she walked out of the building in a group with the teacher and a few of her classmates, but the smile disappeared as she slipped into the seat next to Morgan.

Hidden behind the habitual scowl she wore around her mother was a striking young woman, her red hair a mane cascading down her shoulders and her dark eyes emphasized by high cheek bones, impossibly long eyelashes and thick, dark eyebrows pulled down into an angry scowl. Years of Krav Maga classes had instilled in her a grace of movement and inner poise entirely hidden by the deliberately baggy, dull clothes.

Morgan had already tried to pick her up immediately after school, forgetting as usual that Jessie took an advanced college-level electronics class every Monday afternoon. The two hours wait for the class to end while she tried to get work done in the driver's seat of the car had long since crushed her good mood.

"You're late," Morgan said as she pulled the car into traffic.

"Same time as every Monday," Jessie muttered as she inserted her earphones into her ears, started Pandora on her phone and selected Joe Bonamassa. The clean guitar riffs sliding across the heavy syncopated bass rhythm quickly drowned out any attempt Morgan might have made to say anything further as she turned towards the restaurant.

After a few minutes Jessie looked up and noticed that they were not headed back to the apartment.

"Where are we going?" she asked, pulling one of the earpieces out.

"Ted's. I want you to meet someone."

41

"Another flavor of the month? What's that, six this month?" Jessie said bitterly as she re-inserted the earpiece and then ignored her mother again.

Gritting her teeth, Morgan decided not to rise to the bait.

"She'll be out of my life for good in a few days," she thought. "I can put up with her for another thirty minutes."

The tires splashed through the potholes as she turned onto Chrystal Drive, irritated by the glare of an SUV running up close behind her with its lights on high beam.

As she passed the Chick-fill-A she started to slow down, hoping for one of the few parking spaces on the right side of the street. The city had opted not to add parking spaces on the other side, much to Morgan's increasing irritation as she saw all the available spots on her side of the street were already occupied. In front of Ted's she decided to ignore the "No Left Turn" sign and turn into the driveway around the park on her left. She stopped in front of the restaurant, waiting for a gap in the on-coming traffic, before turning left into the driveway.

The rude bright lights behind her followed closely so she deliberately took her time angling the BMW into a parking spot, hoping to irritate the other driver as much as they had irritated her. Morgan never missed the opportunity to give back worse than what she got.

As she pulled in she did not notice that the SUV behind her had not moved. She was in too much of a hurry to meet Talbot so that she could get rid of Jessie.

"We're here," Morgan said, turning off the ignition. Twisting in her seat she grabbed her attaché case from the back seat and hopped out of the car. Her cellphone rang as she dropped her keys into her handbag.

She dug out her phone and glanced at the Caller ID. It was Andy, Williams' intern. She answered the call as she started walking along the path circling the park and back toward the cross walk in front of the restaurant. She didn't bother looking back at Jessie to make sure she was following.

"Yes, Andy?" she said.

"He's dead!" Andy shouted into the phone.

"Stop shouting. Who's dead?"

"The Senator! It was awful!"

Morgan paused, stunned. She could hear Andy sobbing almost hysterically on the other end of the line.

"What do you mean, he's dead? What happened?" Morgan asked, trying make sense of the call.

"We were sitting in the Senate and he started coughing. He asked me for some water. He looked as white as a sheet. I tried to pass him a glass, but he stood up instead like he was trying to leave. He started choking and blood came out of his mouth. Then he collapsed face first into the tile. He started having a fit or something, blood came out of everywhere, and then he just went limp! It was horrible!"

Morgan took a deep breath. She felt like the world had lurched under her feet and put her career path in jeopardy.

"Was it a heart attack?" she asked, forcing herself to focus.

"Don't you get it? He was leaking blood out of everywhere!" Andy shouted hysterically. "It wasn't a heart attack! The blood was even coming out of his eyes!"

Morgan closed her eyes, taking a deep breath as she tried to stop the planet from reeling under her. The picture Andy had painted certainly did not sound like a heart attack. Slowly the whirling sensation settled down and she was able to focus.

"Where's he now?"

"I don't know. They took him away in an ambulance."

"Okay Andy, I need you to focus. Can you do that?"

"You didn't see it!"

"I know, but I need you to get your act together right now!" she snapped. "Pull it together!"

She could hear him on the other end taking deep breaths.

"Okay?"

"No, but what do you need me to do?" His voice was already starting to sound firmer, more resolved. Morgan could almost see the wheels turning in his head as he tried to figure out how this could be played to his advantage.

"Collect his briefcase, papers, anything else of his still there and take them back to the office. I'll meet you there later and we can figure out what we need to do. Can you do that?"

"Okay."

Morgan hung up the phone, already angry, plotting her next career move.

Suddenly realizing where she was, she looked impatiently around for Jessie, still trailing about fifteen yards behind. A tall man in a dark coat hurried past Jessie, bumping her hard enough to knock her back pack to the ground.

"Hey! Watch were you're going, you moron!" Jessie said as she reached down to pick up her bag. The man stopped in front of Morgan, his back towards Jessie, and reached into his coat. He pulled out an evil-looking 40 caliber Glock with a short-barreled suppressor custom-threaded to the barrel and pointed it at Morgan.

"The folder," the man said. "Now."

"Have you lost your mind? This is confidential government material!"

Reaching quickly with his free hand, the man grabbed at the attaché, trying to pull it free. Morgan hung on, screaming for help. Jessie came up fast behind the man and slammed her pack into the back of his head, knocking him staggering as Morgan pulled free. He spun around to face Jessie. As his gun lined up on her it coughed twice, the sound so quiet as to be lost in the background noise of the city. The bullets never made it to Jessie as Morgan threw herself between them, screaming at Jessie to run. Her voice was abruptly cut off as the bullets hit her high in the chest and knocked her back into Jessie.

Morgan collapsed to the ground, coughing up blood. Keeping his gun lined up on Jessie, the man reached down to grab the attaché, but Morgan still clung on desperately. He never saw Talbot coming until it was too late.

From his vantage point across the street, Talbot saw Morgan on the phone and watched as Jessie's back pack was knocked off her shoulder. Already walking in their direction, he broke into a sprint when he saw the gun, dodging passing cars as he crossed the street. Car horns yelled angrily at him as he sprinted across the street, drivers jamming on their brakes to avoid running him over.

He was just a few steps when the attacker shot Morgan in the chest again. As he wrenched the attaché out of Morgan's desperate grasp he heard Talbot's pounding boots on the concrete. Talbot smashed into him with a pile-driving tackle into the small of his back before he had time to turn. Staggering, he dropped the attaché to turn and fire at Talbot. The bullet barely grazed him, laying open a burning hot streak across the top of his trapezius as he lunged at a glancing angle at the attacker. His body flooded with adrenaline, Talbot knocked the gun to one side and, with a seamless transition from defense to offense, smashed his knuckles with vicious force into the gunman's trachea. He could feel the cartilage crunch into fragments under his fist.

Choking, the man collapsed to his knees. Talbot stepped in close, grabbing his hair to pull his head back, and smashed his fist repeatedly into the throat before dropping him man to the concrete. He stood over the lifeless form for a moment. The, never even noticing as the blood started to trickle down his arm and off the tip if his little finger.

Having made sure that the man was dead, Talbot turned from him and knelt beside Morgan. Jessie was desperately trying to stop the blood bubbling and frothing from her chest and mouth.

Morgan reached for the attaché case, dragging it closer, and then pushed it into Talbot's hands. Then she looked up at Jessie and tried to speak, but the blood choked her. She grabbed Jessie's hand, holding tight before the light faded. The falling snow settled lightly on her face and open eyes. Jessie wept as the snow melted, rocking Morgan's head back and forth in her lap.

Without warning the sidewalk next to Talbot spat fragments of concrete up at them. More bullets buzzed past as Talbot shoved Jessie flat on the ground and dived for the dropped Glock. As he rolled to the side to keep Jessie out of the line of fire he could see the muzzle flashes from the driver's window of the black SUV which as facing away from them. The gunman was twisting backwards out of his window to get a better shot, but the angle was too awkward. He swung the SUV door open and stepped out, lining his gun up on Talbot.

Talbot raised up on one knee with the other leg extended straight out in front of him and took an extra second to take deliberate aim. He automatically compensated for the additional weight of the suppressor and pulled the trigger twice in quick succession.

The man stumbled in mid-stride, dead before he hit the ground. Leaping to his feet, Talbot sprinted obliquely towards the SUV, gun at the ready. As he ran he glanced back to check on Jessie, but she looked unharmed.

He could still hear her crying behind him as he reached the SUV, the Glock held high and close at the ready, the sights lining up where-ever his eyes went. As he got close he fired once more into the head of the driver to make sure, then checked the SUV. It was empty. Talbot turned back to check through the dead driver's pockets. There was no identification of any kind, but he was wearing a military-issue throat-mic and ear piece.

Puzzled, Talbot removing the earpiece carefully to make sure he got no blood on it and held it up to his ear as he collected the driver's spare ammunition.

"Alpha Six, do you copy?" There was a pause. "Alpha Six?"

"Alpha Six, do you copy?"

"Copy," Talbot said and waited.

There was a pause.

"Who is this?"

"Alpha Six. What's the status?" Talbot said, fishing.

There was another pause before the voice spoke again.

"Alpha team, be advised Comm is compromised. Move in and secure."

Talbot dropped the earpiece and walked quickly back to a Jessie, still distraught and sobbing, Morgan's head limp in Jessie's lap. Holding the Glock low and close to his leg to keep it as inconspicuous as possible in the dim street lights, he scanned the area around them. Four men in dark overcoats were converging on their location from different directions. Their hands were concealed in their pockets.

"C'mon Jessie, we gotta get out of here."

Jessie didn't seem to hear him.

"C'mon Jessie, we gotta go!" Talbot said, more urgently.

Jessie stared blankly up at Talbot.

"C'mon, it's gonna be okay," he said, taking her gently by the arm and lifting her to her feet. "But there's more of them coming. We've gotta go NOW."

Quickly Talbot helped her shrug into her back pack, grabbed up the attaché case, and guided her stumbling down the path, almost blinded by tears. Talbot quickly threaded their way into the center of the park and away from the shooting.

One of the over-coated men was hurrying down the path in their direction. His eyes were searching the scene behind Talbot and he barely glanced at them as they passed. Suddenly Talbot heard his footsteps stop behind him.

Smoothly, Talbot half-turned and stepped slightly to his left, putting his body between the over-coated man and Jessie, the Glock still low against his thigh. The man was already talking urgently into the mic. His gun was starting to come out of his pocket when Talbot raised his hand quickly and pumped two bullets into his chest at close range. The man staggered back, cursing as the heavy slugs slammed into the Kevlar vest under his clothing. He lined up his gun again so Talbot shot him in the head. He turned back to Jessie, grabbed her hand and started to run down the path.

Glancing back over his shoulder he saw the other three headed purposefully in their direction.

Jessie was just barely starting to think for herself.

"What's going on? Why did he kill my mom?"

"I don't know yet, but I see three others headed our way and there may be more. We've got to keep moving. They don't know me, but that last guy recognized you."

"Me?!"

"Yes. We've got to get off the street. I don't know who they are or how many so they have the advantage. I don't like that."

Jessie was still a little dazed, her body functioning on autopilot while her brain tried to come to grips with what she had just seen. The worst of the shock had started to wear off, but she was a long way from getting a full grasp on what had happened.

Talbot glanced at her as they hurried along the sidewalk, trying to gauge how she was doing. She seemed to be adjusting fast. It wouldn't be long before she started to ask questions about him, but for now at least his insistence had managed to cut through the initial fog in her brain with something tangible to do.

As soon as they stopped running she was going to start wondering who he was and why she should follow him. In the meantime he had to get them out of sight. Quickly he guided her north along the tree-lined sidewalk on the east side of Chrystal Drive. Just five minutes from the park they walked through the gates of the Water Park Towers apartment complex.

Safely out of sight for the moment, Talbot stopped, took Jessie by the shoulders and turned her to face him.

"Okay, Jessie. Take a deep breath and focus on me."

She breathed in, holding it for a moment before letting the air out of her lungs.

"Good. Let it all out and take another one. Hold it while you count to twenty."

She took another breath, deeper this time, and started to hold it.

"Okay, breathe out slowly," he said, after a few seconds.

Slowly, after a few more deep breaths, Jessie was focusing directly on Talbot.

"Good Jessie," Talbot said. "Now we need to get to your apartment and out of sight for a while. You need to lead the way."

Jessie nodded, then turned and led Talbot through the grounds of the complex, into the building and to the bank of

49

elevator doors. When she pressed the button the door to one of the elevators dinged open immediately. They stepped inside and Jessie pushed the button for the eighth floor. The doors slid shut quietly and the elevator started to rise, the soft music an incongruous contrast to the turmoil.

Talbot watched her reflection in the stainless-steel wall of the elevator carefully, amazed that this girl was his daughter. He tried to see how she might resemble him, but the distorted reflection made it difficult.

Sooner than Talbot expected, the elevator stopped with a jerk. The door dinged open and Jessie walked out. Talbot followed her down the hall as she fumbled for her apartment key. She stopped outside one of the apartment doors and tried to insert her key in the lock, but her hands were still shaking so badly that she couldn't line the key up with the key hole. Talbot gently took the key from her and opened the door for her, letting her walk in ahead of him.

The apartment was small and modern. The furnishing was minimalist and there was a complete lack of clutter. No knick-knacks, no framed pictures, no decoration of any kind. Even cheap motel rooms had more personality. Everything about the place gave the sense of transience, as if the owner had no intention of living or staying in the space. Morgan had obviously made no effort to make the apartment feel like a home.

The front door opened directly into a living room on the left flowed seamlessly into the kitchen on the right. A tall round table made of steel and glass was stuck out of the way in the corner to the right. There were two bar stools made with stainless steel legs and a clear acrylic seat pushed up to the table. The kitchen had new stainless steel appliances which added to the anti-septic modern feel.

Against the left wall in the living room was a small entertainment center made of more stainless steel and clear acrylic. It supported a large, high-definition television. Pushed back against the opposite wall was a single white couch, very simply designed, with a couple of cobalt pillows tossed on it. The blues were clearly chosen to tie into the large wall hanging on the end wall above the matching chair. Talbot got the sense that it all came as a set.

Between the living room and kitchen, a dark hallway led down to what Talbot assumed would be the bedrooms and bathroom.

Jessie dropped her back pack on the floor and sat on the edge of the couch as Talbot went into the kitchen. He put the Glock down on the counter and rummaged through the cabinets to find a glass. Filling it with water from the refrigerator door, he brought it back to Jessie.

"Drink this, it will help."

Without looking up at him, Jessie took the glass and took a couple of sips. A drop of blood trickled off Talbot's hand and onto the laminate bamboo floor between them.

She glanced up, really looking at him for the first time.

"You're hurt. There's a hole in your shirt."

"Just a scratch, but I need to clean it up. Is the bathroom back through there?" he asked, pointing at the hallway with his chin.

"Yes, first door on the left."

"I don't suppose there's a shirt anywhere I can wear, is there?"

"No, but if you give me that one I'll try to wash out the blood."

"Thanks."

Carefully, the bullet scratch starting to hurt now that the adrenaline had worn off, Talbot grimaced as he unbuttoned the shirt and eased it off. Jessie's eyes widened as she saw two

51

puckered marks high on his chest. The scars were a nagging reminder of a deadly firefight in Central Europe during the Balkan war. Handing his shirt over to Jessie, he turned and disappeared down the hallway and into the bathroom. After a moment Jessie could hear the water in the bathroom sink start to run.

She crossed the living room and into the kitchen to open a cabinet door in the corner. Hidden inside was a compact washer/dryer combination. Clearly comfortable using it, she added soap. Out of years of habit doing laundry she started to check the pocket to make sure it was empty. She felt a stiff piece of paper and her fingers extracted the photo Talbot had saved there. She tossed the shirt into the washer, closed the door and started the wash cycle.

As she turned back to the living room she glanced curiously at the scrap of paper, her breath catching as she recognized herself in the picture. She looked up quickly to check that Talbot was still in the bathroom, then looked back at the picture torn down the vertical, puzzled as to why this stranger had her picture. Something about it was familiar, but she could not quite put her finger on it. As she studied it more closely it clicked... the backdrop was familiar. Suddenly she remembered.

Carefully she picked up the Glock and eased the slide back slightly to check for a round in the chamber. Then she eased her way quietly down the hallway, unconsciously holding her breath as she passed the half-open bathroom door before slipping into her own room. The bedside lamp was still turned on from the morning.

Just under the lamp was a small picture frame. She picked it up, opened the back and removed the picture. The picture was also torn down the vertical and Jessie held the torn edges of the two pictures side by side. They were a perfect match. Confused and angry, Jessie slipped back into the living room. She placed the images side by side on the kitchen counter, then stepped back against the wall. She held the Glock gripped resolutely in both hands as she waited for Talbot to come out of the bathroom.

Talbot had used a small wet wash cloth to wipe the blood off his shoulder and arm. After rinsing it out thoroughly he turned the faucet off, the last of the running water chasing itself down the drain. While the wash cloth was still hot from the faucet he folded it down into a small pad and pressed it down on the graze. The bleeding had completely stopped, but he knew it was going to sting for a while. Besides, if he did not keep it covered the scabbing would dry out, crack and bleed again.

Rummaging through the cabinet under the sink he found a small first aid kit. He soaked a pad of gauze from the kit with rubbing alcohol and carefully wiped the area around the wound. Then he leaned forward over the sink and carefully poured more of the alcohol liberally over the gash, grunting as it burned like a hot poker pressed into his flesh. Gritting his teeth, he patted the area as dry as he could, then waited for a moment for the burn to subside as the remainder of the alcohol evaporated.

He squeezed the entire contents of a small tube of antiseptic cream all over the gash to keep the wrap from sticking to the wound and opened a roll of gauze. Awkwardly he wrapped the site until he was satisfied that he would be able to move freely without the bandage slipping around too much. Satisfied he flipped the light switch off and wandered back into the living room.

Jessie was waiting for him, the .40 aimed at his chest.

"Who are you?" Jessie demanded.

"Careful with that," Talbot said. "I can explain."

"Then you better explain that," Jessie said fiercely, nodding at the pictures on the counter. "Why do you have a picture of me?"

53

"You don't remember me, do you?" Talbot answered sadly. "I remember you. I remember the day you were born like it was yesterday. You had red hair even then."

"How do you know that?" Jessie demanded.

"I'm your dad, Jessie. I was there. I cut the cord, and when the doctor handed you to me I thought my heart would burst."

"Not possible!" Jessie spat back at him, the gun levelled. "My dad died overseas in combat somewhere. How did you get that picture?!"

"Really, I am your dad. Your mom divorced me just before your sixth birthday. Then she made sure I was never allowed to see you. I spent the last ten years in court trying see you again. I finally won. Your mom was bringing you to see me tonight."

"Then why did she tell me you were dead?"

"Your mom and I had... a difficult relationship," Talbot said, choosing his words carefully. "But I don't know why. I just know it took me ten years to see you again."

"Okay then, if you're my dad, prove it. Tell me something no one else would know."

Talbot thought for a moment. "Do you remember us sitting on the roof of the house after you were supposed to be in bed? You would sit in my lap, and we would study the stars."

"Not good enough," Jessie said, wavering. "That could have been anyone."

"True, but do you remember the Hunter? I used to show you Orion in the stars and you would make me to tell you a different story about him every time."

Slowly the gun lowered, tears welling up in Jessie's eyes.

"I never believed you died," she whispered, trembling. "I knew you were alive."

She started to sob, deep, choking sobs wracking her shoulders. Talbot stepped forward, carefully easing the gun from her hands and wrapping her up in his arms. Gently he stroked her thick red hair, his eyes closed as he breathed in the smell of his daughter for the first time in ten years.

Finally, Jessie's sobbing eased, and Talbot let her go. He poured two glasses of water and joined Jessie on the couch.

"Where have you been all this time?" she asked.

"You mean between court appearances, right?" Talbot said with a smile.

"Right."

"Well, what do you know about me?"

"Mom said you were a soldier and that you died overseas somewhere."

"Some of that's true, anyway. Not the dying part obviously, although I came close once."

"Those scars on your chest?"

"Right. I was an Army Ranger, and they sent me all over the world. After you were born I didn't want to be away like that anymore, but your mom liked being able to tell people her Special Forces husband was away again on a special mission. I think she liked the hazard pay as well. I opted out after my last tour and she got pretty angry. I think that might be part of why she divorced me."

"So, how did you get shot?" Jessie asked curiously, pointing at the two bullet scars.

"All I can tell you is that I was helping someone get away from some very bad people."

"Where?"

"Eastern Europe."

There was a pause, then Talbot spoke again.

"Jessie, can you think why those men attacked you and your mom tonight?"

A shadow passed over Jessie's face.

"I have no clue," she replied.

"Could it have had anything to do with the NSA?"

"The NSA? No! Why would you think that?"

"Because that wasn't a random attack. They were very specifically targeting you or your mom, and I think they were from the government. They were using Special Forces Comm gear."

"But that makes no sense! I've been helping The NSA close the loopholes in their network security!"

"Well, I'm pretty sure they were after your mom. It looked like they wanted her bag. Do you remember anything strange?"

"Not really. Maybe the phone call."

"What call?"

"When we were getting out of the car her phone rang. I think she was talking to Andy, and she asked him who died."

"Who's Andy?"

"He's the intern she hired to work for the Senator. I think they were talking about the Senator dying. She seemed upset." She paused, thinking. "Do you think there's a connection?"

"I'm not sure, but if those really were feds I don't think we can trust anyone right now."

18h30, Phoenix Operations Control Room, Washington, D.C.

La Salle was furious.

Despite killing Morgan, the field team had been unable to retrieve the folder and lost half their six-man team in less than five minutes and the rest had called in to report losing the mark. La Salle had arrived just minutes after the team got back to their station office across town and the mood was grim. The debriefing had not gone well.

"So, let me get this straight," La Salle ground out, his voice dangerously quiet as he spoke over the phone. "You kill the woman, but you can't get the attaché case because an unarmed random stranger comes along, kills three of you with your own guns, disappears completely with the girl and the file, and you have no idea what happened?"

"No sir."

La Salle took a deep breath, struggling to keep a lid on his anger. His first reaction had been less than productive.

"Okay. You had your mic's on, right?

"Yes sir."

La Salle turned to Tremaine, the Mission Operations Chief. "Get me the tape."

"It's already queued up to play."

Tremaine was a non-descript man in his late sixties wearing tan slacks and a zip-up cardigan stretched to capacity over a belly he had spent years nurturing. Quiet and completely loyal, he had ridden a desk for most of his life and what he did not know about surveillance techniques had not been invented yet.

"Play it."

La Salle closed his eyes, listening intently to the audio to the end.

"Was that Saunders with the woman?" La Salle asked as the audio started.

"Yes."

"Why is the audio so lousy?"

"The teams hide the mic's in their clothing so that nobody spots them. That noise is the fabric rubbing against the mic."

"Start it again."

The audio played over the speakers again, the muffled voices difficult to distinguish. A voice started speaking clearly, urgently calling for back up.

"Who is that?" La Salle asked, taking the remote from Tremaine and pausing the audio.

"Brighton. He was behind the wheel."

"And he started shooting first?"

"After the woman was shot, yes."

"Who was he shooting at?

"We don't know, but whoever it was shot back. Really good shooting, too."

La Salle glared at him. "How long of a shot?"

"Not too far, about twenty-five yards, but he was shooting under fire."

La Salle started the audio playing again, then paused the audio again the moment Talbot spoke into the mic.

"Who was that?"

"We think it was the guy who took out our guys."

La Salle nodded and hit play again. The voices of the backup team were urgent and loud as they converged on the scene, almost drowning out the muffled sounds recorded on the mic of the original shooter, dead beside Morgan's body. Concentrating carefully on filtering out the overlay of voices, La Salle focused on the background noise trying to hear any clues.

"Did someone just call the girl Jessie?" he asked, playing back through the segment where Talbot had urged Jessie to get moving.

Tremaine focused on the words, then nodded. "Yes, definitely."

"Okay, so our guy knows the girl."

He played the tape through again, this time concentrating on the last encounter in the park, the moment Talbot had turned and killed the third team member.

"Who was in the park?"

"Simmons."

"So he recognized the girl and tried to call it in?"

"Looks like it."

"Let me see a map."

Tremaine pulled up a detailed street map of the area as La Salle drummed his fingers on the conference room table, thinking.

La Salle mentally traced a straight line from the first shooting through the second, tried to understand if there was a reason why they chose to escape in that direction. Something about it nagged at the back of his mind. Suddenly it clicked.

"They're headed back to the girl's apartment. Send a team in and kill everyone."

"We've got nobody ready, it will take a couple of hours to get them together."

"Send in the rest of Saunders team, then. They have something to prove."

"Yes sir."

59

22h15, Water Park Towers, Crystal City, VA.

The television in the living room flickered against the walls, the colors changing as Talbot watched the ten o' clock news on WTTG, the local Fox affiliate.

Jessie and Talbot had spent several hours talking and it had been even more difficult than Talbot had expected. Jessie's emotions understandably were an epic roller coaster ride. She had bounced back and forth between grief at the murder of her mother, anger that Talbot had not made more of an effort to see her, fear of the future, curiosity about Talbot's life, joy at reuniting with her father, and everything in between.

The ride had been exhausting and she had finally decided to take a shower and get into some clean clothes. Talbot had turned the television on to see if there were any reports about three bodies in the park. He had not wanted to disturb Jessie and had kept the volume turned down low.

The story dominated the news broadcast, with interviews from various self-professed experts spouting their theories, the live camera feed from the scene inserted in a small window in the corner of the screen. It was clear that the authorities were being tight-lipped about what they knew. Even the few eye witnesses had not been able to provide a clear timeline of what had happened.

Opinions varied from a drug deal gone bad to a potential kidnapping, but the consensus was that nobody who actually knew anything was willing to say anything on camera other than the standard sound bites and memorized phrases. The talk was all about "All the weight of our noble police force will be brought to bear" … "No comment"… "We will have more to share at a press conference in the morning".

There was just one detail Talbot found odd about the interview with the police chief. After several of the more pointed questions the chief would glance sideways at an unidentified man in a dark overcoat. It was obvious he was calling the shots as he watched over the interview.

To Talbot's experienced eye the man was clearly a Fed of some description. Just as clearly, he was using the police chief as a front of normalcy, but had taken jurisdiction over the case. Everything about it stank of corruption.

From behind Talbot came the sound of bedroom slippers scuffing down the hall and into the living room. Talbot turned the television off before turning to his daughter. She was wearing black lounge pants and an oversized black t-shirt with a skull logo.

"How you doing?" he asked.

"Better. I was hungry, so I ordered pizza. It should be here any minute." She plopped down into the couch, kicked off her slippers and curled her legs up under her. " Was it on the news?"

"Yes."

"What did they say?"

"Not a whole lot. I don't think they're telling the press everything." Talbot watched Jessie carefully, trying to evaluate how resilient she was. She was quiet, almost brooding, and had withdrawn again. He wasn't sure if it was because she distrusted him, was tired, or if this was who she normally was.

"What?" she asked, looking at him irritably.

"Nothing," Talbot replied. "Just making sure you're okay."

She shrugged, looking away. After a moment she reached for the remote and turned the television back on to the news. She watched in stone-faced silence as the faces spoke into the camera.

"Vultures," she muttered.

"Who?"

"Reporters. They try to hide it, but they love this stuff."

Talbot nodded, waiting for her to say more but she withdrew into her own thought, ignoring him.

Talbot got up off the couch and stepped into the kitchen, opening random cabinets looking for plates.

"Do you order pizza often?" he asked carefully.

She was quiet for a moment before answering reluctantly.

"Almost every night."

"Same place every night, or do you mix it up?"

"Same place."

"I can't think of any food I would eat from the same place every night. Must be really good."

"Pretty awesome."

"Still..."

She flashed an irritable look at him as he watched her.

"Okay, so the delivery guy is from my school. Kinda cute, too."

"Now that makes much more sense. Are you dating?"

"Of course not!"

Oh really?" Talbot chuckled. "Hasn't he asked you out yet?"

"No!" Jessie said, blushing. "I don't think he even notices me."

"Then he's clearly an idiot and not in your class. What does he look like?"

"What do you care?" Jessie asked. "It's not like you've been around."

Talbot paused, adjusting again to the sudden mood swing. Jessie obviously was still bouncing between resentment and curiosity on the subject of her dad.

"Fair enough, but I thought it might be a good idea to know who to expect at the door. Just in case," he replied carefully.

"Oh. Okay. He's got kind of a surfer vibe with wavy blonde hair and dreamy blue eyes."

"Well, I still say if he doesn't notice a stunning girl like you, then he's not worth your time noticing him either."

Jessie looked away, trying to decide how to react.

"Can I get you anything?" Talbot asked as he finally found a couple of plates and put them on the counter.

"Orange soda," Jessie said, reluctantly deciding she liked his compliment.

Talbot reached into the refrigerator and pulled out one can of Coke and one of Fanta Orange. The doorbell rang as he turned back towards Jessie with their drinks.

Holding his finger to his lips to make sure Jessie stayed quiet, he eased over to the door and carefully peered through the peephole. All he could see was the back of someone wearing a T-shirt with the logo of a pizza restaurant logo on the back. The T-shirt was a bad fit. The hair was dark and very short in the back and sides.

Using the fish-eye lens of the peephole, Talbot carefully studied the hallway on either side of the man. It looked clear.

Reaching down, Talbot carefully placed one of the cans on the ground just outside the arc of the door as it would swing open. Then he opened the door, the other can in his hand behind the door.

"Come on in," he said with a smile.

"Thanks," the pizza guy said, stepping in. His foot accidently kicked the soda can over. Startled he glanced down as Talbot's arm came swinging round from behind the door, smashing the bottom of the soda can into the man's head just behind his ear. As the man started to go down, out cold before his knees buckled, the pizza box spilled from his hands and a Glock dropped to the carpet with a thud.

Talbot grabbed the back of his T-shirt and dragged him from out of the open doorway, then dumped him unceremoniously against the wall behind the door.

"Go fetch me something to tie him up with. Belts, scarves, electric cords, anything like that will do," Talbot said. "I want to get some answers from him when he wakes up."

Jessie's eyes were wide in shock, but she hopped up and ran into her room to find something to tie him up with.

Talbot picked up the Glock and tossed it onto the couch out of reach in case the man woke up. Not that there was much chance of that, Talbot knew. He would be unconscious for hours.

As he turned back to the door to close and lock it he saw a shadow pass the gap at the hinges between the door and jam, barely giving him time to react. The door crashed open and two more men burst in fast, guns up in the ready position.

Talbot locked both hands over the first man's gun and tried to twist it free, but the man hung on grimly, grunting as he tried to swing Talbot to his right towards the second gun man. Talbot let him swing him round, faster than expected. The unexpected momentum over-rotated Talbot so that the first attacker's back was to the second gun man again. Talbot moved in close, chest to chest, and let go of the gun with one hand. Rotating his free hand palm up, he drove his rigid fingers like a knife hard up and under the man's bullet-proof vest and into his body just below the sternum. The vicious blow paralyzed his diaphragm and drove the air from his lungs.

The man dropped his gun and folded over and out of the second gunman's line of sight. Talbot was still moving as the second attacker pulled the trigger. His left hand swept across to knock the gun to one side, but not before he felt a hard punch to his ribs as one of the bullets found its mark. The adrenaline kept Talbot moving, completely intent on his attack. He had no time to think about how badly he was hit. He closed his hand around the suppressor on the end of the barrel to get extra leverage and twisted the gun free. Before he could turn the gun on his attacker he smashed the gun out of his grasp, sending it sliding across the kitchen tile and up under the table.

Hands moving fast, the attacker slid a wicked-looking knife out of a sheath hidden in his sleeve, slashing and cutting at Talbot. Talbot backed into the kitchen quickly, keeping his distance from the blade. Talbot held his hands up like a boxer, his palms turned in to protect his inner arms and the grasping tendons of his hands. He parried the blade with the back of his hands, until he reached the counter.

Talbot swept his hand across the table top, slinging the plates he had put there earlier at the knife man and making him duck back just long enough to give Talbot time to pull a large kitchen knife from the knife block on the counter.

Going on the offensive, Talbot moved forward fast and low, the knife in his left hand as he lunged. The attacker swung his blade to parry, and Talbot smoothly flipped the knife into his right hand, trapping the swinging blade with his left as his right hand slashed forward, driving the blade deep into the attacker's chest.

An arm came around Talbot's neck before he had time to recover, the forearm locked across his throat and cutting off the blood supply to his brain.

Talbot knew he had just seconds before he blacked out. Desperately he swung his elbow back, trying to slam the point of his elbow into his attacker's ribs and drive him off. He missed. His senses spinning already, Talbot could feel his strength slipping as his vision narrowed to a pinpoint. His knees were starting to buckle when he barely heard two soft pops, distant through the roaring sound of blood pounding in his ears. The arm across his throat went slack and his attacker slumped to the ground.

Talbot stumbled to his knees, gasping. His vision cleared as the oxygen rushed back into his brain.

The lifeless body of his attacker was crumpled on the floor behind him and, standing just five feet away, Jessie was holding a silenced Glock in two hands, her eyes wide and hands trembling.

Talbot pushed himself to his feet. Carefully he reached out and removed the gun from Jessie's hands, then pulled her close to hug her.

"I had to do it!" she sobbed. "He was going to kill you!"

"You did the right thing, Jessie," Talbot said holding her close and stroking the back of her head gently. "You did good."

Turning her away from the scene, Talbot led her out of the living room and into the safe zone of her bedroom.

"Deep breaths, Jessie, deep breaths. I need you to pull it together, okay?"

Jessie nodded, the tears still streaming down her cheeks.

"Get into some warm clothes, grab what you need and put it in a bag," Talbot said. "We've got to go right now, okay?"

Jessie nodded and started to move around her room as Talbot stepped out. She grabbed her backpack, tossed out her school books and added a few clothes while Talbot went into the bathroom to check the damage from the new wound.

Carefully pulling off the shirt Jessie had just finished washing, he was surprised at how little blood there was. Then he saw the entrance wound between two ribs, slowly seeping blood. No bubbling, no frothing, and no exit wound... the bullet was still inside him, but at least it had not hit his lung.

Feeling around carefully, he located the bullet just under the skin of his back. Steeling himself against the inevitable burn, Talbot carefully rinsed off the open wound as best he could with some of the remaining rubbing alcohol. Since he had already used up the small First Aid Kit Morgan had kept in the apartment, he unrolled a wad of tissue paper and splashed soaked it in rubbing alcohol. Then he pressed it against the bullet hole and wrapped a towel tightly around his body to hold it in place.

Grimacing in pain, he awkwardly managed to slip back into his shirt using his elbow to hold the towel in place. The finished product was hardly tidy, but it served the purpose and, as long as they stayed in the shadows, the blood on his shirt would be hardly noticeable.

Breathing gingerly he went back to the living room and collected all the spare ammunition he could find from the three attackers. He was still going through pockets when Jessie came down the hall wearing jeans, hiking boots and a warm, black wool sweater, her back pack over one shoulder and a parka in her hand.

"Ready," she said quietly.

Talbot turned her around and tucked Williams' folder and one of the handguns into her back pack, then slipped another into his waist band.

"Let's go," he said quietly. "Stay on my left, just behind my shoulder, and keep about an arm's length away from me. We're going to move pretty quickly. Okay?"

"Almost," she said and walked over to the fake pizza guy. She looked at him for a moment, then kicked him in the face as hard as she could. Without looking back, she walked out, her face hard and angry.

Talbot's eyebrows slid up his brow slightly in surprise, and he couldn't help smiling quietly to himself as he followed her out.

23h00, Crystal City, VA.

The cab driver was a stark contrast to the somber mood on the back seat. He was using the speaker on his cell phone to chat with someone in what sounded Romanian, and the only words Talbot could understand seemed to relate to the Capitols. As cheerful as the cabbie was, he guessed they had just won a game.

Jessie had retreated within herself, using her headphones again as a shield to close off from her surroundings. In contrast, despite the distracting chatter from the cabbie, Talbot was very focused, working the problem. He reached a sudden decision, pulled out his cell phone and dialed a local number. The phone rang on the other end for several minutes before beeping once and switching him directly into voicemail.

"Tango Echo Mike," Talbot said quietly into his phone. "Injured, safe house needed. Current location Crystal City, Virginia."

Hanging up, Talbot glanced over at Jessie. The pain in his side from the bullet in the apartment coiled and writhed through his side like a lava stream, and every breath added to the pain.

Jessie stirred, pulling the earpieces out.

"Do you think he's okay?" she asked.

"Do I think who is okay?" Talbot asked, trying to keep the pain out of his voice.

"Andrew."

"Who's Andrew?"

"The real pizza delivery guy. I mean, they got his T-shirt... do you think he's okay?"

"Oh yes, I'm sure he is. They probably just flashed a badge at him and told him they needed his shirt for a stake out in the building. I bet right now he's figuring out how to start a conversation with you at school, so he can find out if you know anything about it."

She glanced at Talbot.

"He doesn't even know who I am."

"Nonsense. I've been thinking about that. I bet he doesn't even look up at you when he delivers your pizza, right?"

"How did you know?" she asked, puzzled.

"Well, I personally think you get him completely tongue-tied, so he tries to play it cool around you."

"I don't believe it."

"I know it."

Embarrassed, Jessie looked out the window as Talbot's phone buzzed with a text message. Talbot glanced at his phone, then leaned forward.

"Change of destination," he said to the cabbie. "Take us to 907 26th Street South in Arlington."

Then Talbot turned back to Jessie. She pulled the earphones from her ears.

Let me see your phone."

"Why?"

"I don't want them tracking you with it."

Jessie handed him her phone. After a quick inspection, Talbot grunted in satisfaction and removed the battery, killing it completely.

"If this had been an iPhone," he said, "We would have had to smash it because you can't switch the battery out. Do you know why?"

"Because 'Off' isn't really 'Off' so they can still track the phone?"

"Exactly, and how did you know that?" Talbot asked, impressed.

"I don't know, it just made sense," she replied.

"And you're not a secret agent either, right?" Talbot joked as he rolled down the window and tossed both the phone and battery out of the cab.

Jessie ignored the effort to make her smile.

23h15, Surveillance Room, Phoenix HQ, Washington, D.C.

"I don't care what you have to do, I want to know who he is!" La Salle said furiously. "If he can destroy one of my best field teams, he must be someone we should know about! I want to know what I'm dealing with!"

"Working on it," Tremaine said calmly. "I may point out that I suggested you give me time to do this before sending your guys into the apartment, but you were in too much of a hurry."

La Salle glared at the back of Tremaine's head. Knowing Tremaine was right was almost more infuriating than the failure of his team to bring the folder back.

"We got a face hit," Tremaine said after a few minutes. "One of the cameras on the street got a decent picture of the man and girl leaving the park."

With a click of his mouse he mirrored his computer screen onto the large monitor on the wall. A grainy black and white image of Talbot and Jessie popped up on the screen. Tremaine selected one of the tools from the menu bar across the top and drew a box around Talbot's face. Then he clicked a couple of icons and sat back, humming contentedly to himself as the face recognition software worked its magic.

After a few seconds a copy of Talbot's driver's license popped up next to the photo. Working quickly, Tremaine pulled up another screen and typed Talbot's details into the open fields.

"Okay, Mr. Talbot," Tremaine muttered to himself. "Just who are you?"

He drummed his fingers on the table as he watched the sand run out of the egg timer icon in the center of his screen. Then the monitor flashed, and the opening page of Talbot's military dossier popped up onto the monitor, the word "TOP SECRET" emblazoned across it. Even his photo was blacked out.

"Boss," Tremaine said quietly, "This isn't just some guy off the street."

Quickly keying in additional credentials to get access to the file, Tremaine opened the document and the black box hiding the picture of Talbot disappeared.

In the picture he was wearing a red and white scarf and heavy tactical gear. His hair was long and unkempt, and his face masked by a heavy beard. Cold eyes stared back at them from the picture.

Tremaine clicked the picture to scroll to the next. This time Talbot was in dress uniform.

"I don't know what any of those pips and things mean," Tremaine said, "But he sure has a lot of junk on that uniform."

"Dammit, how the hell did Delta Force get involved?" La Salle demanded.

"What do you mean?"

"That arrow head patch with a dagger is a Delta Force patch."

"No wonder he had no trouble with your guys."

La Salle frowned as he read through the file.

"Looks like he's been certified expert in pretty much everything Delta Force can do. But why the hell would he get involved?"

"Checking."

Tremaine did a quick word association search for Jessie's name in Talbot's file.

"Ah, that's the connection," Tremaine grunted in satisfaction. "The girl is his daughter."

La Sale skimmed the rest of the dossier, then leaned back thoughtfully.

"Okay, so even if we just got massively unlucky, at least we know his involvement was accidental. Put out an APB with a picture of him and the girl. Wanted for killing a woman and five cops, stealing Government documents and taking the girl hostage. Armed and extremely dangerous. Use the Amber Alert, push it to every cell phone in a hundred miles, and emphasize the cop-killer thing."

Tremaine started tapping on his keyboard.

"Oh, one more thing," La Salle added. "Get everyone studying all the footage on every camera we have access to. I want to know the minute he walks past any camera on the street. Anything, anywhere."

"Right."

Chapter Three

The small white house at the end of the block was built in a quiet neighborhood on the lot inside the fork between 26th Street and South Ives. The location had been selected carefully, in part because it was built a relatively safe distance from the only neighbor to the west, and in part because it was less than a hundred yards from five different intersections. This provided multiple exit points from the safe house and out of the neighborhood.

The cab pulled up at the footpath to the front door and Talbot paused, studying the layout. There was a light on in the window to the left of the front entrance and the blind was raised six inches. Satisfied, Talbot paid the cab fare in cash and he and Jessie climbed out into the cold air.

Talbot quickly led the way to the door and twisted the handle. The door was unlocked, and he pushed it open. Warm air welcomed them as they stepped into the dimly lit entrance and Talbot closed the door behind them. Talbot lowered the blind back down to the sill.

Flipping on lights as they walked from room to room checking out the house. It was minimally furnished. Marketed as a three-bedroom home with two-and-a-half bathrooms just three years earlier, it no longer bore any resemblance to the original layout. Two of the bedrooms were furnished with beds and night stands.

The third had been converted into a state-of-the-art office. It was filled with high-tech computer and surveillance equipment, including no less than twelve monitors. Every angle of approach to the house was covered in surveillance, including infra-red. One of the monitors showed a red/green status report for a long list of surveillance sensors in and around the house.

The window already pulled up on what looked like the master monitor was flashing red. Talbot walked over and pressed the "Enter" key as Jessie watched.

"Set Visitor Security Key:" flashed up on the screen. Talbot pressed his hand onto the screen and waited a moment.

The screen flashed again.

"Done? (Y/N)"

Talbot pressed the letter "N".

"Set Visitor Security Key:" the screen repeated.

"Jessie, come press your right hand flat against the screen, please."

"What is it?" she asked curiously as she pressed her hand flat against the screen.

"This will record any part of your right-hand print as your access key to the house."

"That's pretty cool," Jessie said, impressed despite herself. "What is this place?"

"It's a safe house some friends of mine keep here in town."

"How did you know it was here?"

"I didn't. I asked a friend for help and he sent us here. He said it would be ready when we got here."

Talbot located the desktop and double-clicked on an icon in the corner. A map of the house popped up with a list of icons down one side. Talbot selected "Store Room" and a red line traced a box around a space between the room they were in and the single bathroom. Talbot hovered his mouse over the outline and a photo of trees in the snow popped up. It looked like an Ansel Adams.

Next Talbot selected icon labelled "Exit" and followed the same process. This time the popup image was a cat sunning itself on a window ledge.

"What was all that?"

"Come and I'll show you."

Talbot led Jessie through the house and into the small bathroom.

"What do you see?" he asked her.

"What do you mean?" she asked, puzzled. "It's a bathroom."

The bathroom was a study in white. White paint, subway tiles, sinks and countertops dominated, and the only color in the room was a stack of yellow towels on a shelf above the toilet seat.

The door to the bathroom swung in against the wall on the right. There was a bathroom sink and cabinet directly across from the doorway and a huge mirror the width and height of the wall above the vanity.

Turning left past the vanity, the toilet was located against the far wall on the left. Also against the far wall was the shower to the right of the toilet. The shower door swung to the right up against the open wall with a single towel rack between the shower and vanity.

Just above the Towel rack was a framed black-and-white picture of Aspen trees in the snow.

Looking closely, Jessie recognized the Ansel Adams photo on the wall. Tentatively she closed the shower door out of the way and studied the picture. Then, with a grin, she placed her right hand flat against the glass over the picture. There was a soft click, and the entire wall between the shower and vanity swung away from her as she kept pushing.

"Clever girl!" Talbot said, grinning at her.

As she walked in she triggered a motion sensor that turned on a bank of harsh overhead fluorescent lights. The room was narrow, with storage space down each side. On the left was a selection of weapons, electronics and ammunition. On the right was a selection of men and women's clothing, all different sizes, but all built around the same wardrobe color scheme... blue and black. Whoever had stocked the store room had assumed no other colors were necessary.

Jessie stood in the middle of the room, her hands on her hips as she looked around, amazed.

"Okay," Jessie said. "Explain. Are you a spy?"

Talbot chuckled. "No, nothing like that. But over the years I made friends with a lot of people who maybe could have fitted that description years ago. They served their country and retired. Some of them still provide security consultation services of different kinds, and we all keep in touch. If we need help, we can call a central number, leave a message, and someone might be close enough to help. I made a call after we left your apartment, and someone text me this address."

"That's so cool," Jessie said, still impressed.

"Take a look through the clothes and see if there's anything you need," Talbot said, grabbing a Medical Kit, a couple of long sleeve shirts, a thick black parka and matching ball cap for himself.

Jessie started looking through her options as Talbot turned to the opposite wall. He selected a Colt .380 in an ankle holster and a Glock 9mm in a concealed carry holster, then picked out three cell phones, unplugging the chargers they were attached to as well. Finally, Talbot opened a briefcase and extracted an emergency pack of hundred-dollar bills, handy for anyone who didn't want to leave a credit card trail. He stuffed it all into a small denim duffel bag.

Jessie had reached the end of the room, a handful of things tucked under her arm. She was looking at the picture on the far wall. It was a cat sunning itself on a window ledge.

"What happens if I touch this picture?" she asked.

"Explosions and smoke all over the house, and a door will open in that wall."

"Nuh-uh!" Jessie said, half disbelieving.

"Uh-Huh!" Talbot replied in kind, grinning. "That's in case someone tries to force their way in. Decoys, diversions and deceptions while we sneak out the escape hatch."

"That's so cool!"

"One-time deal though, so we only use it in an emergency."

"Okay."

Walking out of the store room together, Talbot closed the hidden door again and led the way back into the computer room. With Jessie watching, he turned on the three phones he had selected from the store room. Then he linked the home surveillance system to the App already loaded on the phones and set an alarm on the phone if the security was breached. Turning off the Airplane Mode he handed one of the phones to Jessie.

"Here you go. From now on, this is your phone."

As Jessie reached for the phone it started to buzz for an Amber Alert. Seconds later all three phones were buzzing.

Data had shown that, despite the exponentially greater reach and immediacy of the phone alerts, the vast majority of children recovered through the program had been as a result of a television alert. Research had proven that the images of the child and suspected abductor shown on the television screen had made the pivotal difference.

As a result of the studies the program had added these same images to the phone alerts just a few months before.

Out of habit Talbot cancelled the alert without looking at it, but Jessie was scrolling through the Apps on the phone as the alert came on. The photos staring back at her were her own, and one of her dad in uniform.

"Um, dad?"

"Yup?" Talbot answered, distracted.

"Look." She held up her phone to see.

"This is going to make it very difficult to move around," Talbot said thoughtfully.

"What are we going to do?"

"First things first."

"What?"

"I'm going to need your help. Does blood bother you?"

"No, I like watching ER shows."

"Good. I got shot again."

"Again? Where?"

"In the apartment."

"No, I mean where did the bullet hit you?"

"Oh. Right. In the side," Talbot said, lightly touching his ribs on the left.

She followed him into one of the bedrooms where he removed his shirt, unwrapped the towel, and lay on the bed with the towel folded double under his side.

"We've got to get the bullet out and clean everything thoroughly. Are you up for it?"

"No problem."

He looked at her for a moment, a teasing grin lurking in the corner of his eyes.

"You seem pretty eager to poke at an open wound... should I be worried?"

"Probably."

"Figures. Open that Med-Pac and lay everything out so we can see what we got."

As Jessie started to unpack, Talbot saw a small syringe labelled Lidocaine Hydrochloride. Picking it up, he injected the local anesthetic all around the wound to numb the area as much as possible.

Then he reached over and picked up a large, pre-loaded flush syringe in a sealed pouch along with a box of gauze pads. Opening both, he soaked one of the pads with iodine from a small bottle and carefully cleaned up the drying blood clotting over the wound.

Working gently he pried the clotted blood that was plugging the wound out of the way. Then, gritting his teeth he eased the plastic tip of the syringe into the wound and pressed the plunger to jet the fluid deep into the wound.

The flush started to pour out of the hole, bringing with it clots of blood. Sweating, the pain intense despite the Lidocaine, Talbot could feel the room start to spin and paused to take a deep breath. The local was working fine on the surface but could not reach deep into the wound.

"Did you see how I did that?" he asked Jessie.

"Yes."

"I need you to do that for me again until the drainage has no more clots in it, okay?"

Nodding, Jessie opened another syringe and tentatively inserted the tip into the bullet hole. Glancing at Talbot to gage his reaction, she carefully eased it deeper and started to flush it out further. By the time the syringe was empty, the drainage was clot-free and just slightly pink.

"Okay, good," Talbot said through gritted teeth.

"Now we need to get the bullet out, flush it out again, and sew it back up."

Talbot reached for a set of long-nosed probing forceps. Taking a deep breath, he awkwardly started to slide them into the wound, trying to follow the track of the bullet. Jessie dabbed up the blood that started to leak past the forceps. After a moment he could feel the forceps touching the bullet.

"Can I do something?"

"Yes. The forceps are touching the bullet. If I try to pull it out I might pass out and not finish, so I'm going to let you do this, okay?"

"What do I do?"

"You need to press the tip of the forceps against the bullet, then ease the jaws open. If you get lucky and do it right, the tip of each jaw will slip off and past the bullet. Clamp down and lock the forceps tight. Do you think you can do that?"

Jessie nodded.

"Once you pull it out," he said, pausing as he waited for the spinning room to slow down, "It's going to start bleeding again. You'll have to flush it again, so get a couple of flushes ready. When that's done you'll have to hold some gauze over the hole for a minute or two until the bleeding stops. Then we can tackle the stitches. Okay?"

Jessie nodded again, quickly opened the last two flushes and laid them out ready. Then she gently took the forceps from Talbot. Concentrating, she pushed the forceps slightly deeper to feel the bullet. Closing her eyes, she tried to visualize what she could feel… the narrow bullet track, the tip of the forceps against the bullet, and the bullet itself.

She eased the forceps open slightly, trying to feel the moment when they were open wide enough to get past the bullet. Focused, she ignored Talbot as he groaned, feeling the tips of the forceps suddenly slide forward and around the bullet. Carefully she clamped down on the slug, squeezing hard to make sure of a good grip.

The forceps slipped with a jerk and Talbot passed out.

Grimly she started again, finding the bullet, pushing the forceps past and around. This time, since Talbot was unconscious, she moved the tip around to get a feel for how the slug was positioned. Then she rotated the forceps forty-five degrees and clamped down.

The forceps locked in place.

Taking a deep breath, Jessie carefully started to pull the slug out. She was surprised by the amount of force required, until she realized she was pulling against a vacuum behind the slug

Finally the bullet slid out. Blood started to well out of the bullet hole as she dropped the forceps onto the towel. Then she to rinsed out the wound with the last of the flushes and cleaned the blood off Talbot. Finally she pressed a handful of gauze pads against the wound to manage the slight bleeding as she waited for Talbot to regain consciousness.

After a few minutes Talbot stirred.

"You okay?" she asked.

He looked at her, slightly disoriented, before the timeline fell back into place.

"Okay. Did you get it out?"

"Of course. Piece of cake."

"My daughter is a smart-ass," Talbot muttered, glaring at her in mock anger. "At least the Lidocaine will make stitching easier. Has the bleeding stopped yet?"

Jessie eased the gauze up to check.

"Pretty much."

"Okay, there should be a suture kit in there as well."

Jessie reached over to the Med-Pac and handed him the suture kit. Working carefully, Talbot wiped the surface around the wound thoroughly with more iodine.

"Watch how I do this," Talbot said. Struggling to reach, he managed to finish the first stitch, pulling the knot tight.

"Think you can do that?"

"Duh," she replied.

Taking the suture needle from him, Jessie carefully added several more stitches until the wound was completely closed. Then she gave the area a final wipe clean, slathering the stitches with an antiseptic cream and a pad of gauze and covered the area with what looked like a band aid on steroids.

"Nice work," Talbot said. Taking a deep breath, he sat up gingerly.

Pulling the bloody towel out from under him, he tossed it into a corner of the room with his bloody shirt. Then he eased on a clean shirt before laying back down, his face pale.

"There's another bedroom down the hall for you. Let's try to get some sleep. It's been a long day."

"Okay." She hesitated, about to say something, then turned on her heel and walked out.

09h15, Tuesday January 17th,, 2017, 26th Street, Arlington, VA.

Sleep had all but eluded Talbot. The throbbing in his side and across his shoulder had been a constant and painful reminder of the day before and by seven in the morning he was tired of lying in bed hurting.

Feeling almost human again after a painful shower, he had drifted into the kitchen, made a pot of coffee and rummaged through the refrigerator to see what was available for breakfast.

Deciding on bacon and eggs, he had just pulled the crisped bacon from the skillet and added the eggs to the sizzling fat when Jessie wandered into the kitchen. Talbot watched as, without a word, Jessie found the toaster and started feeding it slices of bread. She generously slathered the hot toast with butter and cut them from corner to corner across the diagonal.

"How do you like your eggs?"

"Sunny side up, runny yolk."

Talbot loaded up their plates and carried them over to the kitchen table. Jessie had already taken a seat, a glass of orange juice in front of her. After reloading his coffee mug Talbot joined her at the table where they took their time eating. Jessie barely picked at her food. Like Talbot she had also spent a fitful night chasing sleep.

"Did you sleep at all?" Talbot asked.

"Not much. Every time I closed my eyes," she started to say, but her sentence trailed off into silence.

Talbot watched as she made a deliberate effort to stay in the now, not allowing her mind to wander back to the night before. Picking up a sliced triangle of toast, she nibbled the points off to make a perfect hexagon and put it back in her plate. Then she started on a second slice.

85

"Do you always do that?" Talbot asked curiously.

"What?"

"The thing with the toast."

"Yeah. Mom said I was weird."

"Well, I cut my toast into perfect bite size triangles, so I can't judge. See?" Talbot said, demonstrating. "It takes me three cuts for every triangle of bread. Weird thing is, I feel like I did a bad job if the triangles aren't exactly the same size and shape."

"I think you're weirder than me," Jessie shrugged.

"Well, I'm older, so I've had more time to practice at it. Want to know something even weirder?"

Jessie nodded.

"I used to try predict the outcome of a mission based on how well the triangles worked out, so I would obsess over making the cuts exactly right."

"Definitely weirder," Jessie confirmed. She picked up her hexagon and used it to swipe up the egg yolk spilled onto her plate, popping it into her mouth. "What's next?"

I didn't get much chance last night," Talbot replied as he started to clear the dishes off the table, "but I need to go through that folder your mom had and see if it can tell us anything."

"Okay, I'm going to take a shower," Jessie said started out the kitchen.

"Hold on," Talbot said. "I made breakfast, at least you can put your plate in the dishwasher."

Jessie rolled her eyes, but picked up her plate and glass, rinsed them in the sink and dropped them into the dishwasher before she wandered down the hallway.

After stacking the rest of the dishes in the dishwasher and starting the wash cycle, Talbot brought the folder out of the office and back into the kitchen. He took inventory of the contents of the folder as he spread all the pages over the kitchen table.

In and of itself, the balance sheet for a company called NeoDine seemed irrelevant. The only point of interest may have been the name Bob Whitfield and a question mark penciled in the corner at the top right of the page. Far in the recesses of Talbot's mind a bell seemed to ring on a memory, but the more he tried to pull it up, the more elusive it became.

There were also two invoices stapled together, both billed to the Department of Defense. Both were cryptic in what the product or service was for, but both were for amounts in excess of fifty million dollars. The first was from a company in Baltimore called GeneSig, while the second was from BioMediCom, located in Arlington, Virginia.

Talbot had spent many years with access to the best and coolest DOD toys. He had even served a stint as a new products specialist, testing the latest weapons and gear the DOD was considering for purchase. He had met hundreds of contractors from every possible company, but neither GeneSig nor BioMediCom rang a bell.

Not that that necessarily means anything, he thought to himself.

Picking up the clipping from the Wall Street Journal, Talbot started to read.

"Will China Impact Your Commodities Portfolio?

China's announcement yesterday that they would halt all export of Neodymium to the West in response to pressure from the IMF to cease their currency exchange manipulations sent shock waves through Wall Street today. China currently controls over ninety percent of the known reserves globally, and the immediate threat of a shortage drove commodity prices soaring for the rare earth metal as manufacturers scrambled to buy up all available reserves in an effort to protect their production lines from a supply-side shortfall.

Neodymium is critical in the manufacture of high-end magnets used in electric cars and wind turbines. Sources stated that, without the two pounds required per vehicle, the critical efficiencies required to make electric cars economically viable may shift sufficiently to drive consumer prices beyond the reach of the average buyer.

More troubling may be the impact on international efforts to reduce greenhouse gases using wind-sourced energy. Every wind turbine requires over two tons of Neodymium-based magnets, without which the energy efficiencies in converting wind power to electricity no longer make sense and the energy generated barely exceeds the effort to produce it.

The global impact of China's decision already has the mining industry scrambling to find alternate reserves, but it may take years to locate viable sources."

Talbot dropped the article back on the kitchen table and sipped his coffee as he tried to make sense of it. The fragrant steam curled up from the mug as he swallowed.

The article seemed just as random as the rest of the pages and Talbot had no expectation that the last document would tie it all together. It didn't.

The last page was just a collection of dots and arrows scattered seemingly randomly over the blank white page. The dots appeared to be arranged in three haphazard verticals.

The left column used three dots arranged one above the other with the center dot slightly wide left. The right column was just two dots and the gap between them seemed roughly the same as the upper and lower dots of the left column.

Halfway between the outer columns was a third. It looked exactly like the column on the left, but the three dots were closer together and the column was sloped slightly downhill from left to right. The middle column was centered between the other two columns, both vertically and horizontally. Together the three columns hinted at an hour glass shape on its side.

Each of the corner dots had an arrow pointing away from it, the four arrows together implying that the entire image was subject to rotation. In the bottom corner was a note in the same handwriting as before.

The not asked a question… "What is Phoenix Dept.?"

Talbot was still trying to understand why the hourglass image seemed so familiar when Jessie walked in from the hallway on his right, dressed in clothes she had picked out from the store room the night before.

"Remind you of anything?" he asked, handing her the sheet.

"Oh sure," she said without hesitation. She turned the page to horizontal format, standing the hourglass up, and slid it back to him.

"Orion constellation. Although I don't know about the Phoenix thing."

It took Talbot just a second, but with the page re-oriented and the image vertical it was immediately obvious… the dots were the stars of Orion the Hunter.

"Well," he said, "That just adds to the puzzle."

He picked up the newspaper article.

"Did your mom do any investing?"

"I know she had a retirement account of some kind through work."

"Sure, but did she do any trading herself?"

"Like on Wall Street?"

"Yes."

"No, I'm pretty sure she wasn't interested." Jessie picked up the other sheets and glanced at them. "You know, you can Google these names, see what comes up."

"Good idea."

As Talbot stood up, the cell phone in his pocket vibrated and Jessie's dinged. Pulling it out of his pocket he checked the screen. Every surveillance trigger on the perimeter of the property had turned red. Talbot touched the lock-down button on the screen and hidden door bolts, built in the style of a gun safe and concealed in the entrance doors to the house slid quietly into place.

"C'mon, Jessie, grab your bag. We've gotta go."

Moving quickly Talbot gathered up the papers and moved into the computer room to get eyes-on the outside of the house. The surveillance monitors hidden in the trees used infra-red and the SWAT team moving into position outside showed up like lighthouses at night.

Keeping an eye on the surveillance cameras Talbot stuffed the papers into the duffel bag, then quickly strapped on both firearms while he waited for Jessie to get her bag. Talbot was pulling on his parka as Jessie came back into the room, her coat on and bag slung over her shoulder. They hurried into the bathroom and Jessie placed her hand over the Ansel Adams picture again. The concealed door swung open and battery-powered emergency LED lights on the floor automatically turned on as they walked in. Talbot hit the large red panic button on the inside wall and the door swung closed and locked.

Talbot grabbed up a handful of cash bundles from the supplies while Jessie went to wait for him at the far wall. Talbot nodded at her and she placed her palm on the second picture. The image changed to show a camera view of a cluttered car port somewhere outside. Inside was a what looked like a run down, older model Ford Taurus. At the bottom of the screen were two icons, one red and one green. There was nobody visible in the carport, so Talbot touched the green button and the wall swung open.

Stepping through, they followed a dimly lit tunnel to another door at the end. There Talbot found and activated another keypad. With Jessie watching he closed the door at the other end of the tunnel behind them. A small digital clock beside the door started counting down from sixty seconds.

Without a second glance Talbot led Jessie to the far end of the tunnel and activated the last touchscreen keypad. The screen showed the same countdown screen, as well as carport, still unoccupied. Talbot paused, watching the seconds count down.

As the clock ran down to zero they could hear the distinct but muffled sounds of distant explosions coming from the far end of the tunnel as the decoy incendiaries in the house started to detonate in sequence, destroying everything inside the house. Taking that as his cue Talbot opened the last door and eased out in to the carport, Jessie behind him.

10h10, South Ives Street, Arlington, VA.

"What are we even doing here?"

Tall and heavily muscled, Special Agent Carter was neither bright nor enthusiastic. He was obviously unhappy about watching the advancing SWAT team from a distance. Lacking any imagination, he was almost comically the classic stereotype of all brawn and no brains.

"Because a cabbie saw the Amber Alert and said he dropped a cop-killing, hostage-taking, secret-stealing bad man off at that house," Special Agent Scott replied impatiently.

"So? What's that got to do with us? It's not like we're going to help them breach."

"Because the SWAT team does not have Top Secret clearance. You, on the other hand and for some reason which completely escapes me, have Top Secret clearance. I have Top Secret clearance. The stolen papers are likely Top Secret. We are here to recover the papers."

"That's just dumb."

Resisting the urge to point out to Special Agent Carter that the only dumb thing about the situation was, in fact, Special Agent Carter, Agent Kelly Scott led them to the edge of the property where they could be concealed behind the brick wall of an old car port with a dirt floor. The carport had been cut deep into the steep slope behind it with the back wall serving double duty as a retaining wall.

Inside the car port was a dirty white Ford Taurus shoved in among the clutter of old paint cans and rotting lumber. The huge oil stain under the engine was a clear violation of city ordinances. A thick layer of dust had settled over the car, the oil stain, and everything else. There were no tire tracks in the dirt leading in and out. It would have taken a very suspicious mind to notice that the tires were almost new and the dust on the windows very light. The car looked abandoned.

"We'll wait here," Scott said.

Taller than average at five feet nine inches, she was dressed in a black pantsuit with a cobalt blouse open at the throat. She wore no jewelry of any kind and, blessed with flawless skin and high cheek bones, did not bother much with makeup. Her auburn hair was pulled back into a pony tail and her eyes were hidden behind dark sunglasses. Growing up competing aggressively with four older brothers, she was fit, lean and much stronger than she looked.

As they watched, the SWAT team ahead of them deployed rapidly into position for a simultaneous front and rear breach. From the outside, at least, the house appeared quiet, even deserted, but the breach teams were taking no chances. The breach would be hard and fast.

Without warning a series of explosions echoed through the quiet neighborhood from deep inside the house, hurling glass from the windows out into the yard and driving the SWAT team to ground in search of cover. Flames started to twist and curl out of the shattered windows, the twisting red and orange in stark contrast to the billowing, acrid smoke pouring out of the place.

A final explosion, much more powerful, shook the house to its foundations as the last explosive device completely destroyed everything in the store room.

Stunned, Scott and Carter could only watch in disbelief as the house started to tilt to one side, the structural integrity severely compromised by the blast. As they watched the assortment of flames through the house started to coalesce into a single, towering flame.

Positioned closer to the carport, Carter heard a slight scraping sound and turned to peer around the corner of the brick wall and into the carport. A portion of the back wall and a pile of rubble and junk was slowly swinging into the carport, pushing a small pile of debris across the dirt floor. Puzzled, Carter stepped into the carport just as Talbot and Jessie stepped through the opening that had materialized in the back wall.

"Hey!" Carter shouted, reaching for his weapon. Without pausing Talbot dropped the duffel bag and moved in fast, getting in close to the much bigger man. Gripping the barrel before it could line up, Talbot twisted down and out, the pressure on Carter's wrist forcing the gun free. Carter quickly smashed the gun Talbot had taken from his hand and threw a wild punch at Talbot's head. Talbot ducked, stepping in as he pivoted fast at the hips, and drove his fist hard into Carter's short ribs three times before Carter could drop his elbows to cover up.

Staying in close, Talbot followed up by smashing the heel of his hand up under Carter's chin, snapping his head back. Carter stumbled backwards, already in trouble, as Talbot followed, his straight left measuring the distance for a fast right cross that connected right on the button. Carter's eyes glazed over, and his knees buckled as he went to the ground.

"Don't move," Talbot heard behind him. Turning his head carefully he saw Scott twenty feet away, her gun lined up unwavering on his chest. Watching how fast Talbot had managed Carter, Scott had immediately recognized the danger of being too close to a man this fast and dangerous. She had backed up far enough away to keep him at a distance and maintain the advantage. Talbot measured the distance in his mind, judging the risks, before he slowly raised his hands over his head.

"Come around here behind me," Scott said to Jessie.

Thinking fast, Jessie realized the woman in black thought she was a hostage. She nodded and moved wide around Talbot, putting the Taurus between her and Scott. With the car hiding her hands, she slid her hand into her backpack to grip the Glock she had kept from the night before.

"Lay down on the ground, spread-eagled," Scott instructed Talbot as Jessie moved around her. Talbot didn't move, keeping Scott's attention focused on him.

Behind Scott Jessie lifted the Glock free and Talbot smiled. His eyes shifted to look behind Scott. "You good?" he asked Jessie.

"I'm good," she replied. "Drop the gun."

Carefully Scott twisted her head and saw Jessie, nervously on edge but poised and ready, the gun aimed steadily at her back.

"Please do as she says," Talbot added.

Slowly Scott lowered her weapon to the ground.

"Take ten steps towards me away from your gun, then turn around, please," Talbot said.

Scott complied, her eyes puzzled. Talbot quickly and efficiently searched her and Carter, removing their handcuffs. Then he dragged Carter back into the back of the carport.

"Step over to your colleague, please, and cuff your right wrist to his ankle."

"I'm not letting a cop-killer shoot me tied up like a dog. Especially not to him," she added, she said bitterly. "You'll never get away with this."

Talbot sighed.

"First, if I wanted to kill you, you would be dead already. Second, if I was a cop-killer, you would be dead already. And third, if I was who they say I am, I would have triggered those explosives after SWAT were inside to kill them, and you would still be dead already."

She frowned, thinking it through.

"Please, just cuff yourself to him so I don't have to knock you out. I would really rather not, but time is wasting."

Scott reached a decision and moved over towards Carter, cuffing herself to his ankle.

"Just surrender. Even if you're not a cop-killer, the cops think you are and you know how they get. You're not going to get far, and I can at least keep you safe."

Talbot studied her for a moment, then he reached a decision.

"Jessie, let me have that gun, please. Then you can choose. You can get in the car and go with me, or you can stay here with the FBI."

Jessie wordlessly handed him the gun and climbed into the car. Talbot dropped the clip out and cleared the chamber. Pocketing the clip and loose round, Talbot placed the gun against the wall, collected his bag and dropped it into the back of the car. Then he faced Scott again.

"That gun killed Amy Morgan in the park last night. She was my ex-wife and she was bringing Jessie, my daughter, to see me. I killed them to defend Jessie and Amy after they were attacked. Do yourself a favor and find out who owns that gun, but I would bet everything it belongs to a government operative. That's why we won't go with you... even if I thought I could trust you, I don't think you have the power to protect us."

Opening the car door, Talbot paused.

"By the way, what's wrong with him?" he asked, pointing at Carter.

"What do you mean?"

"You said you particularly did not want to die handcuffed to him. Why?"

"He's an idiot."

Talbot laughed as he climbed into the car and shut the door. He reached under the console and pressed a hidden switch. The engine started, immediately settling into a throaty, growling idle. The car had clearly never been abandoned and there was equally clearly nothing stock about what was under the hood.

Slipping the car into gear and pulling his ball cap lower over his face, Talbot slowly eased it out of the carport and turned north along South Ives. Scott tried to read the registration plate as he drove away, but the deliberately thick coat of dirt and grime made it completely illegible.

Just up the street he glanced to his right down 25th Street and saw a black Crown Victoria with government plates parked out of view of the safe house. He turned down the street and he pulled up beside the car. Reaching into his bag he pulled out one of the three burner phones from the store room and climbed out of the Taurus. He opened the driver's door, slipped the phone up under the driver's seat, climbed back into the Taurus, and headed east, turning north onto South Eads Street where 25th dead-ended.

21h30, Washington Boulevard, Arlington, VA.

Drifting north along Washington Boulevard through Arlington, Scott was gloomily aware that she needed a life. The problem was that her investigations usually kept her working long into the night, making a social life extremely difficult.

Besides, people were a constant disappointment. The feeling probably stemmed from the fact that work usually exposed her to the worst in people, but nobody matched up to her standards. Whatever the reason, here she was once again, headed back to her apartment in Arlington late in the evening, tired and frustrated.

After querying the FBI database for the owner of the Glock Talbot had left against the wall, her embarrassment at being found handcuffed to Carter had been replaced by a nagging suspicion that there was something wrong with the back story of the case. The gun was owned by a Federal office and issued to one of the agents killed in the park. Ballistics had tied it to the deaths of Amy Morgan, all three agents in the park, as well as a body found in Morgan's apartment.

The official story being circulated among the local cops was that Talbot's PTSD had snapped, he had killed his ex-wife and kidnapped his daughter, and the agents killed had been on assignment to protect Morgan. But Talbot's questions kept nagging at her. The pattern did not fit and nothing about the case made sense.

Her cell phone rang, interrupting her train of thought. Absently she reached for it on the seat beside her, but it was quiet. It rang again, and the sound seemed to come from under her seat. Carefully watching the road she reached down, located the phone and pulled it out. It was not hers.

The phone rang again, and she pressed the button to answer.

"Hello?"

"This is Talbot."

"You know, I'm not even surprised at this point. Is Jessie safe?"

"Of course. There aren't any Feds shooting at her right now."

"Touché. Where are you?"

"Panera Bread on 5th."

"Somehow I don't believe you."

Talbot chuckled.

"Who are you, Talbot?" Scott asked. "I tried to look you up, but the files are marked Secret."

"I used to work for the DOD on some classified projects, but I retired years ago. Why did the Feds kill my ex?"

"They say you did. Not to mention four of her bodyguards."

"Well, there's all kinds of things wrong with that story. I had no motive and besides, why would she need a six-man protection detail? She was just a Senator's aide."

"They say you killed her to steal top secret files and sell them to the Russians."

"Even more stupid. If that was true, I would have brought my own weapon, not been forced to steal one from some bogus security detail."

"Well, there is certainly a lot of hoopla about a missing file."

"Makes sense. It looked like those Feds were trying to take the file from Amy and killed her when she wouldn't give it up."

"And where do you come into it?"

"I was waiting in the restaurant across the street. Come to think of it, I never paid for the coffee, so you should be able to verify that if you like."

"And you saw what happened?"

"I saw them get out the car across the street, so I walked outside to meet them and saw it all. I was too late to save her."

"Do you have the file?"

"Yes, but nothing in it makes sense. All random rubbish and nothing is even marked classified."

"Wait a minute. You said she is a Senator's aide. Do you know which Senator?"

"Williams."

"Senator Williams collapsed and died in the Senate yesterday afternoon." She paused, thinking. "What's in the folder?"

"I can show you if you want to meet alone, but like I say, nothing in it makes sense."

"How do I know I can trust you?"

"Well, for one thing, you're still alive."

"There is that," she conceded.

"Besides, don't you think I am at a greater risk?"

"Meaning?"

"Meaning how do I know I can trust you?"

The light in front of her changed to red, and she coasted to a stop.

"You can choose where to meet."

"Not my city. Suggestions?"

Scott drummed her fingers on the steering wheel, trying to think of a safe place to meet. Suddenly the passenger door opened, and Talbot slid into the seat beside her.

She stared at him for a moment.

"Or we can meet right now in my car in the middle of an intersection."

"Funny, I had the same idea," Talbot grinned.

The light changed, and Scott started to move forward.

"You've been following me?"

"Well, sort of. There's a GPS tracker in that phone I gave you. Take a right here and pull in to that first parking lot on the right. Jessie is behind us and I don't want to lose her."

Scott followed instructions as a set of headlights followed her into the parking lot. Scott parked and waited as the Taurus pulled in beside her. Jessie climbed out, wiping the steering wheel and door handle down before sliding into the backseat.

"Are you okay, Jessie?" Scott asked.

"I'd be fine of the government wasn't trying to kill me," Jessie replied acidly. "Are you sure we can trust her?" she asked Talbot.

"Not entirely, but I don't see that we have much choice right now."

"Well, I don't," Jessie muttered.

She pulled out her ear buds and put them into her ears and turned to face out the window, ignoring them.

Talbot sighed, then decided not to rise to the bait. Jessie's run-in with the NSA had not exactly given her the warm and fuzzies about government to start with and after the night before her distrust was obvious. She had been arguing against talking to Scott from the first moment Talbot had mentioned it.

Talbot had tried explaining that it was most unlikely that the entire government was rogue, but she would not, as she put it, drink his Kool Aid.

"Here's the folder," he said instead, handing the plain, unmarked manila folder over to Scott.

"That's it?" she asked puzzled as she flipped through it quickly. "It makes absolutely no sense."

"Exactly."

"I mean, the invoices *might* be important, but they could just as easily be for toilet paper or paperclips. What's this Phoenix Department?"

"I was hoping you could tell me," he replied.

"Seriously?" Jessie's voice rose irritably up from behind, her voice clearly communicating her current opinion of Talbot. "Why don't you just look it up?"

Scott and Talbot exchanged glances.

"That's a good idea, Jessie," Scott said carefully, "but I was just thinking if they are crooked and we dig too hard into this they might trace the query back to us."

"So use an internet café." She passed her phone to the front. "I googled and found one called Mocha Café and Pastry literally around the corner. We can use their computer and IP address."

Talbot looked back at Jessie, then at Scott. "I think we just got schooled by a youngster," he smiled.

"I think you're right. She's smarter than you, isn't she?"

"Yeah, I'm pretty sure of it," Talbot said with a rueful grin.

They all climbed out of the car into the icy night air and walked around the corner. Half a block down the street they crossed over to the Café. The siren call of pastries and coffee drifted around the door, warm and sweet. Talbot held the door open for them to enter.

"Find us a computer out of the way, please Jessie. I'm going to get us something to eat."

"No way, I'm starving. I want to see what they've got." She walked over to the glass-fronted display cases where a rail thin girl with tendencies towards Gothic tragedy reluctantly put her phone down and came over to take her order. Scott chuckled at the look on Talbot's face and followed Jessie to the counter.

"I'll take a Bear Claw and chocolate macadamia cookie, please," Jessie said. "Oh, and a milk."

"Lemon Bar and small coffee for me, please," Scott said.

"And I'll take a Bear Claw, Chocolate éclair and large coffee, please," Talbot said. "Also we need about 30 minutes on one of your computers."

"Okay. Free to use, so whatever."

Scott exchanged a bemused look with Talbot, but Jessie did not seem to notice the girl's epic lack of customer service.

The girl took her time as she collected their order and rang it up. "Thirty-three dollars and seventy-two cents," she said.

Talbot peeled two twenty-dollar bills out of his billfold and paid as the ladies wandered to the back with their pastries and drinks. He collected his coffee and followed them to find Jessie already in the chair in front of the computer.

"Don't you think I should...," Scott started to say.

Talbot just shook his head with a grin. "You may be good. You may even be very good. But Jessie over there is entirely out of your league."

"For real?"

"Oh yes... she hacked the NSA, then schooled them on how not to get hacked."

"No kidding?"

"Nope."

"What should I start with?" Jessie asked.

"Phoenix. The rest is probably public information and will be easy to research. We can find it from anywhere else without hacking into any servers." Talbot said.

Jessie opened a small window on the screen with a timer on it, then started typing fast. The screen flickered and flashed as she stacked a defensive wall of IP addresses between herself and the target. Then she twisted her way through a series of log in windows, barely pausing as she bounced through DOD security firewalls.

"What's the timer for?" Scott asked, impressed.

"Seriously?" Jessie said impatiently. "We only get a few minutes before the system recognizes a hack and starts hunting us through the stacked IP addresses I routed us through."

Talbot grinned.

"Never mind, I didn't know either."

Talbot and Scott finished their pastries and sipped their coffee, watching as Jessie obliterated the security around the DOD files.

"You sure make it look easy," Talbot said.

"It wasn't easy the first time, but now I can get in and out pretty much at will."

"How did you get into the DOD so easily?"

"I hacked the NSA, right?"

"Right."

"Well, the NSA, DOD, NASA, FBI, pretty much everybody... they all used the same lowest-bid vendor to build their security. He was cheap because he used the same security structure for all of them. I figured the NSA never even thought to warn the other departments of the holes in their security, and I was right."

"Government at its finest," Scott muttered.

Setting up a search interface, Jessie keyed in the word "Phoenix" and hit enter. As the search started grinding through the DOD servers, Jessie munched on her Bear Claw.

"Oh wow," she said.

"'Oh wow' what?" Talbot responded.

Jessie pointed to the domino graphic of stacked IP addresses she was using. The first one had turned red and, even as they watched, the next in line also went red.

"Are they already tracing back?"

"Yes, I just got a hit on Phoenix and someone is already hunting us. We've only got about five minutes and then I'll have to get out."

"Five minutes? That's all?"

"Yes, I've never seen anything hit back so fast."

"See if you can find out what they do."

Jessie kept tapping at the keys, but each window auto-closed within seconds of opening. Typing fast, Jessie launched a script that bombarded the security defense with decoy attacks. As she worked she managed to pull up a chart which outlined the Section Chiefs and who reported where. The window closed almost immediately as Jessie struggled to stay ahead of the defense.

"There's no way this defense is automated," Jessie said, "it's way too reactive."

23h15, Phoenix Headquarters, Washington, D.C.

Lounging deep in his chair and half asleep in the dimly lit cubicle, an anonymous shadow watched the array of dashboards spread out across six large monitors arranged side by side in front of her. Each dashboard was tracking a different set of metrics measuring the security health of the Phoenix network.

The network was already buried so deeply within the government servers and inside so many layers that the security vigil was typically the most boring assignment within the team. In the eight years since the department had been established the dashboards had never gone red, so the shadow was startled when the color shifted.

Jerking upright, she started tapping on the keyboard, running system checks to verify that the breach was real. She picked up her phone, dialed an extension and waited for the call to be picked up.

"Boss, we're being hacked."

"Chase it down, I'll be right there."

Working fast, the security technician triggered a tracking software to locate the source and started isolating the unidentified pings, blocking access to the screens and folders as fast as they were being pulled up.

Tremaine arrived, peering over her shoulder.

"What do we know?"

"Whoever it was didn't bounce off the outside firewalls much before getting in. They've hacked in before."

"Into us?"

"No, not us specifically. We would have known."

"What are they after?"

"I don't think they know for sure, they're all over the place."

La Salle walked in.

"Any key words?"

"Not really anything I recognize. Mostly just about the work we do. Oh, and they pinged a couple of company names I don't know."

"What companies?" La Salle asked sharply.

"BioMediCom and GeneSig."

"Where are they hacking from?"

"Not sure yet, but the search has narrowed it to within twenty miles."

"Where?"

She pointed to a map on one of the screens. It showed a circle with a twenty-mile radius hovering over Washington Boulevard.

"Tremaine, text me the exact address as soon as you know," La Salle said as he turned and walked out.

"You heard the man," Tremaine said. "How long?"

"Almost there. Our protocol runs about twenty percent faster than anybody else's."

Even as Tremaine watched, a window popped up on the screen. Tremaine reached for his phone and sent a text.

"Mocha Café at 2720 Washington Boulevard in Arlington."

23h20, Mocha Café, Washington Boulevard, Arlington, VA.

The stop watch Jessie was using to mark when she absolutely had to get out still had thirty seconds left when she started to shut down her efforts. Talbot tapped her on the shoulder.

"Let it run to the end, Jessie."

"They'll be able to track us here," Jessie replied, her tone making it clear her opinion of Talbot was not particularly favorable.

"Right, but if they come here I might I be able to see who they are."

"We're the bait?"

"Yes, but they won't see us. Stay busy in there and try to time getting out to exactly after they bust that last IP address. I want them to think we pushed the envelope just too far for our own good."

Jessie shrugged and started a search on the assassination of Kennedy as she watched the domino graphic.

"Kennedy?" Scott asked, puzzled.

"Sure, every hacking conspiracy theorist would dig for that. Maybe it will throw them off who we are."

The last IP address went red. With a few quick keystrokes she shut it all down, leaning back in the chair.

"They were better than anybody else I've hacked," she conceded.

"Well, you tried," Talbot said. "Pity we couldn't get anything, though. Those screens closed so fast I never got a chance to read anything."

"We-e-e-ell, not exactly," Jessie said, her self-satisfaction spilling over into a grin.

"Why, what do you have up your sleeve?" Scott asked curiously.

"I ran a script in the background that takes high-speed screenshots and then stitches them together into a video. We can pause the video on any screen shot we want."

Scott looked at Talbot.

"She's smarter than both of us put together," Scott conceded, "But we may only have a couple of minutes."

Jessie opened up the default video player on the PC, found the file her script had created, set the mode to half-speed and hit play. Silently they watched as the video provided a play-by-play of Jessie's work.

"Go back a couple of frames," Talbot said suddenly.

Jessie clicked backwards one frame at a time until Talbot stopped her. One of the opened windows on the screen had a layout of the reporting hierarchy for Phoenix.

"Why does the name 'Bob Whitfield' ring a bell?" Scott puzzled out loud, pointing to the name at the top of the hierarchy.

"Same name on that Balance Sheet in the folder they're after," Talbot said. "What puzzles me is that Phoenix looks like it has no congressional oversight beyond Whitfield."

"But that's a direct violation of every rulebook we've got," Scott said. "The whole point of the government is that there needs to be some level of oversight at least."

"Exactly. But it certainly explains why they think they can operate outside the law."

"If those guys are here in D.C. they may be headed to us right now," Jessie said. "As good as they were, they may have started a team in our general direction before they had a final address. They could get here a lot sooner than you think."

"Good call," Talbot said. "Let's get outta here and find some place to lay low. While we try to figure this out."

Collecting their jackets, they quickly left the café and crossed the street heading back to their vehicles, their breath in the cold air a faint ghost around them.

"Follow me to my apartment," Scott said suddenly, reaching a decision. "We can work on this there and you can stay out of sight."

"Okay, good idea" Talbot said.

"Can I ride with you?" Jessie asked Scott, turning her back on Talbot.

"Of course, but don't think I don't know you want to keep an eye on me to make sure I don't make a call or two," she smiled.

Jessie's shrug said a silent "whatever". Talbot frowned at Jessie but decided to keep his opinion to himself. As they arrived at the vehicles, he paused, his hand on the driver's door.

"Before we go, I'm going to drive around the corner to where I can sit for a minute and see who shows up looking for us."

"Okay," Scott said as she climbed into her car, Jessie joining her. "We'll wait here."

Talbot climbed into his seat, started the engine and slipped into gear. Driving around the block he found a small parking lot for a construction business across the street from the café. He backed into a parking space next to an assortment of other older vehicles and turned the car off.

Within minutes two black Tahoe's with tinted windows slid to a stop in front of the café and disgorged a fast-moving SWAT team. As they crashed through the door and into the café,

Talbot thought of the Goth girl no doubt on her phone behind the counter as the team burst into the empty shop. He could almost see her finish her text, look up, say "whatever", and start tweeting the event to her following of five. Talbot chuckled to himself at the thought.

As the last of the team pushed into the café, the front passenger door of the lead Tahoe swung open and tall man dressed in an expensive suit and coat stepped out. There was an almost palpable air of power and authority around him. As he turned his head to look up and down the street, he was lit up clearly in the headlights of a passing car. Swarthy and dark skinned, a faded scar started a little above the bridge of his nose and ran up into his hairline where it made the hair around it blaze white.

"Now just who are you?" Talbot wondered to himself.

After a couple of minutes, the SWAT team started to trickle out again, one of them joining the man with the scarred face on the sidewalk. After a brief conversation, both cars finished loading up, and they all drove quietly off down the street. Talbot waited a few minutes more.

He was just about to start the car when another black Tahoe cruised slowly past shining a spotlight into the dark corners of the street. Talbot ducked down below the dash, waiting for them to pass. After a few more minutes he drove back around the corner, pulling up with his driver-side window beside Scott's. Scott rolled down her window.

"Did you see anything?" Scott asked.

Talbot quickly described what he had seen.

"They must have been close to get here so fast."

"Not just that, but they run a very high tech, sophisticated operation to get the address that fast. At least the guy with the blaze will be easy to spot again."

"Sounds like it," Scott agreed. "You didn't want to follow them?"

"Thought about it, but I'm glad I decided not to. That sleeper at the end would have spotted me."

"Just as well you have a suspicious mind."

Talbot grinned at her, the lines around his eyes deepening.

Scott had a sudden, unbidden thought of "if only". Irritated, she shook off the feeling.

"Ready?" she asked.

"Sure, lead the way. Jessie, you good?"

"Okay," Jessie said, not bothering to glance up.

"Okay. I'll be right behind you."

Scott slipped into gear and eased forward as Talbot followed. Turning east on North Pershing, Scott led the way to her apartment at the Virginia Square Towers on Fairfax, just minutes away.

Chapter Four

"Good news and bad news," La Salle said, sitting at his desk with the phone cradled between his ear and shoulder.

"It's after midnight, so get to the point," Whitfield snapped.

"Okay. Bad... we got hacked. Good... we managed to keep them out and track them to an internet café. Bad... they were gone by the time we got there. Good... the place had cameras on the computers, so we know who they are. Bad... it was Talbot and his daughter."

"How could you let this happen?" Whitfield's voice demanded, jumping out of the phone at La Salle.

"There's more," La Salle added, calmly. "There's three of them now."

"Who is it?"

"We don't know. It was a woman, but we never got her face."

"What were they after?"

"They were searching on Kennedy's assassination, Phoenix, BioMediCom and GeneSig, but they got no hits. Only thing they learned is that Phoenix is part of the DOD."

"What's with the Kennedy thing?"

"Probably smoke screen."

"And all they got was that Phoenix is a part of the DOD?"

"As far as we can tell, yes."

"Nothing to brag about," Whitfield said acidly.

"True, but we know something else. We know that folder has something in it about BioMediCom and GeneSig."

"Do I need to tell you this is priority one?"

"No sir."

Whitfield broke the connection. Putting the encrypted desk phone back in its cradle, La Salle thought for a moment. Then he dialed Tremaine's number. The earpiece clicked as Tremaine picked up.

"Yes sir."

"Don't you sleep?" La Salle asked irritably.

"Figured you might need me."

"Get everyone in. Everyone. I want every video from every camera around that café, traffic cameras especially. I want to know who that woman was, what they're driving, anything. They may be hiding out with her."

"On it."

"One more thing. I want an hourly review of any footage coming in from GeneSig and BioMediCom."

La Salle hung up.

Scott's Apartment, Virginia Square Towers, Arlington, VA.

"I like your apartment," Jessie said to Scott, wandering around.

"Thank you. Make yourself at home."

The single bedroom apartment was slightly over five hundred square feet with an open format. The bathroom door was immediately to the right as you went in the main entrance, with a set of accordion-style doors just past it which concealed the built-in washer and dryer. A coat closet was set into the wall across the bathroom door, with the bedroom door beside it across the hallway from the washer and dryer. As you walked further into the apartment through an open galley-style kitchen, the living space opened out behind the bedroom. The entire far wall was floor-to-ceiling windows looking out over the city lights.

Rising above the dark laminate hard-wood flooring, the subtle blue walls were trimmed out with white baseboards and crown molding to make the rooms feel larger and more opulent than they really were.

The décor was light with pops of color, but the apartment looked more staged than lived in. It was clear that Scott was something of a workaholic and didn't spend much time at home.

Jessie opened the refrigerator. Almost empty, there were just a few bottles of beer, a half box of canned Sprite and several boxes of leftover Chinese food.

"How old is the Chinese food?"

"From last night, it should be good."

Jessie popped a box of Lo Mein into the microwave for a moment and carried the steaming box over to the couch. Tilting the box over slightly to slide the food to the edge, she used a fork to shovel a large bite into her mouth.

"Beer?" Scott asked Talbot as she pulled open the refrigerator.

"Please."

Scott pulled a couple of Blue Moon's out of the refrigerator and passed one over to Talbot. He winced as he reached for it. Opening the bottle, he took a swig. Scott held out her hand to take the bottle cap from him.

"You okay?"

"He was shot," Jessie said as she finished the food. "He probably needs to change his bandages."

Scott raised an eyebrow. "Shot?"

"Twice."

"I'm okay for now," Talbot said. "Just stiff. Jessie, you think you can get some sleep on that couch?"

Jessie measured it with her eyes. "Easily."

"Where were you planning to sleep?" Scott asked Talbot.

"Floor is fine if you've got an extra pillow."

"If Jessie is okay with it, I've got a big bed. We can share, and you can get the couch."

"That okay with you, Jessie?" Talbot asked.

"Whatever. I'm going to grab a shower after I eat and crash."

"Let me get the First Aid kit out of the bathroom first," Scott said.

Jessie nodded past a mouthful of Lo Mein. Scott disappeared down the hallway and into the bathroom where she started rummaging through the cabinets.

"You rode with her, Jessie. Think we can trust her?"

Jessie looked at him and swallowed before answering.

"Probably."

"So maybe I was right?"

"Maybe."

She stood up and walked into the kitchen with the empty Chinese food box. She tossed it in the trash and pulled a Sprite out of the refrigerator.

She popped it open as she walked back in to the den and picked up her back pack. Then she turned to walk out, stopped, and half-turned back to face Talbot.

"I like her."

Scott walked back into the den with the First Aid kit, passing Jessie on her way out. The bathroom door closed and a moment later the shower water started running.

"Come here to the kitchen and let me see what we're dealing with," Scott instructed as she unpacked the medical kit onto the high table in the dining area. "The light is better."

"You have experience?"

"Some."

Talbot removed his shirt and sat in one of the bar stools at the table beside Scott's stack of medical supplies. Scott's eyebrows lifted slightly as she noted the old bullet scars in his chest.

"She's a great kid," Scott said as she peeled the bandage away from the shoulder wound.

"She is, although she's not showing it too much right now. One minute she likes me, then next she wants me dead."

"I think she's a very angry young lady. She told me a little about you not being around, but she was sketchy on some of the background," Scott replied. "So who exactly are you?" she asked.

"Retired Delta Force."

"That certainly explains how you managed to do so much damage in the last couple of days. And the scars?" she asked, pointing at them.

"Which ones?"

"The bullet holes will do for a start," she said as she worked on his shoulder.

"My team was sent into a hot zone for a hostile extract ahead of a general offensive on Kabul. He was a bomb maker and brass wanted to get hands on him before the he could disappear. Bad Intel as usual. They underestimated the numbers on the ground and we were mown down. I was shot twice in the chest and wound up with a collapsed lung. I managed to hide among the dead until the Rangers found me a few hours later, barely alive."

"The bomb maker?"

"They hit him with a drone as he tried to get out of the city."

"And the other scars?"

"Cigarette burns."

"You were tortured?"

"Yes."

Scott shifted her attention to the wound in Talbot's side.

"Who did the stitches?"

"Jessie."

"Nice job."

"Never fails to impress."

Carefully, Scott wiped the area down with alcohol before she started wrapping the wound again.

"So why were you tortured?"

"Another extract and more bad Intel. We made the grab, but the primary extract was compromised. I took rear guard headed to the secondary and managed to lead the chase away before I got caught. Some ex-Spetsnaz figured to make me tell them where the extract was."

"What happened?"

"The boys made it to the extract, delivered the package and came back for me. Surprised the hell out of him."

Scott finished wrapping the wound in Talbot's side and moved over to one of the bar stools. She perched herself up on it and watched as Talbot pulled his shirt on. Catching herself watching how he moved, she frowned in irritation at herself. She could not remember the last time a man had captured her interest, and the circumstances were hardly ideal.

"What happened with Jessie?" She asked, redirecting her thoughts.

Talbot grimaced.

"Long story."

"I've got time."

Talbot paused, thinking, trying to find a simple explanation.

"Her mom only married me to get an advantage in her career. She figured being married to a Special Ops guy would be something she could brag on. I was just a check mark on her resume'. Jessie was an accident, and she always resented Jessie for it."

"Why didn't you see Jessie all those years?"

"Her mom figured to get a sympathy bump in her career dealing with a supposed abusive relationship, so she claimed I had PTSD and was a danger to them. The judge made sue I would go to jail if I went near them. It took years, but a different judge finally ruled in my favor two days ago."

119

"And were you?"

"Was I what?"

"A danger."

"No, but I did have PTSD. I wound up on the streets for a few years until a buddy of mine tracked me down and helped me get straight."

"One of my brothers has PTSD. He was in Afghanistan, so I learned quite a lot about it. How you doing now?"

"Still good."

Scott watched as Talbot went quiet, remembering. Shaking his head to clear out the cobwebs, he reached for his beer and took a swallow.

"What happened after that?" she asked.

"He put me up for a few months while I got on my feet again."

"What were you doing?"

"Stocking shelves in Walmart at night."

"And now?"

"I got an idea while I worked there and sold the patent. Now I live off that."

"What was the idea?"

"Part of the sale is that I can't talk about it, sorry."

"Oh, okay." Disappointed, she took a sip of her beer.

"What about you?" Talbot asked.

"Not much to tell, really. Only daughter, four older brothers. My dad and his brothers were all cops. All except one of my brothers and all my cousins are cops. Even my oldest nephew is in police academy. I always competed with my brothers, so I joined the FBI instead to outdo them."

"Picking up on a theme here," Talbot joked.

"You think?" Scott laughed.

"And not married, I take it?"

"No. I guess my standards are too high. My brothers don't help, either."

"How so?"

"I know they want the best for me, but they do tend to make it tough on anyone I introduce to the family."

"And their opinion matters?"

"Sure. My brother's and cousins wives all went through the same family scrutiny before they married. Something must be working because they've all got happy marriages. No divorces, happy kids, the whole thing. We're a close family, so I guess having a lot of eyes looking for a deal breaker helps to protect the whole family."

"How do you mean?"

"Well, cops see too many domestic disturbance calls. Nobody wants that in our family, so the whole family has to approve of the future spouse."

"That can make it tough."

"Sure, but divorce hurts the extended family as well, especially with kids in the mix. They're just trying to improve the odds for everybody."

"Never thought about it that way, but it makes perfect sense."

"What about your family?"

"I never knew my parents. I started in a foster care as a baby. My foster parents were testing the adoption waters because they couldn't have kids. Turns out they were trying to use me as the glue for their marriage. It didn't work."

"What happened?"

"They fought and argued so much for eight years that they made me a tough kid to be around. When they finally broke up I wound up in the foster system again. Nobody wanted to adopt a kid like me, so I joined the army as soon as I could. Turned out I was really good at it."

"Delta Force? I would say so."

Talbot shrugged.

"What did you find out so far?" Jessie asked walking back in from the bathroom.

"Find out about what?" Talbot asked.

"The stuff in the folder, of course."

"We didn't get that far yet," Scott said. "I just finished patching your dad up again."

"Oh," Jessie said, disappointed. "Well then, I'm going to bed."

"Good night then," Talbot said, standing up.

"Good night," Jessie said, pausing awkwardly before turning and heading into the bedroom.

"That didn't look awkward at all," Scott teased. "Why didn't you hug her good night?"

"It's not like I know what I'm doing with her anymore," Talbot said defensively. "She definitely doesn't like me much and she barely knows who I am."

"Maybe not, but she knows who she wants you to be."

"Touché," Talbot acknowledged.

"So now what?"

"What do you mean?"

"So be who she wants you to be, dammit. Go in there and say good night properly."

"It's not that simple."

"Actually, yes, it is. She's afraid you're going to leave again, so she's keeping you at a distance, so she doesn't get hurt again. She's also hoping you will close that distance."

"Sounds complicated," Talbot muttered gloomily.

"She's a girl who hasn't even figured out who she is yet. What do you expect? Now get in there before you lose the moment."

Talbot followed Jessie into the bedroom and found her laying on her side already under the covers, the light out. Sitting on the edge of the bed in front of her, he hesitated, looking down at her in the light spilling into the room from the hallway.

"How you doing, Jessie?"

"Fine."

"Now I'm not too smart, but I know when someone says they're fine, it probably means they're not."

Jessie watched him silently from the corner of her eyes, offering no clues.

"Thing is," Talbot said after a moment, "I spent so much time planning on how to get back into your life that I never spent much time on the 'then what' question. Agent Scott just asked me that, and I'm a bit at a loss."

"Kelly."

"What?"

"Her name is Kelly."

"You like her?" Talbot asked, carefully.

"She's nice," Jessie acknowledged.

"Yes, she is, isn't she?"

Jessie had withdrawn into silence again.

"You know, I did everything I could to stay in your life."

"I don't believe you."

"You know I watched every tournament you fought in. You're very good."

"Liar. I would have seen you."

"If I had shown up in person your mom would have had me arrested and I would have lost any chance of seeing you again forever."

"Then how did you watch?"

"Your trainer is a close friend of mine. Jim recorded all your fights for me. How many new students joined his classes after you started going there?"

"What do you mean?" Jessie asked, puzzled.

"Jim doesn't take on new beginner students, only advanced. You were the only beginner in the last eight years. He only took you on as a favor to me."

"I wasn't a beginner."

"From his perspective you were. But he took you on as a favor under one condition."

"Did mom know?"

"No. If she found out she wouldn't have allowed you to train with him."

"What was the condition?"

"He said he would only work with you for six months. If you didn't learn fast in that time he was going to refer you to one of his students. Like I said, you're really good."

"Why did you make him do it?"

"You're my daughter, the best part of my life."

"I don't believe you." Jessie rolled over, turning her back to Talbot.

Talbot hesitated, then stood up, looking down at her. Very gently he reached down and stroked her hair, then leaned over and kissed her on the temple before walking to the door.

"I love you, Jessie," he said, turning back to face her. "Good night."

Pulling the door closed behind him, he walked back into the living room. Behind him Jessie snuggled deeper under the covers, a smile playing in the corners of her mouth as she felt a warmth start to expand in her chest.

"How'd it go?" Scott asked from the couch, her laptop open on the seat beside her and the folder in her hands.

"Bad," Talbot said, gloomily. "She hates me."

"Did she say anything at all?"

"Yes, she grilled me."

"Then you're doing fine. She's just testing you."

"You're sure?"

"Absolutely. Classic stuff. You know, for such a smart guy, you're not too bright."

"It's that obvious?"

"I'm afraid so." Scott teased, resisting the sudden impulse to tell him she found it inexplicably endearing. "I just started googling some of the things in the folder."

"What did you find?" Talbot asked, taking a seat next to Scott on the couch.

"You crashed and burned in there so fast you didn't give me time to look."

"Your brothers didn't exactly teach you to cut much slack." Talbot said, smiling.

"Did I take it too far?" Scott asked, handing him the folder and picking up the laptop.

"No, it's well deserved." Talbot said. He flipped through the pages for a moment. "How about we start with these company names."

"Sure. What's first?"

"Let's take a look at the NeoDine P&L."

Scott typed the names NeoDine and Whitfield into the Google prompt and hit enter. Within a couple of seconds, the screen pulled up a list of entries, including a company website. Talbot leaned in to read with her. Unconsciously Scott leaned closer as well, until her shoulder lightly brushed up against Talbot. The light touch surprised her, radiating a tingling warmth down her arm. She flushed and leaned away to pick up her beer, careful not to lean in that close again. Keeping her head tilted down to read, she managed to hide her face behind her hair as it cascaded over her shoulder.

Talbot leaned in slightly, breathing in the delicate scent of her shampoo as he tried to concentrate on the screen.

"So they're a mining company in Transnistria focusing on Neodymium," he said, concentrating on staying on point.

"Transnistria? I've never heard of it."

"Tiny place that's trying to get independence from Moldova."

"Now how on earth would you know that?"

"They had a little civil war and I wound up in the middle of it. Remember the cigarette burns?"

"That was in Transnistria?"

"Yup. They hired a few Russians as military advisors."

"And now?"

"Last I heard they were trying to get NATO to recognize their sovereignty."

"And how's that working out for them?"

"I don't know. Not too well, I expect." Talbot thought for a moment. "What I don't get is why Senator Williams has a copy of their P&L?"

Scott frowned, concentrating. "More to the point, why would the leader of Phoenix, a secret government agency with no Congressional oversight, be listed on the board for a mining company?"

"What do you mean?"

"It's just a short line item, but it says Bob Whitfield is the Chairman of the Board," Scott said, pointing at the screen. "And why would Senator Williams care about that?"

Talbot thought for a moment, puzzled. Then an idea struck him. "Pull up the names of the committees Senator Williams served on."

Scott typed in the query and waited.

"I thought so," Talbot said, pointing at the screen. "Williams was on the 'Ways and Means Committee'."

"Headed up by a certain Senator Bob Whitfield," Scott added.

"I smell a possible conflict of interest," Talbot said. "Looks like Williams had questions about why the head of the 'Ways and Means Committee' would have such close ties to NeoDine."

"Sure, but that's not too uncommon. As long as there's full disclosure there's no issue," Scott said.

"Okay, so how about this? Why does the Senator who put this folder together die on the same day his aide gets shot to death by government operatives while carrying the folder?"

"True," Scott agreed. "Especially when the name of the leader of those operatives is in the folder."

"If Williams thought there was something wrong with Whitfield, and then both he and his aide dies, I suspect he might have been on to something," Talbot said.

"But what?"

"No clue," Talbot admitted.

"So what about the invoices? Do you think that would help?"

"I don't know. Let's see what we can find out. First one of BioMediCom."

Scott typed it in and the screen popped up the results. Scott speed read through a few paragraphs before settling on an article in the *British Journal of Cancer*.

"Lot's of blah-blah mumbo-jumbo here, but essentially the company is owned by a geneticist named Gavin Mansfield. The company published an article on their research into using engineered viruses to rewrite genetic code in the cells for cancer treatment."

"How's it work?"

"Not sure, but if I understand them correctly, they can isolate the genetic code that triggered the cancer and overwrite it with healthy code. Once you replace all the bad code, the good code takes over and ends the cancer cycle."

"Pretty slick, although I don't see the connection."

"Neither do I. What was the other company name?"

"GeneSig," Talbot said, referring to the folder.

After a minute of typing and reading, Scott looked up.

"Also a private company, this time owned by someone named Todd Castle. This company is also working with genetics, but they took a different track. They isolated a part of the human chromosome that acts as a genetic fingerprint."

"Meaning?" Talbot asked.

"They found a way to uniquely identify every human being, with no duplicates, from a signature locked in our chromosomes."

"Okay, I can see how the DOD might be interested in a genetic signature to identify human remains after a bomb explosion, so I understand the contract with GeneSig, but as far as I know the DOD has no interest in cancer research."

"Well, what else could they use it for?" Scott puzzled.

"That's the million-dollar question," Talbot said, nodding.

"The question I keep coming back to is why Williams put all this together," Scott said.

"Jessie said something about Amy getting a call telling her Williams was dead just before she was shot. It's too much of a coincidence. Do we know how he died?"

"Yes, he collapsed and died in the Senate chambers during session. Apparently, it was pretty ugly. He had what looked like a massive epileptic fit and then died bleeding from his eye sockets. The rumor was that they suspected poison."

"Now how did you know that?" Talbot asked, surprised.

"I was assigned to the case after both of them died. Like you say, too much of a coincidence."

"If they were testing for poison, would they have the test results back yet?" Talbot asked.

"I can check," Scott said, tapping away at the keys.

Using the secure VPN connection to her office, Scott logged into her work station and accessed the case file. The days of shuffling folders full of papers were long gone... updates, notes and even file attachments could be added by any department directly into the digital case file.

"Odd," she said. "Toxicology came in clean, but they moved him to the CDC. Something about a 'hemorrhagic event'."

"As in *'Centers for Disease Control'* CDC?" Talbot asked, startled. "Why would they send the body to the CDC?"

"I don't know, and unless they add to the case file I can't see their data. Maybe something to do with the 'hemorrhagic event' comment?"

"Still too much of a coincidence," Talbot muttered.

"Especially when you add in the BioMediCom engineered virus angle." Scott hesitated. "Remember I said pretty much all my family are cops?"

"Yes."

"I have a nephew."

"I would imagine you have several."

"Smart ass," Scott said with a smile. "Zach is a research grad student specializing in cancer therapy. I never paid too much attention to what he did, but I seem to remember it had something to do with genetics because we teased him about engineering super cops."

"Think he can help?"

"I don't know, but I can ask."

"Good idea. Another beer?" Talbot asked as Scott reached for her phone.

"Sure."

Talbot walked into the kitchen and returned with a couple of beers while Scott dialed her nephew's number.

"It's almost two in the morning. Think he'll answer?"

Scott waved him into silence as the phone clicked.

"Hello?" Towering both physically and intellectually over his peers, Zach Michaels was a big man. Standing six feet five inches in his socks and built like a defensive end, his size disguised what was usually a gentle heart. Slow to anger, it took a lot to provoke him, but there were several who could attest to the fact that he was particularly dangerous in a fight.

"Hi Zach, did I wake you?"

"Oh hi. No, I was just going over some results. Everything okay?"

"Sure, I just thought I could use your input on something."

"You need input from a genetic scientist on a case?"

"No," Scott said, smiling into the phone. "I need input from the best genetic scientist on a case."

Michaels chuckled. "What do you need to know?"

"Any chance you have access to CDC testing on a current case?"

"Sure, but how would the CDC be involved in something you're working on?"

"I don't know yet."

"Okay, what you got?"

"Senator Landon Williams collapsed and died in the Senate chambers Monday afternoon. The way he died they suspected poison of some kind, but toxicology ruled it out and sent the body to the CDC. The case note referenced a 'hemorrhagic event'. That's all I know."

"When did they move the body to the CDC?"

"Late this afternoon."

"Okay, they'll not have had time to do much of anything yet. I'll see what I can find out tomorrow and give you a call."

"Thanks. And Zach?"

"Yes?"

"This is a little outside the usual line, so if anyone asks why you're digging in the case..."

"No problem. I'll just say it flagged as hemorrhagic and that fits right into my research interest. I can play it off on that. I'll call you later."

As Zach hung up, Talbot handed Scott her beer and sat back down on the couch beside her.

"Well?"

"He said he'll do some research and call me back later in the afternoon."

"Okay, so what's next?" Talbot asked, rifling through the pages from the folder. "We need to know more about these companies."

"Well, we can make an official FBI visit to two of them, anyway." Scott said. "GeneSig is in Baltimore, and BioMediCom is right here in Washington."

"Good idea. Maybe we can learn something new that way," Talbot said.

"What about NeoDine?" Scott asked. "They're in… where now?"

"Transnistria."

"Right, Transnistria."

"I've got a friend," Talbot said. "Maybe he can help."

"You've got a friend in Transnistria?" Scott asked, half joking.

"Almost. Last time I spoke to him he had moved to Odessa."

"I'm guessing you don't mean Odessa, Texas."

Talbot grinned as he pulled out his phone and dialed the same number he had called to find the safe house. The line clicked directly into voicemail.

"Tango Echo Mike. Need to contact Odessa."

Talbot hung up and looked up to find Scott giving him a look.

"What?" he asked.

"What do you mean, 'what'? You don't think that was a little odd?"

"Oh you noticed that, did you?" Talbot said, smiling.

"So what's the deal?"

"Some friends of mine with backgrounds of an odd sort from around the world got together and set up a phone number any one of us can call if we need the odd kind of help."

"And what kind of help is that, exactly?"

"I guess you could call it security consulting."

"Sounds like a little more than just security consulting to me," Scott said with a suspicious look at Talbot.

"Well, it's rather upscale, edge of the envelope stuff, I guess," Talbot said trying to play it down. His phone rang.

"Yes?" Talbot said into the phone.

"Well, well, Matt Talbot. I haven't heard from you in over a year!"

"Hello Alexis, I was hoping it would be you. How you doing these days?"

"Bored, my friend, bored. It's not like the old days."

Alexis Zaytsev had spent the better part of his life as a Russian undercover agent, and despite having spent most of his life working on the opposite side of the fence, so to speak, his heavy mid-European accent and cheerful bon homie carried real pleasure in hearing Talbot's voice on the phone.

"Are you still in that little Dachau overlooking the Black Sea?" Talbot asked.

"Oh yes, you know how I like to go fishing."

"Of course, although I seem to remember fish were not always your main interest."

"True, true, but we all have to grow up eventually. Is that why you asked for me?"

"Yes."

"Okay, my friend, what do you need?"

"Ever been to Chisinau?"

"In Moldova?"

"Yes, although they are trying to get independence."

"I know, and what a silly little name they picked for their country. Transnistria. It doesn't exactly roll off the tongue."

"There's a company in Chisinau called NeoDine. I'm trying to find out everything I can about them."

"What is my risk?"

"I'm not sure yet, but I'd play it safe if I were you. I think they are connected."

"CIA?"

"Not much different. They don't seem to care about rule of law much."

"Okay, not a problem, my friend. Are you looking for anything in particular?"

"See if you can find anything they might be trying to hide. Maybe key on Neodymium, Phoenix, Whitfield, GeneSig and BioMediCom."

"Okay, I will see what I can do. Anything else?"

Talbot glanced at the sheets in front of him and picked up the image of the Orion constellation.

"Long shot, but see if anything pops up about the Orion constellation."

"What kind of deep game are you playing, my friend?"

134

"I don't know, but they killed Jessie's mom in front of her."

"Eto piz`dets!"

"I know it is."

Scott raised her eyebrow questioningly, and Talbot covered the phone with his hand.

"He said it's messed up."

"Sounded a little more emphatic than that," she said.

"It was," Talbot said with a grin. "He has an epic capacity for cursing in about thirty different languages."

Talbot returned his attention to Zaytsev.

"When do you think you can get something?"

"I text you my number when I get something, okay?"

"Thanks, Alexis," Talbot said.

Ending the call, Talbot looked up to see Scott leaning back in the couch, arms folded.

"I don't think you've told me everything," she accused.

"Sorry, it's just a bunch of retired guys with special skills. We've all worked in a similar business and we like to help each other when we can. The greater the need, the more help you get. That's how I got Jessie in to Krav Magra."

"This is more than just asking someone to teach your kid a class as a favor."

"Sure, and Alexis knows that if I'm asking for something like this, it's pretty serious. I expect we can hear from him within a few hours."

08h10, Scott's Apartment, Virginia Square Towers, Arlington, VA.

The smell of bacon and eggs lay thick in the air as Talbot stacked the dishwasher with the dishes Scott brought him from the dining table. After only six hours of sleep, there had been very little in the way of conversation around the table. Scott had discovered to her surprise that Jessie was an active sleeper, and her constant movement had made sleep a fitful companion.

For his part, Talbot had quickly learned that the couch, while certainly soft enough, was just a few inches too short. As accustomed to sleeping in difficult conditions as he had been in years past, he no longer adapted as easily. He had not slept well.

The news that Jessie would have to stay in the apartment while Talbot and Scott visited the two companies had done nothing to improve the mood at the table. Jessie had finished her breakfast in stony silence, freezing out all efforts to engage her, and had immediately disappeared into the bedroom and turned on the TV.

Digging into his bag, Talbot pulled out a small button. Using his pocket knife, he cut a small slit into the tip of the tongue on Jessie's sneaker and slipped the button inside.

"What was that?" Scott asked curiously.

"Satellite marker."

"A tracker? You think that's necessary?"

"I know I might be a little paranoid, but I'm taking no chances. I would rather be able to track her if something happens."

"Actually, I thought it was a good idea under the circumstances," Scott said as she pulled on her jacket and picked up her keys.

"Jessie, we're leaving now. We'll be back in a few hours, okay?" Talbot said, poking his head into the bedroom.

Still angry, Jessie turned the TV volume up to shut them out.

Talbot sighed and followed Scott out.

10h55, GeneSig Headquarters, Baltimore, MD.

Covered in dark glass, GeneSig's headquarters in Towson just north of Baltimore was located on the edge of a neighborhood just west of the Baltimore County Circuit Court. It was a non-descript five-story building lacking any signage. Scott's car slid to a stop as she parked on the street in front and dug in the console for change for the meter. The drive to Baltimore had taken less than an hour, and the conversation between Talbot and Scott had been comfortable and easy without any awkwardness.

Stepping out of the car, Scott fed the meter as Talbot scanned the surroundings. Since all the parking for the building was around the back, at this time of day the street was almost empty.

"Ready?" Scott asked, dropping the last coin into the meter.

"Lead on, Agent Scott", Talbot smiled.

With Scott in the lead they followed the walkway to the glass front doors and pushed their way in. Just inside the doors was a tall reception desk. A well-dressed man in a dark suit and tie stood behind the desk. The close-cropped hair and bulge under his arm advertised to both Talbot and Scott that his role was less about welcome and more about security.

"Can I help you?"

"I'm Agent Scott of the FBI and this is Agent Adams," Scott said, showing her badge and nodding at Talbot. "We're here to see Todd Castle."

"Do you have an appointment?"

"I'm afraid not."

"And can I ask what this is about?"

"Sorry, it has to do with an active investigation."

"Yes ma'am."

Picking up the desk phone, the man dialed an extension and paused a moment.

"The FBI is here to see Mr. Castle." He paused, listening. "They just said it relates to an active investigation."

After a moment he hung up and turned back to Scott.

"Someone will be down in a moment if you care to take a seat?"

"No, thank you," Scott replied politely.

After a few minutes during which Talbot, by habit, located each of the five hidden cameras overlooking the lobby, the tall double doors on the far end of the lobby clicked open. Another poorly disguised security specialist stood holding the door for them.

"Agent Scott? Agent Adams? I'll take you up now."

Scott followed him into a second lobby, Talbot on her heels.

The guard pressed the button to call the elevator and the doors dinged open immediately. Ushering them in, he waved his identity badge in front of a reader next to the floor number buttons and pressed five. The doors slid shut and the elevator glided to the top floor before gently jerking to a stop. The doors opened to a room with a single desk on the far side manned by yet another dark suit. Stepping around the desk, he approached the group.

"Mr. Castle has about thirty minutes for you, if you will follow me?"

Leading the way past his desk and down a wide hallway he walked them to the double doors on the end, opened one side and ushered them in.

A very short, broad man with male pattern baldness and designer glasses with lenses tinted slightly pink ambled out from behind a massive desk scattered with papers. His red and blue striped tie was pulled loose, the top button of his starched white shirt undone, and his sleeves partially rolled up his forearms.

"Good morning! I'm Todd Castle, owner of GeneSig. And to what do I owe the pleasure of a visit from the FBI?" he asked cheerfully, shaking their hands in a warm welcome.

While his Texas drawl went well with the ostrich leather cowboy boots, neither matched his surroundings at all.

"We're collecting some background information to help with an active investigation, and we thought you might be able to help us," Scott said.

"I would be more than happy to help. Take a seat. Can I get you something to drink? Tea? Coffee? Soda?" Castle asked, ushering them over to an arrangement of cow hide armchairs and sofa.

"Not for us, thank you," Scott said. "We just had a few questions. We shouldn't take up a lot of your time."

"Shoot."

"We understand your company has found a way to read the unique genetic fingerprint of every human being?" Scott asked.

"Yes, very exciting stuff! Of course, the sequencing is pretty complex, but completely accurate."

"And how did GeneSig get to this point?"

A shadow passed over Castle's face.

"My background was originally software development and I was working on funding for a new program which Emergency Response agencies could use that made it possible to link people who need help to people offering help."

"Any success?"

"Not immediately. In fact, it was struggling. So I stayed home to work and my wife went alone to visit my son in his offices at the top of World Trade Center One on 9/11. They never made it out, and nobody was ever able to identify any remains."

"I'm so sorry for your loss," Scott said quietly.

"Thank you, it's been a long time now, but I still feel the guilt. In any case, I made it my life's work to make it possible to positively identify the victims, even from the smallest piece of genetic material. It took me seven years before I sold the software I finally finished, and it gave me enough to finally finance GeneSig. Seven years later we have the solution I wanted."

"Impressive."

"Thank you," Castle nodded. "I just hope the work we've done here can save other families the heartbreak of not knowing."

"I'm guessing the tests are pretty expensive?" Talbot asked after a moment.

"Very," Castle agreed. "So much so that we can't get a lot of traction finding anyone in the private sector as clients."

"I imagine you would get a lot more success getting a state agency to buy in?" Scott probed.

"You would think so, but we had some difficulty initially. The government isn't very good about recognizing a beneficial product or service when someone brings it to them. They usually respond out of need, then put out bid requests and deliberate for a couple of years before making a decision."

"I imagine the DOD would be interested now that they have to deal with IED's so much in the Middle East?" Talbot asked.

"Exactly. Hopefully that success will trigger other agencies to look at us as well."

"Do you see any other applications for this technology?" Scott asked.

"Sure. We're working with several pharmacological giants to develop cancer treatment protocols custom engineered for each patient, but we're probably decades away from human trials. Of course, we provided them with free licensing on the process while they're in development. It's a good incentive and besides, I don't want money to get in the way of doing that much good. It's not like I'll ever need the money."

"How would it work?" Scott asked curiously.

"The business model or the science?"

"Science."

"Well, the basic idea is that you can redesign a virus to invade your chromosomes and rewrite the broken code that triggered the cancer. They've had some trouble with the initial work because one size does not necessarily fit all."

"So the more specific you make it the better the results?" Scott asked.

"That's the theory right now, yes."

"Sounds like you're doing amazing work here," Scott congratulated him.

"Thank you, it's important to me."

"Just a thought," Talbot mused, "Have you considered selling the service as a rider on insurance policies?"

"What do you mean?" Castle asked, curiously.

"Well, it occurs to me that, if you can sell access to the test to anybody with health or life insurance, you can spread the cost across multiple buyers based on a risk analysis. Basically, they buy peace of mind for their survivors if they die in a way that makes their body unrecognizable, and no single person has to pay for the total cost. I would imagine every airline and many manufacturing companies would be interested if the price was low enough."

Scott and Castle exchanged glances.

"If you ever want a job in the private sector," Castle said, "come see me. You can head up my sales team."

"No thanks," Talbot chuckled. "I'm no salesman. Does the name 'Phoenix' mean anything to you?"

"Mythologically speaking, yes. And did you know they were originally going to call the first Pontiac Firebird a Phoenix?"

"Why didn't they?" Talbot asked, his interest piqued.

"They realized the idea of naming a fast muscle car after something that dies in flames to be reborn might give the wrong message," Castle said smiling.

"Probably a good marketing decision," Talbot said. "Nothing else on the name, though?"

"Sorry, I'm afraid not."

"How about NeoDine or BioMediCom?"

"Nothing on NeoDine, but I believe BioMediCom is one of our licensees. They're doing research on gene therapy for cancer treatments."

"Are they making progress?" Talbot asked.

"They're the ones still years from human trials, but their work certainly shows a lot of promise."

"How so?"

"They've been able to customize a virus to rewrite the genetic code for a single gene sequence on a single chimpanzee without any impact to other chimps."

"So the treatment is as unique as the signature?" Talbot asked.

"Exactly."

"Very impressive. Anything else on them?"

"I'm afraid not. They're understandably very secretive about it."

"Well, that's all I needed to know," Talbot said.

"Same here," Scott said. "I know you're short on time, so we will let you get back to it."

"You're very welcome, and good luck with your investigation," Castle said as he walked them to his door. "One of my guys will make sure you can get past all this security we have to have."

"Thank you," Talbot said, shaking Castle's hand at the door.

19h30 Local Time, ODESSA, UKRAINE

"Miserable dogs."

Muttering under his breath and chewing on a mint-flavored toothpick, Alexis Zaytsev was deeply engrossed in his efforts to hack into NeoDine. Everything about his looks made him instantly forgettable, a fact he had leveraged to his benefit for decades working underground in counter intelligence. Now, after years of hiding in plain sight and wearing the most boring of browns and greys, he was enjoying a sartorial awakening. His bright red jeans and blue-themed Hawaiian shirt were so loud even the dimly lit room could not mask their colorful exuberance.

The bank of computer monitors on the wall in front of him flashed and flickered as he bounced his probes against the NeoDine firewall from every angle at the same time, routing every attack through over a thousand IP addresses scattered around the world.

Finally, he grunted in satisfaction as he pried open a digital window and slipped behind the NeoDine firewalls. Setting his timer to keep track of how long he was inside, he started digging through their servers, searching on the keywords Talbot had given him.

He worked fast, not bothering to read what he captured. He figured he could review the downloads later at his leisure. As he worked his new set of dental implants destroyed one toothpick after another in quick succession. Each file that satisfied the search criteria was downloaded one after another and saved to an encoded thumb drive on his computer.

Keeping an eye his timer, he finally pulled the plug and completely powered down his router, destroying any chance of back tracking his hack to his location.

"Alright then, my little beauty" he muttered, mentally rubbing his hands together in anticipation, "What do you have for me?"

11h45, BioMediCom Headquarters, Alexandria, VA

Located at the east end of 19th Street in Arlington, the building was shaped somewhat like a futuristic fighter space craft, and the BioMediCom office suites on the upper three floors provided a splendid view of the Potomac River.

The building entrance served multiple businesses and, as such, required no particular security measures, but as the elevator doors opened on the nineteenth floor, Talbot and Scott stepped into a large, open private lobby. Visitor seating was scattered along the walls on either side of the elevator doors facing the curved reception desk. The man behind the desk was clearly cut from the same cloth as the first face they met at GeneSig.

Talbot wandered over to the corner as Scott approached the desk.

"Good morning, ma'am, can I help you?"

"Special Agents Scott and Adams of the FBI to see Gavin Mansfield, please," Scott said politely and firmly, showing her badge.

"Is Mr. Mansfield expecting you?"

"No and we have no appointment. This relates to an ongoing investigation."

"I'm afraid Mr. Mansfield is not available unless you have an appointment, ma'am."

Scott stared at him coldly for a moment.

"Why don't you communicate to Mr. Mansfield that we're investigating a murder. He can meet with us now, or we can return in a few hours with a warrant and a couple truckloads of people to start carrying every file and computer out of this building and into federal custody."

"Yes ma'am," he said unfazed, calmly reaching for the phone. He spoke quietly into the receiver for a few moments, hung up, and looked back at Scott.

"Mr. Mansfield will see you in a few minutes, ma'am."

"Thank you."

Scott joined Talbot in the corner.

"I'm impressed," Talbot said admiringly, keeping a straight face.

Scott grinned at him, her back to the lobby desk.

"Not quite the same welcome as GeneSig, is it?" Talbot said.

"Not exactly, although that doesn't mean much on its own."

"True. By the way, did you see how deep the doors are set in the wall?"

Scott glanced over to the single door on the far side of the room. Instead of the standard depth of door jamb, the framing for the door showed an additional four inches of framing depth.

"Does that mean what I think it does?"

"Yes, the walls are much thicker than usual. Either the wall in the other side has a brick facade, or that wall is bullet proof."

The door they were studying swung open and yet another dark suit appeared. His name tag announced him as Voss.

"Do they clone them or something?" Scott muttered.

"Mr. Mansfield will see you now. Please follow me."

Voss ushered them through the door and led them silently down a long corridor to another set of doors. Pushing them open, he led them into a spacious corner office in the west corner overlooking the Potomac. Considerably wider than deep, everything about the room was designed to give the impression of power. The left end of the office was given over to a living room-style seating arrangement, with sleek, contemporary furniture in black leather arranged around what was clearly an authentic polar bear pelt. An HDTV was mounted above a small, gas-burning fireplace against the far wall, and a well-stocked wet bar was built into the wall opposite the vast bank of windows which spanned the width of the office and around the corner to the right.

The entire office to the right was designed around a massive, dark walnut desk on a raised six-inch platform. Gavin Mansfield sat in the oversized, plush leather office chair behind the desk annotating a single, multi-page document. Except for a sleek silver iPhone, the rest of his desk was empty. There were two simple chairs facing the desk at the bottom of the platform, designed to place anyone seated in them at a psychological disadvantage.

"Take a seat," Mansfield said without glancing up. "Voss, you can wait. They won't be here long."

Standing a little over six feet tall, Gavin Mansfield was a well built, handsome man with striking features that never failed to turn heads. Dressed in his usual tailored navy pin stripe suite, light blue button-down shirt and red and navy striped tie, the large gold signet ring and cuff links gleamed in the ample light from the windows.

Unimpressed, Talbot and Turner took a seat as Mansfield worked his way to the end of the paragraph. Everything about his demeanor was a calculated effort to put these low-ranking government lackeys in their place.

Talbot glanced at Scott, his eyebrow raised quizzically, before turning his attention back to Mansfield.

"Yes?" Mansfield said coldly, laying his pen down on top of the document. Abruptly, harshly, his cell phone started ringing. Glancing at it, he hesitated, then reached for it.

"Yes?"

The faint sound of a voice on the end of the phone carried across to Scott and Talbot, but the words were indistinguishable.

11h30, Phoenix Headquarters, Washington, D.C.

Tremaine pushed La Salle's office door open.

"Got a minute?"

"Is it important?"

"Probably."

"Go ahead."

Tremaine walked in carrying a printout and dropped it onto La Salle's desk.

"What is this?" La Salle asked, picking it up.

"That's a screen shot from video surveillance of the woman we believe was with Talbot in the coffee shop."

"When and where did you get the footage?"

"From the surveillance cameras in Castle's office. She was there about an hour ago."

"How do you know it's the same person?"

"Talbot was with her."

"You have my attention. Who is she?"

"Her name is Special Agent Kelly Scott of the FBI. She was asking Castle about what they do there."

"No risks at GeneSig. Do we know where they are now?"

"No, but I can guess."

"Where?"

"Mansfield. They seem very intent on digging into those three companies."

La Salle gave him a thoughtful look.

"There's something else," Tremaine added.

"Go on."

"We were able to get surveillance footage of their vehicle leaving. She's driving an FBI vehicle."

"Was the kid in the car?"

"No."

La Salle tapped his fingers on the desk, deep in thought, as Tremaine waited.

"Seems likely Talbot and the girl spent the night with this Scott woman. Do we know where she lives?"

"Not yet, but we can get that in a couple of minutes."

"Send a team to her place and grab any documents that seem relevant. Bring the kid in as well if she's there."

"The kid?" Tremaine said, uncertainly.

"Of course. We won't hurt her, but we can use her as leverage to get Talbot to give himself up. Leave a note for him to call my cell."

"I'm still not comfortable with that," Tremaine said uneasily.

"I'm not asking you to feel comfortable, I'm telling you to do your job," La Salle said staring Tremaine down.

"Yes sir," Tremaine said after an awkward hesitation. He closed the door behind him as he left.

La Salle reached for his cell phone, scrolled through his contacts list and pressed a button.

"Yes?"

"Mansfield, we may have an issue. There are a couple of FBI agents probably headed your way. The woman is the real deal, the man is not. They will have a lot of questions, probably about Senator Williams' death."

"That probability you referenced is a current fact," Mansfield said, carefully.

"Are they there right now?"

"Correct."

"Stall them."

"Any suggestions on how?"

"I don't care. Give them a tour or something." La Salle hung up, reached for his desk phone and dialed. After a moment he spoke. "I need a team ready to go in thirty minutes."

11h50, BioMediCom Headquarters, Alexandria, VA

Talbot watched Mansfield put his phone down thoughtfully. Then Mansfield looked up, smiling warmly. Scott could not shake off the sudden, uncomfortable feeling of being watched by a crocodile.

"So, Agents Scott and Adams, is it? What can I do for you?"

"Just a few questions," Scott responded. "What can you tell us about Phoenix?"

Mansfield's eyes flickered briefly, looking away from Scott for a split second, before replying.

"Never heard of it."

"How about NeoDine?"

"No, I'm afraid not."

"And BioMediCom?"

"Also nothing," Mansfield said suavely. "Should I?"

Scott glanced at Talbot, hiding her surprise. Talbot shook his head very slightly to confirm her instinct that she not dig too much deeper yet.

"Can you tell us a little about what you do here?" Talbot asked, changing the subject.

"In broad terms, sure, although I need your promise not to discuss it outside these walls," Mansfield smiled urbanely. "We design virus-sized couriers that we can introduce into a living body. These couriers are designed to rewrite very specifically selected segments of genetic code. The idea is to overwrite the cancer message and kill cancer."

"Sounds difficult."

"It is."

"How do you make sure the rewritten code is right for the specific person that needs the therapy?" Scott asked.

"We haven't figured that out yet, and we may be years from solving that problem," Mansfield said. "Look, I'm very busy, but I can arrange for a tour of the place if you like."

Talbot and Scott exchanged a surprised look.

"Sure," Talbot said.

Mansfield glanced behind them.

"Voss, introduce them to Dr. Hampton, then have one of the techs give them the tour."

"Yes sir."

"Good luck. I hope you find out who killed Senator Williams. Now, if you will excuse me?"

"Follow me, please," Voss said, guiding them out.

Standing, Talbot and Scott followed Voss out. Mansfield was reaching for his phone before the door clicked shut behind them. Voss led them silently through a series of corridors and badge-controlled doors to a large, open-concept lab surrounded by glass-walled cubicles. He tapped briefly on a door labelled "Dr. Andy Hampton" and pushed it open without waiting for a response.

"Mr. Mansfield needs you to answer any questions Special Agent's Scott and Adams might have about the cancer research while I find an intern to give them the tour."

Voss turned and walked off as Hampton glared at the back of his head.

"Muscle without manners," Hampton said, apologetically. "Please, take a seat." There was clearly no love lost between Hampton and Voss.

Hampton was a slightly built man about five-and-a-half feet tall. His thick white hair and matching overgrown white

155

eyebrows and mustache made a bold statement. His office was a cluttered mess with books and papers scattered on every level surface, and the only concessions to individualism was a single small pot plant and a piece of pottery side-by-side clinging desperately to the corner of his desk.

Talbot picked up a stack of papers and books from each of the two metal chairs across the table from Hampton and carefully placed them on the floor before he and Scott took a seat.

"Don't tell anyone," Hampton said, his eyes twinkling, "but those stacks of papers and books are completely useless. I just put them there to discourage the idiot managers around here from taking root when they come to bug me."

Scott chuckled.

"I see you favor African Violets," Talbot said, nodding at the pot plant. He had taken an immediate liking to the irreverent doctor.

"I do. It reminds me of my years in Tanzania."

"Stunning country," Talbot said.

"Yes, it was a beautiful country spoiled by politics," Hampton agreed. "You've been to Tanzania?"

"Yes, I had the chance to spend a few weeks there about ten years ago. Sometimes I'd walk through the markets. I liked watching the potters. Is that one of their pieces?" Talbot asked, pointing to the pot on the corner of Hampton's desk.

"It's supposed to be," Hampton smiled. "But I bought it on eBay."

"What were you doing in Tanzania?" Scott asked curiously.

"I was working for the World Health Organization keeping an eye out for any new or emerging viruses, pathogens, that sort of thing. We were tasked with preventing any major pandemics."

"Is that your field of study?" Talbot asked.

"Only partially. I specialize in understanding the genetic makeup of viruses, and how they work."

"And how did you wind up here?" Scott asked.

"Tanzania went through a civil war and I had to leave. Mansfield knew of my work from an incident in South Africa a few years earlier and offered me a job when I had to leave Tanzania."

"So what are you working on?" Talbot asked.

A shadow crossed Hampton's face, more imagined than seen. Frowning, he studied Talbot for a moment. As if reaching a decision, he smiled.

"What did Mansfield tell you?"

"Just that the company has had some success using a virus to rewrite a small piece of genetic code with the end game of fixing the code that triggers a patient's cancer," Scott replied.

"Did he say anything about our work around making it specific to the needs of each patient?"

"He said you were years from solving that challenge," Scott said.

"I suppose progress is always relative," Hampton said, hesitating.

Before he could add anything further, Voss' voice interrupted from the door.

"We are ready for your tour."

"It was a pleasure meeting you, Doctor," Talbot said as he stood up. "I hope you get a chance to go back to Tanzania some time."

As Talbot and Scott started to leave his office, Hampton made a decision.

"Agent Adams?"

Talbot turned back to catch Hampton's eyes staring at him hard.

"Before you leave, would you mind stopping by my office again? You're the first person I've met that has also been to Tanzania, and I wanted to get your opinion on that piece of pottery before you go."

"Sure," Talbot said, puzzled, as he followed the intern into the lab area.

Hampton thought for a moment, then reached into his pocket and pulled out a small thumb drive. Inserting it into one of the USB ports on his computer, he started selecting files from the network and copying them over to the thumb drive. Working quickly, glancing up on occasion to keep an eye on his surroundings, he finished copying the files he wanted, removed the thumb drive, and reached for the fired clay pot on the corner of his desk. Removing the lid, he taped the thumb drive to the bottom of the lid and put the pot back on the corner of his desk. Then he copied the files to a second thumb drive which he slipped into his pocket before going back to his work.

About an hour later there was a tap on the glass next to his open door. Looking up, Hampton saw Talbot smiling through the glass. Voss was hovering nearby watching as Scott chatted to the intern who had given the tour.

"You wanted me to look at that pottery piece?" Talbot asked.

"Yes, actually. When I bought it on eBay it came with a certificate of authenticity, but I'm not entirely sure I believe it."

Talbot picked up the pot and turned it over in his hands, studying it as Hampton continued.

"I don't seem to remember their pots having lids," Scott commented.

"Exactly," Hampton agreed. "It's the lid that has me wondering. This one has a marking of what looks like a small bird on the inside which supposedly identifies where it came from."

Talbot lifted the lid and peered into the hollow of the lid. The thumb drive was nestled inside the bowl-shape, taped in place with a note to take the drive. Smoothly Talbot palmed the drive as he studied the lid carefully.

"Sorry, I don't recognize the marking. Not that I'm an expert on the subject." Talbot handed the pot back to Hampton. "It does remind me of the pottery I saw there, though."

"Ah well," Hampton said meaningfully, "I wasn't sure if you could help, but it was worth a shot."

"Well I must admit, I don't remember when last a piece of pottery attracted my curiosity quite like this one. The lid was more interesting than I expected."

"Ready?" Scott asked. "We have to get going."

"Right," Talbot replied. "Pleasure to meet you, Doctor."

"Same to you."

Hampton glanced behind Talbot as he turned to leave.

"Voss, you may escort them back out."

Walking quickly, Voss guided them through the building and back to the elevators. Pushing the button, he followed them in and stood in stony silence as the elevator glided back down to the ground floor.

"Do you think we need an escort out the building?" Scott asked.

"It's lunch time," Voss replied politely.

The door dinged and slid open. Talbot and Scott walked out the building and down the stairs.

"Mind if I drive?" Talbot asked.

"My driving makes you nervous?" Scott teased as she tossed him the keys.

"Not in the least," Talbot chuckled, "but I get bored just sitting."

Back in the car, Talbot pretended to fiddle with his rear mirrors. Getting the angle just right, he watched Voss standing just inside the door, talking into his sleeve.

"Zach texted me about the CDC report," Scott said as she checked her phone.

"Oh?"

"He said, and I quote, 'This is weird. We need to talk.' Unquote."

"Speaking of weird, do you remember mentioning Senator Williams to Mansfield?"

"I'm certain I didn't."

"So why did Mansfield mention him specifically?"

"You noticed that as well?" Scott asked as Talbot pulled the car away from the curb and into traffic.

"Yes."

"Do you think they were on to us?"

"I'm certain of it."

"How so?"

"I just saw Voss talking into his sleeve, and three black Taurus Interceptors just pulled into traffic behind us."

Scott twisted around in her seat to see three government-issued Taurus Interceptors with blacked out windows trailing three cars behind.

"Let's find out if they're really following us," Talbot said.

He accelerated east on nineteenth Street, gunning through two intersections before making a hard left and merging into the one-way traffic headed south on North Fort Myer Drive. Watching in the rear-view mirror, he could see all three Taurus Interceptors follow.

"Matt? If they've figured out who I am, they may send a team to my apartment. They might find Jessie."

Talbot reached for his phone and handed it to Scott.

"Find the App called Tracker. It'll locate that button I put in her sneaker."

Accelerating hard into a left turn on Fairfax, he drifted the heavy car through the turn and round into the one-way traffic on North Lynn. Braking hard before the Taurus Interceptors reached the corner, he spun the car into the entrance of the public parking garage on the corner and followed the lane up to the next level. Quickly he backed the car into a space between two large trucks, the engine still running, and rolled down his window.

"She's still in the apartment," Scott said.

"Call her," Talbot said urgently, "tell her to get out immediately."

As Scott dialed quickly, Talbot listened to the sound of squealing tires coming up from the smooth concrete of the parking lot at street level.

"Good, only one followed us in here. They don't know where we are for sure."

Talbot pulled out his Glock and jammed it within easy reach between the seat and center console.

"Jessie?" Scott said as the phone connected. "The bad guys are on their way to get you. You need to get out of the apartment right now. Don't wait, just go."

She paused as Jessie asked a question.

161

"No time. Turn right as you leave, go to the end of the hallway, and take the stairs down. Go out the back of the building and turn left on Fairfax. There's a Starbucks two blocks down on your left. Go in there and go to the back. We'll find you, okay?"

She paused again as Jessie spoke.

"We're okay. Don't waste time, just go. We'll be there in ten minutes."

Hanging up, she glanced at Talbot. His eyes, usually warm and kind, were hard and his mouth was set in grim lines.

The pursuing Crown Vic careened around the corner at the other end of the parking garage and raced towards them.

"Hold on," Talbot said.

Startled, Scott grabbed the dashboard with one hand and the handle over the door with the other as Talbot gunned the engine and rammed the trunk of the car as it passed in front of them, spinning it violently around to line up parallel with Talbot before smashing into one of the concrete pillars.

Talbot reached for his Glock and coldly, deliberately, fired twice in rapid succession, the bullets smashing through the window of the other car and instantly killing the driver. Hopping out fast, Talbot moved around to the front of the other car and fired twice more, killing the stunned passenger as he struggled to lift his Mach 10. Poised and ready, he quickly checked the car for any further threats before reaching in and turning off the engine.

Then he reached in and grabbed the Mach 10 and checked the magazine.

Satisfied Talbot slid back behind the wheel and handed the Mach 10 to Scott. She took it without a word as he put the car in gear and eased it back down to the parking entrance. Glancing quickly left and right, he eased back into the traffic on

North Lynn. Following Wilson Boulevard back around to the left and merging into North Fort Myer again, Talbot headed south to merge into the east-bound traffic on Arlington Boulevard.

"Jessie is on the move," Scott said as she studied the screen on Talbot's phone. "She's on her way to the Starbucks."

"Good," Talbot said grimly, focused on his driving. Glancing back in his rear-view mirror, he spotted the remaining two Taurus Interceptors weaving fast through traffic trying to catch up. Holding his speed steady, he handed his Glock over to Scott to reload as the pursuit pulled up behind them.

The lead car slammed into the trunk, forcing Talbot to wrestle the wheel to keep the car under control. Accelerating, Talbot pulled away, but the car behind them crept up and rammed them again several times in succession.

Talbot crowded the road to the right, leaving space in the lane to the left. The car behind took the bait, whipping around and drawing up beside Talbot, the passenger leaning out to aim his Mach 10.

In a single, smooth movement, timing it perfectly, Talbot jammed his brakes hard once so that the other car spurted past. Before the car was completely past, Talbot swerved hard to the left and gunned the engine, slamming the heavy nose into the back-quarter panel. The rear tires of the pursuing vehicle lost traction with the concrete. As it swung broadside to the road at ninety miles an hour, the tires of the leading wheels collapsed. The rims dug into the concrete and the car started to flip and roll down the highway. The passenger was ejected from the window and flew over Talbot to land in the road behind them, rolling like a broken doll. The second pursuit vehicle braked hard to avoid the body but was too late and plowed right over him.

The car in front flipped and rolled in front of Talbot. Seeing his chance as the car spun up on one end, Talbot gunned the gap. Glancing in his rear-view mirror, he could see the second car also clearing the wreckage and accelerating after him.

Still focused on the phone, Scott hung on grimly.

"She's in the Starbucks now."

Talbot nodded, watching the car behind them coming up fast.

"How good are you with your gun?"

"Top of my class."

"Okay, get ready. You take the driver."

Waiting for some open space around them, Talbot suddenly flipped the car around to face the opposite direction, driving one-handed in reverse as he reached for his Glock. Levelling it, he started firing rapidly through the windscreen at the passenger. Scott lifted the Mach 10 and directed a short, controlled burst at the driver. Their slugs punched through the pursuing car's windshield, hitting both driver and passenger. Immediately out of control, the car swerved hard and slammed into the road divider.

Dropping the Glock into his lap, Talbot spun the car back in the direction they were travelling. As he glanced in the rear-view mirror he could see a tendril of black smoke lift up out of the wreckage before it erupted in a single, vast fireball. The fire rolled and boiled, lifting ever higher as the superheated air picked up the oily black smoke to cast a shadow over the road behind them.

The flames were still climbing when Talbot took the exit ramp for Tenth Street.

"I think we're clear," he said, "but no chances. If they thought about putting a tracking device on this car while we were with Mansfield they'll be on top of us in no time."

164

"We're just five minutes from Starbucks," Scott said. "You get Jessie and I'll get your car. Mine is toast. I'll meet you in the parking lot of the church next to Starbucks."

"Okay." He glanced at her, watching her hands start to shake. "You okay?"

"Yes, why?"

"Your hands are shaking."

"Just the adrenaline."

"Okay," Talbot nodded.

"By the way, is that why you wanted to drive?" Scott asked.

Talbot nodded.

12h45, Starbucks, Fairfax Drive, Alexandria, VA

Breathing deeply as she tried to catch her breath after walking so quickly, Jessie huddled out of sight at a table in the back of Starbucks. She had bought a small cup of hot coffee in a Styrofoam cup to blend in with the clientele sipping their over-priced lattes and surfing the free Wi-Fi. She removed the lid and pretended to sip the coffee as her eyes darted nervously around studying the people around her for threats.

No-one seemed to have followed her, but she couldn't relax. Glancing out the window and towards the apartment, she saw four men in dark coats exit the apartment complex. Two turned away, but the other two started walking purposefully in her direction, their eyes roving around them.

Jessie huddled lower, her head down to hide her face. One of the men stared hard into the window, searching, before he looked away. The two men passed on out of sight.

Breathing a sigh of relief, Jessie resumed her vigil, watching the street towards the apartment again.

A heavy hand came down on her shoulder.

"Jessie Morgan? Please don't make a fuss. Stand up quietly and come with us."

Startled, Jessie looked up to see the same two men in dark overcoats. She hesitated, then nodded. Standing up she seemed to stumble over the chair leg. Pretending to get her balance she leaned on the edge of her table. As her hand came free she grabbed the cup of hot coffee and hurled into the face of the man across from her. He stumbled back, bellowing in pain as the hot liquid scorched his face.

The man behind her clamped his hand down hard on her shoulder, but Jessie spun in close and tight. Her left hand swung up hard to knock his hand off her shoulder. Her right hand grabbed the back of his neck for leverage as she slammed her right knee high and hard into the man's body. He grunted as the knee drove the air from his body, staggering back, but Jessie staying in close. Her knee lifted hard and fast three more times before she let go of the back of his neck. Shifting tactics she slammed her fists as hard as she could into the softer tissue of his face and throat.

The soft, preppie Starbuck's clients scattered away from them, some screaming, knocking tables and chairs over as they scrambled to get away.

Ducking his head, the man regained his balance and pulled a knife from a sheath concealed in his sleeve. Holding the blade low, he started to crowd his way in Jessie's direction. She backed up fast as he came forward, looking around for anything she could use as a weapon, but the second man came up behind her and wrapped her up, pinning her arms to her sides and bodily lifting her off her feet.

Frightened and angry, Jessie stabbed her fingers over her shoulder, her fingernails scratching bloody trails across his face. He grunted, throwing her hard against the wall and knocking her breath out.

Staggering to her feet, shaky but ready to do battle, she saw a fast-moving shape ripping through the tables behind the men.

Talbot one-stepped onto a table, somersaulting through the air above the first man. As he went over-head he grabbed the man's neck from behind, locking tight. The rotation carried him through the air so that his feet slammed down into the knife man's back, driving him forward. Talbot finished his rotation and landed on his feet still holding the man's neck. Talbot twisted hard and there was a sickening crack as the first man's neck broke. He crumpled into an inert pile at Talbot's feet.

Turning fast, Talbot dodged the slashing knife as the second attacker regained his balance and moved in quickly. Using short, fast slashes and stabs, the attacker drove Talbot back as he dodged and blocked the knife. Talbot skittered a chair across the floor at the attacker, trying to tangle his feet up, but he kicked it aside and moved in, crowding Talbot against the back corner. Grabbing a colorful silk scarf left on a table by one of the fleeing patrons, Talbot wrapped the ends around his fists and pulled it tight to make a moving shield. Leaving an opening in his defense, he baited the knife in close and wrapped the scarf around the attacker's wrist.

Jerking him forward and past his own body, Talbot turned, using the attacker's momentum as leverage to pull the knife hand up to head height. Quickly Talbot wrapped the scarf around his throat, trapping the knife hand against his ear.

Talbot pulled backwards trying to choke the man out. The attacker drove himself backwards, driving Talbot over a table, but Talbot hung on, dragging him over on top of him as the table collapsed under their weight. Twisting his powerful hands in the scarf, Talbot pulled tighter and tighter, feeling the strength fade from the attacker as he choked him out. Within seconds, the blood supply to his brain cut off, the attacker went limp. Talbot kept up the pressure until he was satisfied the man was dead.

He shoved the body away and staggered upright, gasping. Turning to check on Jessie he saw she was staring at him, her hands on her hips.

"Took your time a little, didn't you?" she said with a shaky smile.

"Just wanted to see how you would manage," Talbot answered, still sucking in great lungsful of air to catch his breath.

"And?"

"Not too shabby for a girl... against two trained operatives with years of experience. Not too shabby at all."

"I could have taken them," she said.

"Think so?"

"Two trained operatives with years of experience? Uh... no!"

Talbot grinned.

"Let me guess," she said, "we gotta go?"

Talbot nodded. Picking up her backpack, he led her outside. As they walked down the sidewalk towards the church parking lot, Talbot stole a sidelong glance at her.

"Only because you got me into Jim's Krav Magra classes."

"Well, I may have gotten you in, but you stayed in all on your own. I'm very proud of you."

Jessie smiled up at him. "For real?"

"For really real," he smiled back as they turned into the church parking lot.

Scott pulled up beside them.

"Any trouble?"

"Nothing Jessie says she couldn't handle," Talbot boasted.

Jessie punched him in the arm.

15h45, Ulysses S. Grant Memorial, Washington, D.C.

The bitter west wind coursed unhindered across the Potomac. It pushed down the length of the Lincoln Memorial Reflective Pool and the National Mall and slipped unwelcome tendrils of frozen air inside the collar of the few stalwarts determined to take selfies with the Ulysses S. Grant Memorial in the background.

With their backs to the wind, the conversation between Whitfield and La Salle went completely unnoticed by anyone around them. Nobody gave them a second look.

"Something off track came up. I don't really think it's a part of this, but I don't want to take any chances."

"What is it?" Whitfield asked.

"There's a doctor in Memphis who's been digging through the CDC test reports on Senator Williams."

"Do we know why he'd be interested?"

"His research is in genetic therapy for cancer, so it's possible he's just keeping a lookout for viruses he might be able to manipulate."

"To do what?"

"Rewrite genetic code that causes some cancers."

"Feasible." Whitfield thought for a moment. "It's probably nothing but do a little digging just in case."

"Okay."

"Is that why you dragged me out here?" Whitfield asked.

"No."

"What then?"

"We found out the woman helping Talbot is FBI."

"So why is the FBI helping this guy?" Whitfield asked, irritated.

"No idea, but she's acting alone. Her boss thinks she's out sick."

"How did you identify her?"

"They showed up together talking to Castle and Mansfield. We sent a six-man team to BioMediCom to intercept them, and a four-man team to the woman's apartment after the girl."

"And?"

"Dead."

"What do you mean, dead?" Whitfield asked sharply.

"Talbot killed everyone on his tail as well as the two who had cornered the girl. In a Starbuck's, no less."

Whitfield glared at La Salle.

"All the assets he's already eliminated, and you send only ten men?"

"Most of our assets are training Shevchenko's men in Chisinau. At your instruction, I might add."

"Well, he doesn't need them right now. Get our best twelve-man team back here."

"Already on their way. They'll be arriving stateside tomorrow afternoon."

"Good. One more thing," Whitfield said.

"What?"

"I do NOT want the FBI doing a grudge investigation into the death of that agent of theirs. Kill her, but make it look like Talbot did it. Understand?"

"Yes sir."

"Don't screw it up, or I'll find someone to replace you."

Wrapping his coat more tightly around him, Whitfield stepped out of the leeward side of the memorial and into the wind, walking without a backward glance back to the road where his car was waiting for him.

La Salle stared after him.

"Careful, old man," La Salle muttered to himself. "You forget who you're talking to."

22h15, Petro Stopping Center, Exit 369 off I40, Knoxville, TN.

Limited sleep the night before had ill-prepared both Talbot and Scott for a fourteen-hour drive to Memphis, so they had taken turns napping. Now the imperative tug of hunger had grabbed Talbot's attention. He glanced over at Scott asleep in the seat beside him. Despite the bubble of drool on her lip, he could not help but appreciate the view. Reaching a decision, he tapped her lightly on the shoulder.

Her eyes opened slowly, reconnecting her brain with her surroundings before she reached up and wiped the drool from her mouth with her palm.

She looked over at Talbot and saw him grinning.

"Not cool," she said acidly.

His grin just widened.

"Why did you wake me? I was drinking a Tequila Sunrise in Tahiti!"

"I am very tempted to pursue that line of conversation, but we need gas. We should probably get something to eat as well."

"Okay," Scott said, stretching as best she could in the cramped confines of the car as Talbot took the Watt Street exit off I40 in Knoxville.

Curled up on the back seat, Jessie had finally been able to drop off to sleep as well, but she woke up when Talbot and Scott started talking. She sat up, yawning.

"Where are we?"

Talbot glanced back at her in the mirror.

"Knoxville. Sleep okay?"

"Kinda. What time is it?"

173

"Eleven. Hungry?"

"Starving."

Pulling into The Petro Stopping Center, a busy twenty-four-hour operation a few miles west of downtown Knoxville, he parked next to one of the gas pumps. They pulled on their coats against the raw cold and walked inside, passing a young man, painfully thin and obviously cold, shivering at the door with his small backpack at his feet. His worn, faded jeans and threadbare windbreaker did nothing to keep him warm, but the blast of heat spilling out of the station as the door opened at least provided a momentary respite from the cold.

Talbot walked up to the counter to pay cash for the gas while Scott and Jessie found a table in the Iron Skillet in the back.

"That kid been standing out there long?" he asked the elderly man behind the counter.

"Probably five hours or more. He comes in for a few minutes every once in a while, pretending to shop, but he doesn't stay."

"Do you care if he stays?"

"No, I just think he's embarrassed. He was in the restaurant earlier, but didn't stay long."

"Think he ate?"

"Doubt it. Maybe coffee."

"Okay, thanks," Talbot said.

Walking back to the car, Talbot started the pump and watched the young man stamp his feet against the cold. He was standing as close to the wall of the building as he could to keep out of the wind.

The pump clicked off and Talbot pulled the nozzle out of the car, replaced the gas cap and hung the nozzle on the hook.

174

Climbing into the car, he found a parking space in front of the building. He stepped out and walked up to the young man.

"Where you headed?" he asked.

Startled, the young man looked up, not used to anyone talking to him.

"Trying to get home to Lexington."

"Cold to be hitching a ride."

"Very," The young man said with a smile, "but it'll be worth it."

"Really?"

"Yup, my sister's getting married."

"When'll that be?"

"Saturday, so I've still got time to get up there."

"Long wait for a ride, though. You checking with the truckers?"

"I don't like being pushy, but the guy in dispatch said he would ask them if anyone wanted company for the night haul up there."

"Good. Hungry?"

The young man shrugged. "Yeah, but I can wait 'till I get home."

"Okay," Talbot said, "Good luck."

Talbot pushed the door open and went inside. Wandering through the aisles he grabbed up a pile of nuts, jerky, fruit, a couple of Deli sandwiches and several cokes. He carried his collection over to the clerk. The clerk stacked the items in a paper bag as he rang them up. Talbot paid and slipped a twenty-dollar bill into the bag.

"Got another bag?"

"Sure."

Talbot bundled his own jacket into the empty bag the clerk handed over, grabbed up both bags, and walked back to the door. Pushing it open, he stepped out into the cold. He walked back over to the young man hiding from the wind against the building.

"I've had some tough times myself, so I know what it's like," Talbot said as he handed the bags over. "Just do me one favor, okay? Do the same for someone else one day."

"But I can't just take your jacket," the young man objected, seeing the jacket bundled up in the bag.

Talbot smiled. "Sure you can, you need it more than I do right now. Good luck getting home."

Talbot turned and walked away, pushing his way through the door to join Scott and Jessie at their table.

"Everything okay?" Scott asked as he sat down.

"Sure, why?"

"You took longer than I expected. We ordered already. We didn't know what you would want so we just got you coffee so far. That okay?"

"Perfect."

Seeing Talbot sit down, the waiter shuffled over to their table.

"Know what you want, Bub?"

"You serving breakfast?"

"Yup."

"Couple eggs sunny-side up, sausage, toast, and grits."

"Comes with a hash brown if you like."

"Sure."

The waiter wandered off into the kitchen to add his order to the table.

Scott noticed Talbot wasn't wearing a jacket.

"Aren't you cold?" she asked, curiously.

"In here? No, it's like a sauna. They could stand to turn the heat off for a bit."

Talbot changed the subject.

"By the way, I didn't get a chance to show you."

He dug in his jeans pocket, pulled out the thumb drive Hampton had slipped him, and handed it to her.

"What's this?" she said, turning it over in her hand.

"That's why Hampton wanted to talk about the pottery. He had it hidden inside for me to take. I just wish I knew what was on it."

Jessie hopped up.

"I'll get my laptop from the car, so we can see."

"Okay, car's right in front of the door," Talbot said as he handed her the keys.

Jessie turned and walked out, pushing the unlock button on the key fob as she pushed through the door. The running lights flashed at her and she walked over. Pulling open the door, she grabbed her backpack and shut the door. The door to the building opened as she walked back, and the young man dashed out, a huge grin on his face.

"Tell your dad thanks from me and let him know I got a ride!" he called out as he ran past.

Startled, Jessie looked back at him, but he was already gone. She walked back to the table frowning and plopped back down into her seat.

Talbot noticed the odd look on her face.

"Something wrong?"

"No, but some random guy just ran out past me and said to thank my dad, and to say that he got a ride. Weird."

"Maybe he mistook you for someone else," Talbot said, with a smile. "Did you get your computer?"

"Yes," Jessie said, pulling it out.

Scott handed her the thumb drive and she slipped it into the USB port. The Windows File Explorer automatically opened and gave her a view of the files saved on the drive.

"There's one file called Orion and another one called Scribbler," she said.

"Orion? Isn't that in the papers from your mom?" Scott asked.

"Yes, I'm opening it now." She opened the Word document and started scrolling through the pages.

"It looks pretty complicated. All kinds of medical stuff. There's also some pictures that look like they came from a microscope."

Jessie turned the computer so that Talbot and Scott could read it. After a moment Talbot looked up.

"Too complicated for me," Talbot said. "I'm going to need help to even get a feel if it's relevant."

"Too much for me, too," Scott admitted, "but it looks like it may be right up Zach's alley."

"Good thing we're headed to see him then. What about the other file, Jessie?"

Jessie turned the screen back and opened up the second file.

"Same kinda stuff," she said after a quick glance.

"Okay, we'll let Zach tell us what we're looking at," Scott said as their dinner arrived.

Chapter Five

"Well," Jessie said, glaring at the screen of her computer in the dark of the back seat, "I've read both files and I still can't understand it too well, but I think I might have figured out a couple of things."

"Really? Like what?" Talbot asked with a smile, glancing at her through the mirror. Her face was lit up in the bluish light of the screen, intent on reading, and she didn't notice his look.

"So the Orion file is talking about a virus they called Orion, and the Scribbler file is talking about another virus. No prizes for guessing what they called it. The Orion one seems like it changes its own genetic structure when you add genetic material to it. The other one doesn't change itself, it changes the genetic code of the host."

"Wait, what now?" Talbot asked.

"Orion will morph itself, and Scribbler morphs whatever it infects."

"Now why would Hampton want us to know that?" Scott puzzled.

"Especially since it sounds like Scribbler is the cancer-killing solution they have been trying to figure out," Talbot added.

"I don't know," Jessie said. "The rest was way too complicated for me."

Talbot's phone beeped, interrupting the discussion. He pulled it from his pocket and handed it to Scott to check the incoming text.

"It's from your friend in Odessa."

"What's he say?"

"It's just a string of numbers."

"How many?"

"Twenty-eight," Scott said after counting.

"Okay, it's an international phone number in code," Talbot said. "The numbers work in pairs. Add each pair together. If it comes up to anything less than ten, write it down. Anything over ten and you add the two numbers together and, if the result is less than ten, write it down or repeat the process."

"Oh, that's pretty clever," Jessie said. "So if the original pair is a nine and a four, added together you get thirteen, so you add the one and three from the thirteen to get four and write it down?"

"Exactly," Talbot said as Scott decoded the string of numbers. Dialing the number, she put the phone on speaker and handed it to Talbot. The phone rang once before the call was picked up.

"Hallo, my friend!" Zaitsev's booming voice and thick accent filled the car with energy.

"How'd it go, Alexis?" Talbot asked.

"Very tricky. These are very serious people. They use the military-grade security."

"Now I know that just made it fun for you."

"You know me too well, my friend!"

"Did you manage to get in?"

"Now you just make fun of me, right? Of course I get in! Nothing can stop Alexis!"

Talbot grinned at Scott.

"So what sneaky tricks did you use?" Talbot asked.

"Wait... are you on speaker phone?"

"Yes, I'm driving."

"Who is with you?"

"Jessie and Special Agent Kelly Scott of the FBI."

"Jessie, hallo!" Zaytsev boomed in delight. "I have heard so much about you! Your father tells me you genius!"

"Hello," Jessie answered, blushing.

"Yes, he tell me you embarrass NSA?"

"Kinda," Jessie said. "I stole their satellite for a while."

"That is brilliant! Not easy. Well done!"

"Thank you sir."

"And Special Agent Kelly Scott? Matt, why you got the FBI with you?"

"I trust her."

"Her? This Kelly is a woman? And you trust her? This is progress for you my friend! This is good! So you trust her, but the question is, do you LIKE her?"

Talbot caught Scott's eye.

"Yes, Alexis, I like her."

A small smile stole across Scott's face.

"Ha!" Zaytsev exclaimed. "I knew it!"

"But I like you too, Alexis." Talbot said, smiling.

"That is not what I meant. Besides, everybody like me!"

"Not so sure the CIA would agree with that."

"Of course they like me! They just wish they could catch me to tell me how much they like me!"

Talbot laughed.

"So Special Agent Scott, what you think of my friend?"

"From what I've seen since I met him yesterday, he's very capable."

"But of course, everybody know he is capable! He is the best! But do YOU like HIM?"

"As much as you can after one day," Scott said.

"Okay, Alexis, you've embarrassed everybody enough. What did you find for us?"

"Okay, so I already tell you it was tricky. I had to hide behind a hundred IP addresses so they couldn't find me, and when I got in, I only got five minutes alone."

"Only five minutes?" Talbot teased. "Jessie got into their secret department and stayed for fifteen minutes. You're getting old, Alexis!"

"We all know that, so why you bring it up? Besides, I am younger than you. AND better looking! But fifteen minutes? That is very good, Jessie! How you do that?"

"I already had over a thousand blind IP addresses in line from all over the world, so it just took them longer to filter through them all."

"Your daddy was right. You're a very clever one!"

"Did you find anything?" Talbot asked.

"Of course I find something. I am Alexis! I find a recording about mining rights in exchange for help getting Transnistria into UN. I will send it to you."

Talbot and Scott exchanged significant looks.

"Can you play it for us now as well?" Scott asked.

"Of course. Let me turn it on. I play just the relevant piece, okay? Rest is just chit chat."

The phone clicked a few times as they listened to Zaytsev fiddling with controls on the other end. Then a smooth American voice started speaking.

"Shevchenko, how do you expect us to be able to make the UN vote in your favor? Moldova will never let Transnistria get its independence."

"Not my problem, Whitfield," Shevchenko's heavy central European accent joined in, his voice gravelly and hard. "You want to get my Neodymium, then that's what I want in exchange."

"Be reasonable, man. We already got the subject on the agenda, so now it's up to you to persuade the UN delegates."

"I want guarantees, Senator, or I give the rights to someone else."

"Do you know who will vote against you?"

"Some of them."

"Get a complete list to me, and I will see what I can do."

The phone clicked a few more times before Zaitsev's spoke again.

"See? I tell you I find something!"

"You sure did. Nice work. Anything else?"

"No, that was all I had time for."

"Okay Alexis, thanks."

"Not a problem. If you need anything else, just let me know. You remember Li?"

"From China? Of course."

"He retired and comes to visit tonight. I think I take him fishing, but if you need me, just call, okay my friend?"

"Thanks Alexis. Good luck."

"Da. Maybe we catch a sturgeon. Get some caviar!"

The phone went dead.

"Well, he's certainly a character!" Scott said.

"You have no idea."

"So what is Transnistria?" Jessie interrupted.

"Have you heard of Moldova?" Talbot asked.

"Isn't it a small country?"

"Right. It's sandwiched between Romania and the Ukraine."

"What's that got to do with Transnistria?"

"There are some people in Moldova who want independence. They want to their own country, but they can't unless Moldova and the UN agrees. I think if the UN agrees, Moldova will as well. There's nothing there."

"Or there wasn't." Scott added. "If they really do have a lot of Neodymium, it could be a very rich area. Moldova will never let them go then."

"True," Talbot said. "Which is probably why they want to keep all that under wraps for now."

"But how does all that connect to Orion and Scribbler?" Jessie asked.

"I was just wondering the same thing," Talbot said.

07h30, Phoenix Headquarters, Washington, D.C.

Feet propped up on his desk, La Salle quickly scanned the security review of the last twelve hours. There was a knock on the door and Tremaine walked in.

"Found out a couple things for you."

"Yes?"

"NeoDine reported someone tried to hack into their database. They couldn't trace them, but they don't believe they saw anything. Apparently, they were only in for five minutes and didn't have time."

"Is this the first time?"

"Not even close. There's usually someone sniffing around. This is the first time anyone got in though."

"You think it's just a coincidence?"

"Best guess based on probability, yes."

"Okay. What else?"

"We intercepted a standard security report at BioMediCom. One of their scientists copied a couple of files to a thumb drive, so they followed standard process and interviewed him. He said he was going to take the files home to work on them. Apparently, this is the lead scientist and it's not the first time. He often does his documentation at home, so they closed the report."

"Do we know what files he copied?"

"Something called Orion, and something called Scribbler."

La Salle struggled not to react.

"Anything else?"

"One more. You asked for some background on the doctor digging into the CDC report on Senator Williams."

"And? Anything?"

"Yes. His aunt is Special Agent Kelly Scott of the FBI."

A muscle started to twitch in the inside corner of La Salle's eye, a stress-induced reaction to the faded scar that started above the bridge of his nose.

"Anything else?" he asked, under tight control.

"No, that's it."

"Okay. Has the field team from Europe landed at Dulles International yet?"

"No. It will be another hour or so."

"Keep them on the plane, file a flight plan from Dulles to Memphis, and have them wait for me."

"Yes sir."

As the door clicked shut behind Tremaine, La Salle pulled his feet off the desk and leaned forward, slamming the palm of his hand down onto the desktop.

"Damn! Damn! Damn!"

Pacing back and forth in front of the window, he planned his next move. Reaching a decision, he picked up the phone and dialed Whitfield on his secure line.

"Yes?"

"Three more developments."

"What?"

"First, someone tried to hack into NeoDine. We don't think they found anything. They were in less than five minutes."

"Second?"

"One of the research scientists at BioMediCom copied the Orion and Scribbler files to a thumb drive, apparently to work on them. He still had the thumb drive when they asked him about it and gave it back without fuss. It seems he works from home on paperwork a lot, so this may be nothing, but the timing is suspicious."

"And he had access rights to the files?"

"Yes, he wrote them in the first place."

"Third?"

"The doctor in Memphis digging into the CDC files on Williams?"

"Yes?"

"Special Agent Scott is his Aunt."

"That's not a coincidence."

"I didn't think so either. I'm heading to Memphis in an hour with a team. I think that's where they're headed."

"Okay, but don't waste time. You have to be in Chisinau on Saturday."

Whitfield hung up.

La Salle put the phone down and walked over to his office door. Locking it, he walked over to the bank of filing cabinets, opened the hidden door and stepped into the ante-chamber where a bio-suit hung ready for him. Ignoring it, he stepped up to the touch screen key pad beside the safe door and tapped on it a few times. The safe door opened and he reached in, pulling out a small, flat, stainless steel box with a single handle on the top and a battery-powered touch-screen lock on the side.

Tapping the small screen a few times, the top of the steel box popped open with a hiss and puff of vapor. Reaching inside he eased a rubber tray out of the box. The tray had a series of nine custom holes drilled into it. Eight of the holes contained red-capped, steel "cigar tubes" and the last hole contained another, slightly larger, green-capped tube. The holes were drilled to perfectly hold the tubes with a slight compression fit so that they could not slide out on their own.

Carefully opening one of the red-capped tubes, he gently slid a glass vial out. The vial had a red rubber stopper sealing it, and the top had been dipped in wax to further seal it. He slipped the vial back in, replaced the tube, and slipped the tube back into the square steel box with its carrying handle.

Carrying the box back into his office, he carefully shut the hidden door to the ante-chamber, put the box into his leather briefcase, and walked out.

08h30, Zach Michael's Home, Memphis, TN

The garage door opened to reveal Zach Michaels waving them in as Talbot pulled the car into the driveway in front of the new house at the north end of Meegan Drive. Stiff from the hours on the road, they climbed out of the car.

"Come on in!" Zach Michaels said, ushering them out of the garage. "I figured you might want the car out of sight?"

"Good call. We're sorry to barge in on you," Scott said.

"Not at all! Anybody hungry?"

"No thanks Zach, we stopped and had breakfast. This is Matt Talbot and his daughter Jessie," Scott said, introducing them.

"Welcome to Memphis."

"Thanks. Wish it was under better circumstances."

"No doubt. Quite the story Kelly was telling me. I'm sorry about your mom, Jessie."

"Thanks."

"Not to rush you or anything," Talbot said with a smile, "but we really are pressed for time."

"Of course. Let me show you what I found."

Turning, Michaels led them through the house to his computer room, equipped with an impressive array of computers and monitors set up on an enormous desk. The only window in the room was covered with a blackout curtain, and the walls were lined with shelves full of stacked books and papers. There was an odd collection of mismatched office chairs scattered around the room. Obviously it was not unusual for Michaels to have a team working with him in his house.

"Take a seat while I open this file," Michaels said.

Talbot, Jessie and Scott sat down and waited for Michaels as he opened the file and connected his computer to the projector. An image from an electron microscope materialized on the wall.

"So what can you tell me about the person who died?" Michaels asked.

"Not much. What do you want to know?" Scott asked.

"Well, who is he? What's his background? Did he travel overseas much? Do we know how or where he got infected?"

"Well, I really shouldn't tell you anything," Scott said. "How it will help?"

"Normally it wouldn't matter, but in this case, it may go a long way to explain what I found out."

"Okay," Scott conceded. "He was Senator Landon Williams, to our knowledge he has not travelled out of the country in years, and the first indication of infection was when he collapsed and died on the Senate floor on Monday."

"That makes this an even more unusual case than it already was," Michaels said.

"So what can you tell us?" Talbot asked.

"Well, he was killed by a completely unknown hemorrhagic virus."

"You mean Ebola?" Jessie asked.

"No, this looks a lot like a variation of Fulminant Hemorrhagic Smallpox."

"Smallpox?" Scott said, puzzled. "Wouldn't that mean he should have been covered in sores?"

"Normally, yes, but the Fulminant variety kills before those pustules can form. Whatever this is, it makes Ebola look like the common cold.

"Sounds horrible," Jessie said, shuddering.

190

"It is," Michaels agreed. "And no-one else has reported sick?"

"Not that we know about," Scott said.

"Makes no sense," Michaels said, thinking. "The disease process would imply multiple infections and subsequent deaths."

"So what's that picture you're showing us?" Talbot asked, interrupting Michaels thought process.

"Oh yes, right. That's a raw electron microscope image of the virus that killed the Senator. That view doesn't tell us a whole lot, does it?"

"Oh good, it's not just me," Talbot said.

"No, not just you," Michaels agreed. "So our research is to develop mathematical algorithms that we can run against the DNA sequences inside the image. These algorithms look for patterns of recognizable DNA strings and groups them for analysis. That lets you mark the identified segments and color code them for easier analysis."

"Did you run the algorithms against this yet?" Scott asked.

"Yes, that's the next image," Michaels said as he changed the picture on the wall.

A complex set of intersecting curves and lines drawn in 3D space, color coded in red, green and black, appeared on the wall.

"Not sure that helped," Talbot muttered.

"So how much do you know about how a virus works?" Michaels asked, grinning at Talbot.

"Less than nothing," Scott said.

"Okay, crash course. A virus can only infect its host if it can attach itself to the cell wall of that host. So even though there are all kinds of viruses, only some can infect humans because only some have the structure to attach to our cell walls. But once it attaches, the way it spreads in most cases is to penetrate the cell wall. Then it hijacks the DNA in our nucleus as the building blocks to reproduce itself. With me so far?"

All three nodded.

"Now once the virus has made a lot of copies of itself in that cell, the cell ruptures and the copies spill out. They start the process over again by attaching themselves to all the surrounding cells. From there the process just repeats over and over with exponential effect."

"How does this one kill so fast?" Scott asked.

"Well, your veins and arteries have a lining of endothelial cells which stop the blood from leaking out, but hemorrhagic viruses like this one make that layer leak like a sieve. That means you pretty much bleed to death on the inside. With this particular virus, that entire process happens in just a few hours."

"I've never heard of anything that fast," Talbot said.

"Neither have I," Michaels agreed. "Now most of these viruses are quite delicate. They don't survive outside the host long, but smallpox can last a long, long time outside your body. That's why I'm so puzzled that we only have one fatality."

"So what about this picture?" Scott reminded Michaels.

"Okay, so I had already run the algorithms on this sample and combined the results into three color groups. The majority is the red part you see. That's the smallpox variant, but on its own it's actually harmless."

"Why? Talbot asked.

"Because this variant of smallpox has no surface structure that can attach to a human cell. That means it can't infect a human."

"What's the black line?" Jessie asked.

"That's a Rhinovirus derivative from a common cold. Everything about the surface of the Rhinovirus portion is designed to attach to a human cell. That makes it highly contagious."

"Is it the combination that makes it deadly?" Scott asked.

"Not yet, no. Think of it this way. You can't attack an enemy when your back is turned, right?"

"Right."

"The Rhinovirus part makes it contagious but keeps the smallpox element facing away from the human cell. It helps the whole virus move from human to human very easily, but it makes it almost completely harmless."

"Because the orientation keeps the small pox part facing away from the human cell?"

"Exactly."

"So then that green line makes all the difference?" Jessie asked.

"Right. You see how the red small pox portion focuses down to a single line that T's into the green line?"

"Sure." Talbot asked.

"That green line is human DNA, and that's what sets this thing apart."

"How on earth would human DNA make this thing deadly?" Talbot puzzled.

"Well, this green human edge changes everything. First, our immune system doesn't see it as a threat and lets the virus in to do whatever it wants. It never even tries to slow the process down. Second, it re-orients the smallpox to face the cell."

"What do you mean?" Talbot asked.

"Remember how the Rhinovirus keeps the small pox's back turned to our cells?"

"Yes?"

"This strip of human-style DNA lines it up perfectly for attack."

"Sounds very complicated," Scott said. "But does that explain why there's only been one case of it?"

"No, it just makes it more confusing," Michaels said.

"It looks familiar," Jessie said, puzzled. "Can you rotate the image?"

"Sure. On the vertical or horizontal plane?"

"Vertical first."

Michaels started to rotate the image slowly until Jessie stopped him.

"Now the horizontal."

Michaels slowly turned the image.

"Stop," Jessie said.

All three of them stared at the image.

"I'll be damned," Talbot said, stunned. "It looks like Orion. See? The red looks like Orion's body, the black is the belt, and the green is the bow."

"It sure looks a lot like it," Michaels agreed. "Does that mean something to you?"

"We visited a company called BioMediCom yesterday and the lead scientist gave me a thumb drive with some files on it. One was called Orion. It also had a picture from an electron microscope in it," Talbot explained.

"Can I take a look at it?" Michaels asked.

"I was hoping you would," Talbot said, handing it over.

Michaels opened the file entitled "Orion" and paged through it until he came across the inserted image.

"Interesting," he said. Digging through the files, he came across a file in a format Jessie had been unable to open.

"Jackpot."

"What is it?" Talbot asked.

"It's the original data file from the electron scan. I can feed this through the algorithms."

"Will it take long?"

"Couple hours. I can read through the other files while the algorithms do their thing."

"Okay. Do you care if I take a shower while we wait?"

"Not at all. Towels under the sink, help yourself," Michaels said, already distracted.

" I'll shower after you then, dad," Jessie said.

"I'll go after you, Jessie," Scott added as they followed Talbot out. "Do you want some coffee while we wait on your dad?"

"No thanks, just a soda."

10h00, Zach Michael's Home, Memphis, TN

Refreshed after their shower, Talbot, Scott and Jessie rejoined Michaels in his computer room.

"Got anything yet?" Talbot asked.

"Actually, yes I do. Take a seat," Michaels said as he reconnected his screen to the projector. "First, it turns out that a company called GeneSig has identified a piece of our DNA that is our unique DNA signature."

"Right," Scott agreed. "The guy at GeneSig was telling us about that."

"Okay, so you knew that already," Michaels said as he projected a picture up on the wall. "Look familiar?"

"A little, but there's no green," Talbot said.

"Yes, there is," Jessie interrupted, "But it's really small."

"Exactly, Jessie. So after reading through the files, this first image is the initial structure which the file calls Alpha. Now let's look at the one they call Beta," Michaels said, putting another image up beside the other. "See the difference?"

"Of course," Jessie said. "Now it has a full size green bow."

"Right." Michaels said. "Now when I add the image from the CDC... we'll call this one Gamma... you can see it's a match."

"So what's it all mean?" Talbot asked.

"They built the Beta version to kill the Senator."

"Wait, do what now?" Talbot said, stunned.

"Basically, they attached a strip of the Senator's human DNA signature to the Orion Alpha. That coded it to hunt for the person with the matching DNA signature material. Once it found the match in the Senator, it mutated to activate the small pox which killed him."

196

"That's not really possible, is it?" Jessie asked.

"That's not all," Michaels added. "They have supplies of Alphas waiting to be coded for anyone at any time. All they have to do is introduce a complete string of the target DNA and it codes itself to hunt for that person. When you release it, it infects everyone it touches with something as harmless as the common cold until that signature finds its exact match. Then it activates the small pox and kills them."

"That's horrible!" Jessie said.

"It gets worse."

"How can it possibly get worse?" Scott asked.

"If you release an un-coded vial of Alpha into the air, each of the billions of virus spores in that vial will code to the first human genetic material it comes in contact with. It's possible that every one of those could code to a different human. At that point it will mutates and kill. This can kill an entire stadium of people in just hours."

The stunned silence deepened as the implications sank in.

"What I don't get is why they used this to kill the Senator," Michaels said.

"You think they killed him because they're trying to hide Whitfield's connection to a private mining company in a foreign country?" Scott asked Talbot.

"A lot of Senators and Congressmen have connections to private companies though," Michaels said. "Surely it's more than that?"

"I think the answer is probably in that audio segment from Alexis. Whitfield guaranteed a positive vote in the UN for Transnistria. The only way he can do that is to influence the vote somehow," Talbot said.

"How would he be able to do that?" Scott asked.

"If they get a good delegate turnout at the vote and the voting is going to come in close, they can kill a few of the delegates who are going to vote against it without breaking the quorum and the vote would still go through."

"Seems very complicated. Too much can go wrong."

"True, they would have to control a lot of the circumstances."

"Such as?"

"Well, they would have to be able to kill a bunch of them all at once. It would have to look natural, and they would have to make sure it happened as close to the vote as possible."

"Why?"

"So there would be no time to replace those delegates before the vote," Talbot said.

"Makes sense," Michaels said.

"We have to warn them!" Jessie insisted.

"You're right, Jessie, but they won't listen to a few nobodies. Particularly nobodies on the run from the law. Besides, we don't even know who to warn," Talbot mused.

"I think we'll have to go to London," Scott said.

"Why London?" Talbot asked, puzzled.

"You're not the only one who knows a guy," Scott said with a smile.

"How's your guy going to help?"

"He works for the UN."

"Okay, London it is," Talbot agreed.

"Jessie doesn't look too keen," Michaels said, smiling at an obviously delighted Jessie. "She can stay here with me."

"Not happening," Jessie said emphatically. "I'm going to London too!"

"Wait a minute," Talbot said thoughtfully. "No-one builds something like Orion without a backdoor anti-dote. What was on the other file?"

"The Scribbler file?"

"Yes."

"It didn't seem relevant. It described another virus that was designed to change the way we synthesize a specific protein in our cells," Michaels said. "More of a medical solution to a disease process than anything else."

"It must be relevant somehow," Talbot insisted. "Does Orion use that protein to do its thing?"

"Afraid not."

"How does the cell make that protein?" Jessie asked.

"The ribosomes in the cytoplasm outside the nucleus build the proteins."

"So how do they know what proteins to build?" Talbot asked, interested. "Or more specifically, does Scribbler change the ribosomes to make them change the way they build that protein?"

Michaels started grinning.

"What?" Scott asked. "Did you figure it out?"

"I think so. Proteins are built by the ribosomes, but they are told *what* to build by... DNA. The DNA is like a protein blueprint repository. If that protein design is not in the DNA, the cell can't build it."

"So Scribbler changes the blueprint for that protein?"

"Exactly."

"I still don't see how it's relevant with Orion," Scott puzzled.

"The protein itself is unimportant," Michaels said. "But what Scribbler is doing is to change the DNA signature."

"An identity change!" Jessie exclaimed. "So Orion can't find you anymore!"

"Bingo. It's pretty slick, actually," Michaels agreed.

"That's fine and dandy if you know Orion has already been coded to find you. I can see how you can use Scribbler to change your signature before it finds you, but what if you're already infected with Orion?" Talbot asked.

"Theoretically it's all a matter of timing, I suppose," Michaels pondered.

"What do you mean?" Scott asked.

"I would assume the two viruses would be in a race inside your body. As Orion spreads, it would be attacking cells that are still coded with the original gene sequence. So if Scribbler can change enough cell signatures fast enough to get ahead of Orion, you should be able to survive. Very theoretically, though."

"Dad?"

"Yes, Jessie?"

"How much would someone who has this want to keep it a secret?"

"A lot. Why?"

"Do you think they might want to stop anyone digging into the CDC report?"

"She's right," Talbot said, turning to Michaels. "Especially once they figure out your connection to Kelly. You're going to need to disappear for a while. At least until we've sorted this out."

"That serious?"

"Afraid so. You'll have to go somewhere no one knows you and lay low."

"Well, I just started dating someone. Her family has an old cabin in the Appalachians. I can hide out there, I suppose."

"Good. Start at the bank and withdraw as much cash as you can. Then forget you ever had a credit card or a cell phone. I'll let you have one of my encrypted burners. They're untraceable."

"Okay."

"We also need to trade vehicles. They don't know mine, so they can't trace you. We'll take yours and leave it in long-term parking at the airport in Nashville."

"Why Nashville? Why not here in Memphis?"

"If they come by here and see your car is missing, one of the first things they'll do is check the airport here. They'll figure out where we're headed much too soon."

"Makes sense."

"One more favor?"

"In for a penny..." Michaels said with a shrug.

"Can you swing by Walmart and get us a few things? We're going to have to change our looks."

"Sure."

Zach was the designated judge for the success of their disguises, and their transformation was hardly subtle.

Scott had ditched the severe navy pantsuit, ponytail and minimalist makeup and opted for a more flowing look. Knee-high black boots and black tights, a cerulean blue, buttoned blouse open at the neck, and a gray sweater coat with a long, flowing tail were all complemented by an elegant pashmina in blues and silver.

She had added makeup to emphasize her beautiful eyes, and her now auburn hair picked up golden highlights as it cascaded in loose curls over one shoulder, partially obscuring one side of her face.

As expected from an extended family of almost all boys, Zach had teased her on how much of a difference it was, but she was surprised by how much she enjoyed the stunned expression on Talbot's face when she walked into the room.

Jessie had categorically refused to either cut or color her signature red hair. Instead, she had braided it up and away from her face and hidden it away inside an oversized, floppy, black wool beanie. From there she had gone completely Goth. She was wearing an over-the-top study in black. Shapeless black clothes, a black silk choker, long black leather dust coat and clunky black platform boots were all offset by silver buckles, chains and giant safety pins.

There was even a stick-on tattoo of a black widow spider on the side of her neck, crawling out from under the choker. A thick silver nose ring, black fingernails, heavy black makeup smudged around the eyes and black lipstick finished the rather disturbing look she had chosen.

Zach's only comment had been that she looked terrifying and that only hardcore Goths would want to be anywhere near her. She had giggled completely out of character at the compliment.

Talbot's choice to play the role of an aging gay Lothario had started a fit of giggles in both Jessie and Scott. He had shaved his face as close as possible and dyed his hair an almost unnaturally dark black, combing it to sweep across his forehead. He wore skinny white jeans and white leather belt, light pink buttoned shirt with wide collars, partially rolled up sleeves and matching socks. Matching white patent leather shoes were complimented by a baby blue, sleeveless sweater, white cashmere scarf and Sinatra-style fedora. Black eyeliner and a single ear Cubic Zirconia stud finished the look.

But the greatest difference was Talbot's change in mannerisms. His walk, how he stood, how he gestured as he spoke, even the tilt of his head played to every possible stereo-type.

"You laugh," Talbot said, grinning, "But when people see an over-the-top stereo-type, they don't see the person inside anymore. Both of you need to play to the stereo-type of who you're pretending to be. So Jessie, show me who you are."

"Okay, no problem."

Reaching into the pocket of her duster, Jessie pulled out her headphones and inserted them into her ears. Selecting a punk rock track on Pandora, she stalked across to the couch, collapsed into it as if the weight of the world was bearing down on her. She looked at Talbot with utter disdain and rolled her eyes dramatically before she turned her face away and ignored him completely. Utter boredom oozed from her every pore.

Jessie stole him a look.

"Zach was right... you're a little terrifying."

She laughed.

"Where did you learn all that?"

"There's a girl at school. Everybody stays away from her, but she's actually got a really nice side when you get to know her."

"Well, as long as you don't show your nice side, that should do the job very nicely," Talbot said. "How about you, Kelly? Who are you?"

"I'm a liberal college professor who loves to read. I'll be constantly hurt by my daughter's attitude to everything I say, and I'm trying to use a trip to Europe to reconnect with her."

"Hear that, Jessie? Roll your eyes at Kelly or say 'whatever' to everything she says, okay?"

"What-ever-r-r-r-r."

"No need to play the role quite yet."

"Who says I was?"

Zach snorted into his soda.

"Be afraid, Matt. Be very afraid."

"No kidding," Talbot grinned. He turned back to Scott.

"One more thing, if you're a college professor, you must either teach something so obscure no-one will be able to call you on anything you say, or you need to know the subject inside out. What will it be?"

'Oh, that's easy. I'm a Forensic Archeologist specializing in facial reconstruction. I'll even be reading a thick book on the subject."

"And what exactly is a Forensic Archeologist specializing in facial reconstruction?"

"I'm so glad you asked! Let me show you!" she gushed, slipping into character and opening her book to a page filled with pictures of clay.

"I look at the tiny little bumps on a skull to figure out how much soft facial tissue to attach and where. See?" she said, pointing at the pictures. "That way I can rebuild what a face probably looks like to help police identify the remains."

"Wow, straight into character. But if you're going to jump into a conversation about it, you need to really know what you're talking about."

"As it happens I wrote a paper on it for my Master's in Criminal Science."

Talbot looked at her for a moment.

"Okay, I got nothing!"

"I'm telling you, she's amazing!" Zach added.

She grinned.

"So what do you think, Zach?"

"I think no-one will ever look at the three of you and connect that look to who you really are."

"Good. Now we need to get some passport pictures. Jessie, you first. We'll use that wall as a backdrop. Try to put as much disdain and boredom as you can into your expression."

15h15, Michaels Home, Meegan Drive, Memphis, TN

The black shadows hidden in the field of trees behind Michaels home were silent, patiently waiting. As they watched the house, two black Tahoe's pulled up in front of the house from opposite directions. Before they coasted to a stop the doors opened to disgorge a fast-moving tactical assault team.

Before the Tahoe's rolled to a stop, the team in the field fired tear gas through the windows in the back of the house, then rushed forward quickly in support of the breach team in front. Within less than sixty seconds the team had cleared every room in the house. The squad leader walked out of the front door, the tear gas spilling out behind him, and removed his mask as a third black Taurus pulled up to the curb smoothly.

La Salle stepped out, impeccably dressed as always, the winter sun gleaning in the blaze of white hair over his forehead. He walked up the path to join the squad leader in front of the door.

"Anything?"

"House was empty."

"Computers?"

"There's a room full of them."

La Salle turned and waved at the Taurus. An overweight, heavily bearded, scruffy-looking man heaved himself out. The buttons on the red Hawaiian shirt struggled to restrain the jiggling mass. He lumbered over to join them clutching a laptop.

"Show him to the computer room, then report back to me." La Salle said as he turned back to the squad leader.

"Yes sir."

La Salle wandered over to the side, waiting, until the squad leader rejoined him.

"Your computer guy is… different."

"I know. But he knows his stuff. What was he doing in there?"

"By the time I left he was already hooked into those computers and running some sort of scan. Said something about the non-existent security."

"What else?"

"Only hit on his search was for that Senator."

"What about it?"

"He said it just looked like research."

"What kind of research?"

"Something about isolating and identifying gene segments in longer strings. I didn't understand much about it."

La Salle looked thoughtful.

"Anything else?"

"That's all he said."

"And the rest of the house?"

"He had company. Wet towels, dirty dishes, that sort of thing. And if I were a betting man I would say they were working on disguises."

"Why do you say that?"

"Three sets of worn clothes, a trash can full of Walmart bags and a box of hair dye."

"Where there any Walmart receipts in the bags?"

"Didn't check."

"Find out."

The squad leader touched his hand to the throat mike.

"Jake, search those Walmart bags for receipts. Check the trash as well."

They waited for a minute. La Salle could hear someone talking over the radio into the earpiece in the squad leader's left ear.

"And?"

"No receipts."

"Is there a car in the garage?"

"No."

"Find out what he drives. Find out where it is. When you find it, call me. Anything else my guy finds on those computers, call me. I'll be in the air."

"Yes sir."

16h30, Front Lobby, Nashville International Airport

"Okay, now what?" Jessie asked. "How are we going to fly out without passports?"

They were standing in the lobby of the Nashville International Airport after ditching the car they had borrowed from Zach in one of the long-term parking lots.

"I have a sneaky feeling I know the answer," Scott said.

"What?"

"Your dad's going to say he knows a guy."

"Well, I do. And he already dropped a packet off for us at Customer Service."

"Just like that?"

"Almost. I emailed him the pictures we took, he did his thing, and then handed in an envelope for Lost and Found."

"You conspire with some very devious, probably illegal people, you now that?" Scott said.

"That did not sound much like you are unhappy about it."

"Normally you'd be in cuffs by now, but today I have a bit of a different perspective. So where do you get this envelope?"

"Right there," Talbot said, indicating a Customer Service kiosk against the wall. "Go downstairs to Baggage Claim and wait for me there. And from now on, we're in character."

"Okay," Scott said. "C'mon Jessie."

"What-ever-r-r-r-r."

Talbot watched a moment as they drifted off, then turned and sashayed over to the kiosk.

Talbot coughed politely to lift the eyes of the Customer Service Agent up from scrolling through her Facebook page. Her fake eyelashes looked so heavy, he was certain her eyelids were the fittest muscles in her body. When she looked up she saw a dapper gentleman in a stylish fedora, smiling as he waited.

"Yes sir, can I help you?"

"I sure hope so," Talbot said, smiling. "I was trying to get my tickets printed at one of the self-service kiosks. It wasn't working so I had to switch to another one. When I was finished I realized I left my envelope on top of the other ticket kiosk. When I went back it was already gone. Please tell me someone turned in a large, padded Manilla envelope? It had my company name on it, Chisinau, Inc."

"Maybe," she said.

Reaching under the desk she fumbled around for a moment, and pulled out an envelope, hiding it from Talbot so that he could not see any of the writing.

"Can you spell the name of your company, please?"

"Of course. C-H-I-S-I-N-A-U. It should also have three letters handwritten very small in the top left corner on the back."

"And what are the letters?" she asked, turning the envelope over.

"M-T-T."

"Then this would be yours," she said, handing it over the counter. "Is there anything else I can help you with, sir?"

"No, thank you so much," Talbot smiled primly. "You've been very helpful already."

"Not at all, sir. Travel safe and enjoy your flight."

"I will, thank you," Talbot acknowledged as he turned and walked away.

Taking the stairs down to Baggage, he found Scott and Jessie waiting for him.

"Got it," he said as he opened the envelope. Inside were three smaller envelopes. He pulled them out.

"Mrs. Carla Clark, here's your Passport, Driver's License and credit cards. Ms. Rachel Jessica Clark, these are yours. We gave you your same middle name to help avoid confusion in case we call you Jessie by mistake."

Taking their envelopes, Scott and Jessie tore them open and inspected the contents. Talbot did the same. The name beside his new passport picture was Patrick Alan Larson.

"How come my passport shows I've travelled already?" Jessie asked.

"TSA agents pay a little less attention to the face when the passport shows you have travelled safely in and out of the country before. They just check your destination stamps for red flag countries like Syria or Iraq, then hand it back. Your stamps are for places you've already actually been so you can talk about them if you have to."

"I see I've travelled as well?" Scott asked.

"Yes. Same dates and places as Jessie."

"But I've never been to some of these places. I wouldn't be able to talk about them."

"Maybe not, but a distracted professor travelling for a convention dragging her daughter around with her would never leave the convention hotel anyway. Which is another reason for Jessie being mad at you. Again."

"Clever. There's also stamps here for other places I've actually been."

"Exactly. You've travelled without her a couple of times. Having a lot of travel history is its own disguise, especially around bored TSA agents."

"That's not why I mentioned it. How did you know I've been to these places?"

"Oh, I didn't, but my guy knows these things," Talbot smiled.

211

"I just bet he does," Scott muttered.

"Turns out it's a good thing, right?" Jessie said.

"True."

"Okay," Talbot said. "Your tickets are already paid for, and you've been seated next to each other. Go up to the ticketing kiosks upstairs and scan your passports to get your ticket printed, then go check in."

"What about luggage?" Scott asked. "Won't that be suspicious?"

"If anybody asks, you have no luggage because you shipped it ahead. I'll be a little behind you in the line. Remember to stay in character. Kelly, when you get to security, maybe you can be trying to talk at Jessie, and Jessie you should probably make it as obvious as possible that you're ignoring her. They see that every day, so they will barely notice you, okay?"

"Okay, no problem," Scott said.

"There's one more thing I should probably mention."

"What?" Jessie asked.

"They probably already know the car is here, so they may have people watching at the TSA checkpoints. Go all out on the stereo-types, okay?"

Talbot watched Jessie.

"You okay? Nervous?"

"A little."

"Flying?"

"No, I like flying."

"Okay, but if someone asks, just tell them you don't like flying. It's also another reason you're mad at Kelly, okay?"

She still looked nervous.

Talbot hesitated, then pulled her into a hug, holding her as he whispered into her hair.

"Don't worry, I'll be right there. I'll keep you safe, okay?"

Jessie hugged him fiercely, then stepped away.

"Okay."

Glancing at Scott, Jessie grinned.

"I think Kelly might be nervous as well."

"You are?" Talbot asked.

"A little. I hate flying."

"For real, or is that your story?"

"She needs a hug as well," Jessie said, nudging him with a smile.

Scott flushed, suddenly disconcerted by the warmth and tenderness in his eyes as he looked at her.

"I would love to give her a hug, Jessie, but I'm not sure she wants one."

"Oh please. You both want to hug, so quit stalling already!" Jessie said, grinning. "You can pretend it's because she's nervous about flying because nobody would think that," she said, pointing at Talbot's outfit, "would ever be interested in Kelly."

"True," Talbot agreed. Smiling, he stepped forward, his hand reaching for her waist, and pulled her gently into his arms. She tucked her elbows inside, then unconsciously rested her forehead against his shoulder. As the warmth of his hug cocooned her, she resisted the impulse to lift her arms and wrap them around the back of his neck. The energy between them was electric. After a moment Talbot let go, reluctantly stepping back.

"To be continued?" he asked, his eyes locked on hers.

Scott recovered her composure quickly.

"Not while you're dressed in that ridiculous outfit," she said.

"Fair enough," Talbot chuckled. "Now you two need to get going. I'll be a little behind you."

They turned and walked away, Jessie trailing a cloud of attitude. Talbot watched them until they reached the top of the escalator, then followed them. They turned left to find a ticket kiosk, so Talbot turned right, choosing a kiosk on the opposite end of the concourse. He scanned his passport and collected his ticket, watching as Scott and Jessie did the same. He fiddled with his documents until there were several groups of people behind them waiting in line at the check-in counters before joining the queue.

Standing in the slow-moving line Talbot pulled his phone out of his pocket and downloaded a word game to look busy. He kept his head down to discourage anyone from starting a conversation. Out of the corner of his eye he could see Scott and Jessie reach the counter. After a few moments the agent handed them their boarding passes. They turned away and walked over to the line waiting to go through the TSA security checkpoint.

Talbot strolled over to the slightly-built agent at the ticketing desk.

"Good evening sir," he said, smiling. He wore just the slightest hint of eyeliner, and his hands were perfectly manicured.

"Good evening indeed," Talbot smiled as he handed his ticket and passport over.

"Single to London?"

"That's right."

"I wish I was going back to London," he said. "The scene there is so vibrant."

Glancing through Talbot's passport, he looked up, smiling.

"My, my, you certainly get around, don't you?"

"Not as much as I used to," Talbot flirted. "The world is so different now."

"I know what you mean, and the web has changed everything. Not that I like it... I much prefer meeting people face-to-face," the agent hinted.

"Far less ambiguity," Talbot agreed with a smile, playing the role.

"Will you be in London long?"

"I'm not sure yet. I've actually never met him in person," Talbot confided.

"Oh, that can be so tricky. I hear it can sometimes work out, but it never does for me. Good luck in London," the agent said wistfully as he handed Talbot his passport and boarding pass.

"Thank you!"

Smiling, Talbot wandered off to join the line at the security checkpoint. Jessie and Scott were less than a dozen people ahead, and he could see that Jessie was nervous again. There was a black-suited man standing beside the TSA agent. He seemed to be looking for someone in particular.

Pulling out his phone again, Talbot sent a quick text to Zaitsev. After a moment his phone rang.

"Role play ready," Zaitsev said quietly.

Talbot started talking into the phone, obviously upset. A growing range of bystanders quickly got the impression that Talbot was having a rapidly escalating dispute with an ex-lover. As the volume increased, the TSA agent glanced up, watching for a moment before reaching for the Jessie and Scott's passport.

Talbot's volume and bitter diatribe continued to escalate and finally reached an epic level, completely distracting both the TSA agent and the black suit. With barely a glance, the TSA agent handed their boarding passes and passports back and waved them through.

Talbot finished the call with a string of accusations, allegations and snide insults.

"I hate you!" Talbot shouted into the phone before he hung up, his face flushed and his breathing quick. The people around him studiously avoided eye contact as the line moved through the TSA station quickly.

As Talbot's turn came, he handed his passport and boarding pass over, muttering under his breath. The agent barely glanced at him, but the black suit studied Talbot carefully.

Talbot glared back at him.

"And no, I am *not* available!" he said acidly at the black suit. The suit looked at him coldly, then decided Talbot could not possibly meet the description and looked on down the line past Talbot.

The TSA agent handed Talbot's passport and boarding pass back and Talbot walked through. Dropping his phone, shoes and belt into the tray, he watched it go through the screening machine, then took his turn through the body x-ray.

Talbot collected his things and minced his way over to the kiosk across from the security gate where he bought a People magazine to help stay in character. As he paid for the magazine he glanced at the crowd and saw Scott and Jessie coming out of the restroom and turn towards their gate. Scott ignored him completely, but Jessie caught his eye and started to giggle as they walked past.

Taking his time peering into all the expensive shops on the way, Talbot finally reached his gate. The waiting area was crowded, but he managed to find a seat across from Jessie.

He winked at her as he caught her eye and she started giggling again. Scott struggled not to laugh out loud as she kept her eyes focused on her book.

Chapter Six

FRIDAY January 20th, 2017, 12h30, Waterloo Station, London

After years of catching what sleep he could at any opportunity, the flight over had given Talbot plenty of time to rest, although he had woken up stiff from the cramped seat. The train ride from Heathrow to Waterloo Station had given Talbot the chance to watch Jessie's delight as she saw flashes of England pass by the window.

Talbot and Jessie had taken a few minutes at the airport to buy clothing that better reflected who they were, and except for Talbot's black hair, they looked very much the same as they had in Washington.

Scott had decided she liked her look.

Now off the train at Waterloo Station, Talbot was leading them south east down Waterloo Road. After a couple of blocks, they crossed the road and walked into the lobby of the Hampton at Gray Street.

"May I help you?" the well-dressed clerk behind the desk asked warmly.

"Reservations for Larson and Clark, please?" Talbot said at the desk.

She smiled widely, her perfect teeth a dazzling white against the ebony of her skin.

"Welcome, sir, we've been expecting you. As requested, your rooms are on the top floor away from the elevators." Her accent was a curious mix of England and North Africa. "Do you need help with luggage, sir?" she asked as she scanned their door keys.

"Unfortunately, the airlines lost our luggage, so nothing to carry yet. We'll pick up a few things later. Thank you, though."

"I'm sorry to hear that, sir," she said as she handed over their keys. "Are you familiar with London, or would you like some ideas on where you can buy some clothes?"

"Thank you, but I know London quite well."

"Of course, sir. The elevators are around the corner, and breakfast will be served in the morning through that hallway to your left. Enjoy your stay!"

"Thank you," Talbot smiled as he turned away, leading Scott and Jessie to the right and round to the elevators.

Their rooms were side-by-side on the top floor. Talbot pushed into his room to check it out while Scott and Jessie went into the room next door. After a moment there was a knock on Talbot's door. He opened it and Jessie bounced in, followed by Scott.

"So cool! You have to use your room key to turn the electricity on in the room!"

Talbot chuckled. "Yeah, it's a good idea for saving electricity, but not a good idea in summer. The room is hot when you go in and takes a while to cool off after you put your key in."

"Oh, I never thought of that!" Jessie said.

"So what's next?" Scott asked.

"Well, ideally we need you to talk to your guy at the UN. How well do you know him?"

"Pretty well. We dated for almost a year when I was stationed in London."

"Oh really?"

"Dad's jealous."

"No, I'm not!" Talbot protested unconvincingly. "I'm trying to figure out if there's enough history that he would be okay with giving you classified information without telling him why."

"I still say you're jealous," Jessie teased, grinning.

"Well, be that as it may," Talbot said, glaring at an unrepentant Jessie, "we need to figure out how to get in touch with him."

"No problem, I have his number," Scott said, smiling widely at Jessie.

"Sure, just happened to have his number handy," Talbot muttered under his breath with feigned disgust.

"Of course I do. I googled the International Maritime Organization where he works and there it was." Scott laughed as she dialed. The phone rang a moment before the operator answered.

"Nathan Fulham, please."

"Who should I say is calling?"

"Kelly Scott."

The phone clicked a few times before Fulham, his voice crisp and his Eton accent evident, answered.

"Good morning, Nathan Fulham speaking. How may I be of service?"

"Hello Nathan, its Kelly."

"Well, well, they said it was you, but I wasn't sure if I should believe it or not. How are you?"

"Well, thank you. And yourself?"

"Excellent! Very busy and very happy!"

"I'm so glad to hear it. I heard you got married?"

"I certainly did. Do you remember Mary Lee? She was the paramedic that helped me when I broke my ankle getting off the bus?"

"Of course, although I never met her."

"Well, we were married about six years ago, and we have two boys now."

"Congratulations!"

"And you?"

"Oh, still stuck on work."

"That's no surprise. I take it this is not a social call?"

"It isn't. Can we meet?"

"Sure, come on by the office anytime this afternoon."

Scott caught Talbot shaking his head.

"Can it be outside your office, perhaps?"

Fulham paused before answering.

"I usually have a table at the Wolseley at three Friday afternoons. Would that work?"

"Perfect. See you there."

Hanging up, Scott looked at Talbot, her eyebrow raised quizzically.

"I take it you did not want to meet in his office?"

"No chances," Talbot said. "I don't want anyone to know we're here if we can avoid it."

14h55, The Wolseley, Piccadilly, London

Jessie was in English heaven.

Their waiter had just left and the small table between Talbot and Jessie was covered in a white linen tablecloth and matching serviettes. The three-tiered silver cake tray was loaded with scones, cookies, small sandwiches and slices of cake, and a pot of steeping tea with two delicate china tea cups and saucers finished the elegant spread.

Talbot's eyes wrinkled in a smile as he watched her pour their tea. She carefully selected some items from the cake tray before delicately biting into one of the beautiful pastries.

Talbot reached for one of the sandwiches, biting into it as he looked across the room. Scott was waiting at the door for Fulham to arrive. At that moment, exactly on time, the heavy glass door pushed open. A tall man impeccably dressed in a navy pinstripe suite joined a smiling Scott. Feeling a little foolish at the sudden surge of jealousy, Talbot measured the man as they were shown to their table, his eyes taking in the Cambridge tie and classic English brolly.

Across the room, Scott and Fulham took their seats across the table from each other.

"Your usual, sir?" The waiter asked as he seated them.

"Yes please."

"And for you, madam?"

"The same will be fine, thank you."

"Certainly, madam."

The waiter disappeared as Fulham studied Scott.

"Well, time has certainly been kind to you," he complimented. "I don't think I ever saw you dress like that."

"Thank you. Time as treated you well, too. And congratulations again on your family."

"Thank you."

Almost immediately the waiter returned with a tray of sandwiches, a pot of tea and two cups.

"That was quick," Scott commented as the waiter walked away.

"Standing order. That way I can get in and out in under twenty minutes."

"Efficient as always," Scott said, pouring their tea.

"So what can I help you with, Kelly?"

"I need a list of the UN Delegates, where they are, what their schedules are, and the agenda for their meetings for the next three months."

Startled, Nathan looked up from selection of sandwiches.

"Now why on earth would you need something like that and, more to the point, why do you have to ask me for it in a public tea room?"

"I believe it has bearing on a murder investigation back home."

"I'm afraid I'm going to need a little more information than that."

"I'm investigating the murder of a Senator, and some of the tentacles point to some of the UN delegates being at risk."

"Not good enough."

"I don't think I can tell you more than that."

"Come on, Kelly, you're going to have to give me more to work with than that."

"I need you to trust me."

"I would have trusted you years ago, but the world has changed. People change. I have no idea what you might be up to these days."

Scott hesitated, then came to a decision.

"Complete confidentiality?"

"Of course."

"Someone used a weaponized small pox to kill him because he knew too much. We think he had stumbled on a plot to influence an upcoming vote, and they may use this virus to do it."

Fulham studied her carefully for a moment.

"Seems farfetched. Wouldn't a virus like that go rogue?"

"Normally, yes. But this one is special."

"How?"

"It's designed to be customized."

"What do you mean?"

"They can program it for a specific person."

"Oh come now, Kelly. Too much like a bad science fiction movie. Try again."

Scott sighed and pulled out her phone. She unlocked the screen and handed it over to Fulham with an article from the Washington Post already pulled up.

Fulham read it through to the end.

"This doesn't say anything about a weaponized small pox."

"It wouldn't. Zoom in on the body in the picture."

Fulham zoomed in. The body was badly contorted, and there was blood at his eyes, ears and nose. Fulham put his cup down, his appetite gone.

"Hemorrhagic?"

"Yes. It only took a couple of hours."

"And nobody else got sick?"

"Nobody."

"Who else knows?"

"A lot of people know how he died of some sort of Hemorrhagic disease, but not that is was customized for him."

Fulham drummed his fingers on the table, thinking.

"Why not just warn the UN and let them protect their people?"

"The people we suspect are involved have powerful ties in the government, and we don't know who can be trusted. That's why I came to you."

Scott watched as Fulham turned the information over in his head, examining the angles.

"Something else," she added.

"What would that be?"

"There's a surveillance risk."

"What do you mean."

"I mean that this is so deep that if you start digging into anything related to their schedules, it may trigger a red flag for them."

"How likely?"

"Very. Can you help?"

Carefully he took a sip of tea, deep in thought. Scott waited as he processed the information.

"Alright, I can help."

"Thank you."

Fulham sipped his tea once more, then placed his cup down and fastidiously dabbed his mouth with his serviette.

"Very well. I can put the information you need on a thumb drive and meet you after work on my way home. Shall we say quarter-past-five at the base of the London Eye?"

"What will be your cover story if they ask?"

"I will say I am finishing up a project investigating ways to reduce plastic in the oceans. I can say I am looking at the schedule to find time to add a resolution to the agenda."

"And are you?"

"As it turns out, yes."

"Thank you."

Fulham nodded as he stood up.

"My bus will be stopping outside in a moment. I'll see you this afternoon, then."

Scott watched as he left, waiting for him to step outside and board his bus before joining Talbot and Jessie at their table.

"Well? How'd it go?"

"Good. He wanted to know why, so I had to tell him a little more of what we know than I wanted, but he'll give me a thumb drive with the information after work at the Eye."

"Can you trust him to keep it quiet?"

"Absolutely. Once he decides on the right thing to do, he is utterly dependable."

"Did you explain the risks?"

"Yes. Turns out, we could not have been any luckier on the timing."

"So what are we going to do for the next hour while we wait?" Jessie asked.

"Kill time, I suppose. Any ideas?" Talbot said.

"Yes!" Jessie said excitedly. "Fortnum and Mason!"

"Whozit and what?" Talbot asked.

226

"Fortnum and Mason. It's an upscale department store that opened the year after Benjamin Franklin was born, and it's just a couple of blocks down the street. Kelly said I have to see it!"

"Oh she did, did she?" Talbot said.

17h00, The International Maritime Organization (IMO), Albert Embankment, London

They split up after leaving Fortnum and Mason. Jessie and Scott had gone directly to wait at the London Eye while Talbot had opted to wait discretely outside the IMO waiting for Fulham to exit his offices. Standing across the street, Talbot studied the three-story grey building on the Albert Embankment, almost directly opposite Lambeth Bridge.

The tall tower on the corner of the Palace of Westminster and the Clock Tower housing Big Ben added to the setting but, with one exception, the IMO building was bland and non-descript.

The exception was a two-story sculpture of the prow of a ship that seemed to be sailing out of the building. A sailor wearing a hard hat and carrying a coil of rope was standing on the prow looking over the street. Talbot was making every effort to melt into the tourist landscape by taking pictures aimed in every direction.

As Big Ben struck five o' clock, the front doors opened, and a horde of civil servants spilled out. Some turned immediately left or right down the street, some crossed the street to wait at the bus stop, and the rest chose to walk along the embankment that lined the River Thames.

Talbot saw Fulham exit the building, walking briskly. He crossed the street and opted to walk to the Eye, following the path north along the Thames under Lambeth Bridge. As Talbot watched, one of the tourists who had been taking pictures started following Fulham north. Talbot hesitated, watching to make sure no-one else followed before falling in behind, frequently pausing to take pictures of the historic landmarks across the river.

As he trailed along, Talbot called Scott.

"Hey, looks like someone else is following your boy."

"Not good. And he's not 'my boy'."

"You and Jessie get out of sight until I get there."

"Okay."

Knowing Fulham was headed to the London Eye, Talbot picked up the pace. By the time Fulham and his tail reached the pedestrian underpass at Westminster Bridge, he was able to jog up the stairs to the road level, and dash across the bridge and back down to the embankment on the other side to get ahead of Fulham. Walking quickly, he found Jessie and Scott waiting around the corner of the ticketing office at the Eye.

"Jessie, we're going to need you."

"Okay."

"When he gets here, you need to walk over and ask for directions to the London Eye Hospital. Tell him your GPS brought you to the wrong place."

"Is there even a London Eye Hospital?"

"Oh yes," Talbot said.

"And how would you even know that?" Scott asked.

"I knew a guy," Talbot grinned before turning back to Jessie. "Then when you get close, tell him Kelly sent you, that he's been followed, and to get on the bus to Westminster Abbey, okay?"

"No problem."

"When you get up to him, stand to the side so I can see him, and be sure to tell him he's been followed, okay?"

"Okay."

As Fulham arrived at the entrance to the Eye, glancing around in search of Scott, Jessie walked over to meet him.

"Excuse me sir, can you help me? I'm trying to find the London Eye Hospital, and my GPS brought me here."

"Certainly," Fulham said, reaching for his phone and pulling up his mapping app.

Jessie lowered her voice as she stepped closer to look at the map.

"A lady said to tell you that you were followed. She said to say her name is Kelly, and you should take a bus to Westminster Abbey."

Startled, Fulham glanced around. Unconsciously his hand reached for the pocket where he had placed the thumb drive was to make sure it was still there.

"Well aren't you clever," Scott said under her breath to Talbot as they watched from cover.

"What do you mean?"

"You just made him show you where he put it."

Talbot grinned.

Jessie redirected Fulham's attention back to the map.

"So it's all the way up here?" she asked.

"I'm afraid so."

"I'd better hurry then. Thank you!"

Jessie turned and walked back around the corner and out of sight to rejoin Talbot and Scott. Fulham glanced around as he turned and headed back the way he had come. Just before Trafalgar Bridge he climbed the stairs off the Queens Walk embankment and walked the few yards to the bus stop.

"Right," Talbot said. "You two head back to the hotel and I'll meet you there. I'm going to get that thumb drive."

"Don't mug him, he may surprise you."

"Well of course I'm not going to mug him," Talbot protested. "I'm going to pickpocket him."

"Well, I didn't know your plan, and given the stack of bodies in your wake you can see why I might not expect such finesse or subtlety. Besides, Nathan may look like a pushover, but he isn't. Are you any good at pickpocketing?"

"You have no idea," Talbot said as he walked off after Fulham.

Taking the stairs, Talbot followed Fulham to the bus stop. He weaved through the mostly Japanese tourists waiting for the bus. He wanted to study the posted bus schedule and keep an eye on Fulham in the process.

After a few minutes, the 211-bus pulled up and disgorged a host of tourists eager to add yet another picture to their camera. The exiting crowd thinned and Talbot crowded up behind Fulham. As he had expected, the excited crowd of Japanese tourists crowded and jostled around them as they boarded. Talbot noticed Fulham's tail slip on board on the other end of the bus just before it pulled away from the curb.

The bus was already full at this time of day, allowing for standing room only, so the addition of this many tourists made even standing room crowded. As the bus lurched forward it threw the standing passengers into each other, giving Talbot the opportunity to bump into Fulham.

Slipping the thumb drive from Fulham's pocket, Talbot replaced it with a single United States one dollar bill. If Fulham was as smart as he seemed, Talbot expected that he would see it as an impromptu sign that the drive was in Scott's hands.

Within minutes the bus pulled up at the stop on Parliament Square to deposit onto the curb the excited Japanese tour group, Fulham and, after a moment, Fulham's tail. Talbot stayed on board.

Standing on the sidewalk Fulham reached into his pocket to check on the thumb drive. The bus lurched forward as Talbot watched Fulham pull the dollar bill from his pocket and stare at it for a moment before glancing around, smiling and striding purposefully away, his brolly swinging.

Switching buses at the next stop, Talbot headed back towards Waterloo Station and the Hampton. Glancing around he noticed a thin young man sitting in the back of the bus. He was hunched low behind the seat in front of him, shivering in a T-shirt and threadbare jeans.

It looked like he was trying to hide out of sight of the bus driver so that he could use the heated bus to keep warm. Looking up, the young man noticed an older woman standing beside him. She looked tired, and here flat, sensible shoes looked worn the way shoes do when you stand in the all day.

He tapped her on the arm and smiled as he offered his seat. Gratefully the woman sat down. The young man tried to make himself as inconspicuous as possible, careful to keep the crowd between himself and the driver.

As the bus approached his stop at Waterloo Station, Talbot slipped a twenty-pound note into the pocket of his jacket and took it off. When the bus stopped, Talbot draped the jacket over the young man's shoulders and slipped off the bus, disappearing into the cold.

18h45, The Hampton, Waterloo and Gray, London

"Wait, weren't you wearing a different jacket earlier today?" Jessie asked as Talbot walked into the hotel room.

"Was I?" Talbot asked, digging into his pocket and handing her the thumb drive.

"Your father has a habit of giving his jacket away to cold people less fortunate than he is," Scott explained as Jessie inserted the thumb drive into the USB slot of her laptop.

"Really?" Jessie asked Talbot.

"I've no idea what she's talking about," Talbot said, smiling. "So what did Fulham find for us?"

Jessie opened the files as they gathered round the screen.

"This looks like a schedule with agendas," Jessie said, scrolling through the first file.

"Can you search the document for any reference to Transnistria?" Talbot asked.

"Sure."

With a few quick keystrokes, Jessie jumped the file to the first mention of Transnistria.

"Looks like a fact-finding tour of Transnistria for these six delegates this weekend, and then a vote on sovereignty in Paris on Tuesday," Jessie said.

"Do you suppose these are the delegates they know will vote against the motion?" Scott asked.

"Maybe. If that's the case, they may be at risk already. When do they arrive in Transnistria?" Talbot asked.

"They got there today. They're staying at the Hotel Chisinau. They're booked solid with tours and dinner. Then they fly to Paris Sunday night in time for the vote on Tuesday," Jessie said.

"We need to get to Transnistria," Talbot said.

"I'll check flights," Jessie volunteered.

"No flights. At least not until we're out of England," Talbot warned. "We need to keep a low profile. Check the train schedule across the channel."

"Okay," Jessie said.

"Any trouble getting the thumb drive?" Scott asked as they waited for Jessie.

"Not at all. I traded a dollar bill for the thumb drive, so he would figure you got it safely."

"And your jacket?"

Talbot shrugged. "No problem. I picked up a new one on my way back."

"Okay," Jessie said, "the train to Chisinau in Transnistria will take over three days. Driving would take at least two days. But if we take the train to Paris and then fly, we can be there tomorrow."

"Good, when do we leave?" Talbot asked.

"Earliest train is in the morning just after six. Paris before ten in the morning and fly out a little after one. We'll get to Chisinau around nine tomorrow night."

"Okay, good work. Go ahead and book the tickets. You and Kelly can sit together again, and I'll sit alone."

Chapter Seven

The dapper Frenchman sitting next to Scott on the train was an irritating itch Talbot could not reach to scratch. From the moment he sat down beside her he had made his interest very obvious, and the longer he watched, the more irritated Talbot became. Jessie's knowing grin as she had walked past earlier to find the restroom had done nothing to appease his mood.

Finally, irritated past logic, Talbot stood up, walked down the aisle, and stood over the Frenchman.

"I think you're in my seat," Talbot said politely.

"Non, non, monsieur. This is my seat," he replied, reaching for his ticket and handing it over to Talbot.

"That may be your ticket, but that's my seat. That's my daughter," Talbot said, indicating Jessie, "and they're travelling with me."

The Frenchman studied Talbot for a moment, taking him in, then smiled knowingly.

"Of course, monsieur. It is clear you are in love. Who am I to interfere in such a thing? Might I suggest we trade tickets?"

"Thank you."

The Frenchman winked at Jessie as he traded seats with Talbot, then walked away whistling to himself. Talbot sat down and avoided looking at either Jessie or Scott. After a minute of silence, Jessie spoke.

"Told you so."

Talbot sighed.

"Okay, you did. Satisfied?"

"Nothing to do with me," Jessie grinned. "You'll have to ask Kelly."

Talbot cast a reluctant eye over at Scott, then grinned sheepishly.

"Well?" he asked.

"Well what?" she teased.

"Well, are you satisfied?"

"You mean, am I satisfied that you came over here scowling and chased off a very nice, good-looking Frenchman with excellent conversation?"

"Yes, although I would have described it differently."

Scott looked up at him, then smiled warmly.

"Yes, I'm very satisfied. I might even say infinitely so," Scott replied, leaning her shoulder against his.

Talbot grinned. Taking her hand in his, their fingers twined together as he quickly kissed the top of her head. Talbot smiled across the small table at Jessie, then mouthed a single word at her… what-ever-r-r-r. Jessie giggled.

19h30, Hotel Chisinau, Chisinau, Transnistria

The lobby of the Hotel Chisinau was a two-story affair with an odd mix of styles. Despite the building itself comfortably pre-dating communism, the dominant style of decorating was strongly reminiscent of the Stalinist era.

Marble walls and pillars, large black and white checked tiles and a sweeping staircase directly in front of the lobby doors were all designed to impress, but the trappings were, for the most part, utilitarian and bleak. Despite the relatively early hour, the bar to the left of the entrance was deserted. The only concession to the creature comforts was the large fireplace in the corner surrounded by an eclectic selection of comfortable chairs.

"I can't believe we had to walk down the steps off the plane and across the runway," Jessie said as she plopped down into a deep arm chair facing the fireplace. "I'm exhausted."

"Don't get too comfortable," Talbot said. "I'm going to get us checked in."

"Okay."

Talbot and Scott, their footsteps echoing off the tile floor, walked up to the front desk to be greeted by the hotel receptionist. He was wearing a red, button-up, sleeveless vest over a white shirt. His name tag identified him as Danislav and his beaming smile proudly announced him to be a people person.

"Good evening sir, madam, and welcome to the glorious Hotel Chisinau!"

"Thank you, Danislav," Talbot smiled.

"I hear you speak English as you walk in, so now I practice! How you like Transnistria?"

"We just landed, so we haven't yet had a chance to see anything, but I hear it's a beautiful country," Talbot said. "We have reservations."

"Of course, of course! Your name, please?"

"Patrick Larson," Talbot said, using the name on his passport.

Flipping through a small stack of papers on the desk in front of him, Danislav pulled out a sheet.

"Here you are, two of our very finest rooms, side-by-side."

"Are you full this weekend?" Talbot probed.

"Not full, but we have extra-special guests," Danislav boasted.

"Really?" Talbot said. "You mean like a famous musician or something?"

"Ha! Better than that," Danislav said beaming. "The United of Nations is here to visit our glorious country, and they stay here!"

Talbot glanced at Scott, his eyes twinkling.

"You have the whole United of Nations visiting here?"

"No, no, no, not all of them. Six. They have whole top floor."

"I had hoped we could get rooms on the top floor?" Talbot suggested.

"I am so sorry, sir," Danislav said, the smile unwavering, "but they took whole floor."

"Six people took over the whole floor?" Scott asked.

"It is six top people," Danislav explained, "but they bring a lot of people to help."

"They must have a lot of security then," Talbot said.

"No, they pretend to be nobody. I think they not want people to know who they are, but I know," Danislav bragged.

"They here to find the fact so we can be independent country. It is great day for us."

"I'm surprised none of them are enjoying a drink in your fine bar," Talbot commented.

"Ah, they not in hotel now," Danislav replied. "They enjoy state dinner and symphony. We have excellent symphony."

"Well, congratulations," Talbot said.

The phone on the desk rang softly as Danislav was getting their keys ready. Glancing at the LCD display on the phone, Danislav straightened almost to attention.

"Please to excuse me," Danislav smiled, reaching for the handset. "It is China!"

"China?" Scott whispered to Talbot.

"I assume someone from the Chinese delegation," Talbot replied.

"Good evening sir! How can I be of service to you?" Danislav said, answering the phone.

Straining to listen, Talbot could only hear Danislav's side of the conversation, but it was clear the guest was unhappy.

"I am so sorry you still feel bad, sir. Can I get doctor?"

Talbot could barely hear a voice on the other end of the phone.

"Yes sir. Our street food, it taste very good, but sometimes it does that," Danislav commiserated. "I bring you Vodka, you feel better in morning."

The voice on the other end garbled through the speaker.

"No Vodka?" Danislav looked hurt. "It is best Vodka."

Talbot strained to listen in on the conversation without success.

"I am sorry, sir. I thought that is why you called."

239

The phone garbled again.

"But I do not understand, sir. We do not have anyone cleaning just bathrooms at night. That is very strange."

The voice on the other end was clearly getting more irate.

"I understand sir, but I am certain. We do not clean rooms at night. What she look like?"

The caller's response was brief.

"She is he? No sir, never have we used a man to clean bathroom. This man, did he steal anything?"

Talbot could not make out the response, but it was clearly angry.

"He steal nothing? That is strange. You like I call police, sir?"

Even without making out the exact words, Talbot could easily pick up on the intended message in the tirade that followed… the guest was clearly not going to recommend the Hotel Chisinau to anyone he cared about.

"Very good, sir," Danislav said dejectedly before hanging up the phone and turning back to Talbot. "So sorry for delay, sir."

"No problem," Talbot said. "What was that about?"

"It is no problem, everything A-OK!" Danislav said, regaining his composure as he inserted their room keys into a paper sleeve with their hand-written room numbers. "One of our special guests get sick two days ago and missed some of tour."

"Really?" Talbot said, curious. "What did he miss?"

"He miss Circus and hospital. My sister is nurse there, and they practice two months to take blood for the United of Nations guests, but he miss tour."

"So we should stay away from the street food, I take it?"

"Street food is good, but some places not so clean."

"Same thing all over the world," Talbot nodded.

As Talbot chatted with the clerk Scott's attention was distracted by the sound of leather-soled shoes tapping quickly down the stairs behind Talbot. Shifting her body slightly to see past Talbot, she saw a man in sanitation overalls and expensive dress shoes came down the stairs, the blaze of white hair over his eye in stark contrast to his dark hair.

"Didn't you tell me the main guy at the raid on that internet café was tall, dark hair with a streak of white in the hair over one eye?" she asked Talbot softly.

"Yes, why?" Talbot asked, reaching for the room key.

"I think he just came out of the Chinese delegate's bathroom and is coming down the stairs behind you."

"Has he spotted us?"

"No."

"Danislav?" Talbot said quietly.

"Yes sir?"

"Call the police. I think the man that was in your guest's bathroom is coming down the stairs. I'm going to stop him."

Talbot handed his room key to Scott as he turned and recognized La Salle as soon as he saw him. La Salle also recognized Talbot immediately and, without hesitation, broke into a sprint for the door.

Talbot launched himself in pursuit, smashing through the door a half beat behind La Salle. Pausing in mid-stride, Talbot saw La Salle had turned left at the bottom of the stairs and was headed south west past a collection of small shop fronts looking out into the square.

Talbot leapt the stairs and raced after La Salle, following him fast around the corner to give him no time to set up an ambush. With a hard lunge, he tackled La Salle from behind, bringing them both tumbling to the ground. La Salle was fast, jumping to his feet as Talbot straightened up. La Salle lunged

241

forward, his hands a blur as they slashed out, but Talbot kept his feet moving and managed to slip his punches and keep himself just out of reach.

Spotting an opening, Talbot moved in fast and managed to get inside La Salle's longer reach. He slammed two fast body blows just under La Salle's ribs. La Salle grunted, stepping quickly out of reach. He started throwing a fast combination of punches at Talbot's body and face to keep him at a distance, but Talbot crouched low, weaving his body as he covered up, the blows glancing off his arms and shoulders.

Stepping quickly forward and to his left, Talbot used his jab to tattoo La Salle's face, measuring the distance for a hard right cross. La Salle rode the punch and slipped inside to pound at Talbot's ribs, but Talbot closed in, grabbing La Salle's lapel to pull him down and into a fast knee strike. La Salle staggered back. Talbot's fist was still wrapped up in La Salle's clothing and his overalls tore. A small, bubble-wrapped manila envelope dropped to the ground.

La Salle's eyes dropped to follow the envelope, his body following his eyes as he moved fast to grab it up, but Talbot dove forward, knocking him away and tackling him to the ground. They rolled around in the trash on the street, throwing fists, elbows and knees in a battle of attrition. Talbot maneuvered for an arm bar, but La Salle slipped the hold, rolling to his feet. Talbot followed him upright, standing over the envelope.

The sounds of running feet approaching distracted Talbot for a moment and La Salle snapped a front kick into Talbot's chest, knocking him backwards and driving the air from his lungs. Before Talbot could get rest La Salle he turned and disappeared around the corner.

"You okay?" Scott asked as she came to a stop beside Talbot.

"Yeah, just winded," Talbot nodded. Looking around, he spotted the padded envelope La Salle had dropped and picked it up.

"What's that?" Scott asked as she helped him dust his clothes off.

"No idea, but he tried really hard to get it back after it fell out of his pocket, so it must be important," he replied, studying the sealed envelope carefully. The upper left corner had a curious logo on it, and in the center, someone had handwritten a name in black ink. Gently squeezing the envelope to see if he could tell what the contents might be, Talbot grunted.

"Feels like it could be a small tube. Let's get it to the hotel and see what we've got."

Walking back around the corner together, Talbot breathing carefully to get his breath back, they walked up the steps and back into the hotel foyer.

"You okay?" Jessie asked Talbot, concerned.

"Yeah, just winded," Talbot said.

"Hotel Security came looking for you. They want to ask some questions. They said to wait here for them while they call the police."

"Okay," Talbot said, discreetly handing the envelope over to Scott. "You two go to our rooms and wait for me there. I'll join you after I'm done."

SATURDAY, January 31st, 2017, 21h30, Hotel Chisinau, Chisinau, Transnistria

Talbot knocked on the hotel room door. After a moment the light glowing through the peephole went black. Talbot winked at the peephole and a moment later he heard the door unlock. Scott swung it open and Talbot walked in to see Jessie engrossed in her laptop.

"How'd it go?" Scott asked.

"No problem. They thought I was just another harmless journalist."

"Journalist? Why not a tourist?"

"That would be less likely."

"Why?"

"Transnistria is not exactly a tourist attraction, but with the UN Delegates here, a journalist would not be too out of the ordinary."

"Makes sense. Did you mention the envelope?"

"No, I want us to look at it before we hand it over to anyone."

"Well, Jessie has already got us something to work with, and we haven't even opened the envelope yet."

"Great! What did you find out?" Talbot asked Jessie as he joined her on the couch.

"Not a whole lot. The logo on the envelope is for that mining company in mom's papers."

"NeoDine?"

"Yes."

"What else?"

"Li Han is one of the UN delegates here in the hotel."

"Who?"

"The name on the envelope."

"Oh, right," Talbot nodded. "Anything else?"

"Not until we open the envelope," Scott said. "In the meantime, Jessie was trying to see what she could learn about NeoDine."

"Okay. Where's the envelope?"

Scott handed it over. Carefully, Talbot scrutinized the seams and glue-down flap, then gently squeezed to get a sense of the shape of the contents.

"Doesn't seem to have an air-tight seal. We can probably open it, don't you think?" Scott asked.

"I think so," Talbot agreed. Reaching into his bag, he extracted a pocket knife with a locking blade, opened it up and carefully slit the envelope open. Squeezing the edges towards each other with his hand to open the envelope without putting his fingers inside, Talbot peered carefully inside.

Grunting, he reached inside and pulled out a small test tube with a rubber stopper and, inside, the bristled head of a toothbrush. Holding it up, he showed Scott.

"What do you make of this?"

Her puzzled look faded almost instantly into comprehension.

"DNA."

"Exactly."

"Do you think he has a pocket full of those?" Jessie asked.

"I doubt it," Talbot said. "I think the plan was to get DNA from all the delegates when they did the blood draw demonstration at the hospital tour. Han got sick and didn't go, so they couldn't get his blood. This was plan B."

"That voice recording Alexis sent makes a lot more sense now."

"So are they collecting DNA from the UN Delegates so they can code Orion?" Jessie asked.

"I think so," Talbot agreed.

"How long would the DNA be viable?" Scott asked.

"No idea, but I would guess the sooner they can do the coding, the better," Talbot said.

"I was pulling up more information about NeoDine, and I found an article that talks about the Bio-Hazard lab they have," Jessie said.

"What's the article say?"

"Biologicheskaya_opasnost' laboratoriya," Jessie said, stumbling through the Russian pronunciation with a grin.

"Of course it does," Scott said. "But how did you know what it meant?"

"I ran a page translation on any web pages that mention NeoDine in Europe, and this is one of the pages that came up. It's basically saying the glorious politicians of Transnistria made NeoDine put in a max security-style bio-hazard lab the local doctors can use as a condition of paying no taxes."

"Sounds like the article was a smoke screen," Scott said.

"What do you mean?"

"I think NeoDine wanted the lab here, but that type of place is high risk and not too popular. So they greased a few palms and came up with a cover story."

"Well, well, well," Talbot said thoughtfully. "Whatever the reason, that's probably where those samples are headed. Jessie, can you get access to floor plans of the building??

"Are you thinking of an after-hours tour of their operations?" Scott asked.

"Seems like the next logical step, don't you?"

"Yes, but we know nothing about their security."

"That's not going to be a problem," Jessie said smugly as she turned the computer screen towards them.

The screen was split into six separate screens, each showing a different view of a building. With a couple of quick clicks, Jessie switched to a different set of windows.

"Did you actually hack into their security cameras in the last ten seconds?" Talbot asked, impressed.

Jessie just grinned.

"I'm going to have to keep a very close eye on what you do with this skill set of yours," Talbot said. "Does it give an overview?"

"Yes," Jessie said, tapping the keys. "I can keep the layout screen open in one of the six windows, and then switch between cameras on the other five."

Talbot and Scott watched as Jessie used the layout screen to select camera views and toggle from one angle to the next.

"How many cameras are there?" Talbot asked.

"The place is covered in them," Jessie replied. "You can pretty much see into every corner."

"That's not too good," Talbot said. "That means they can see everything we do in there. Unless we can hijack their system. What do you think?"

"What do you want me to do?"

"Can you tape an hour or so of activity and feed it into the monitors they watch, and then still watch what is really happening on the cameras?"

"I don't know. Probably. Let me play with it for a while."

"Okay, and before you do, take a screenshot of the floor plans and send them to my phone so I can study them."

"Sure."

After a couple of clicks on the keyboard, Talbot's phone dinged and he pulled up the images. Pulling some sheets of paper out of the drawer in the desk against the wall, Talbot huddled with Scott over the phone, sketching out some ideas for gaining entrance.

SATURDAY, January 31st, 2017, 23h00, Hotel Chisinau, Chisinau, Transnistria

"Got it," Jessie said, triumphantly.

Talbot and Scott turned from the sheets of paper on the desk as Jessie walked over from the couch and put her laptop on the desk in front of them.

"Okay, so I wrote some code that will let me feed a recorded session into their security monitors while I can see what the cameras see. Will that work?"

"Good! But you will have time your recording carefully or one of the cameras might pick up some guy disappearing in the middle of the room when the footage loops back to the beginning."

"Way ahead of you. I recorded and edited the footage for each camera separately to make sure that does not happen."

"Great! They won't be able to see us, but you can. Very good."

"And I can warn you if anyone is headed your way," Jessie added.

"This is really good work, Jessie," Talbot said.

Jessie beamed at the praise.

"Need one more thing, if you think you can handle it?"

"Sure!"

"We need to a way into the place that uses the cameras so that you can walk us in," Talbot added. "Take a look at these sketches and see if you can track the camera views all the way in and out."

"Oh, that should be easy."

Talbot grinned at Scott.

"Told you so."

Chapter Eight

The cold, misting rain painted the streets with reflected colors from the few neon lights still on. The rain served as a very wet guarantee that any normal person would remain huddled indoors, preferably deep under the covers. Not that either Talbot or Scott were feeling very normal at that moment.

The NeoDine building was a new construction. The land had originally housed what the previous communist regime had called an education facility. In reality it had been a combination prison and asylum where they had used questionable methods in efforts to re-educate citizens who failed to follow the party line.

The last structural reminder of those days was the old brick wall topped with wrought iron surrounding the property. It was six feet tall and at one time had been topped with razor wire. The wire was gone, but there were cameras mounted at intervals along the walls.

Talbot was listening intently to Jessie through his Bluetooth headset as she walked him through her view on the security cameras.

"She can see us," Talbot said. "No-one in sight over the wall."

Scott nodded.

"I was expecting a more serious wall to contend with," she said. "This isn't much of an obstacle."

"I know. I expect they rely on electronic security. Those are very high-tech cameras they use."

Quickly they pulled themselves over the wall and worked their way quietly across the open lawn towards the side of the building. Reaching it, they glided softly along the wall until they came to the main entrance. With so much electronic surveillance in and around the building NeoDine was clearly of the opinion that a man standing guard in plain sight was completely unnecessary.

The door unlocked as Talbot reached for it. Talbot gave Scott a meaningful look as he pushed the door open and ushered her in before him.

"You sure she's just sixteen?" Scott asked.

"I know."

Listening to Jessie's directions, Talbot headed down the corridor to the left with Scott following close behind. Dodging in and out of doors and corridors, they worked their way past the roving guards patrolling the building. Jessie finally directed them to a non-descript door half-way down a long corridor lit with cold fluorescent lights. Talbot paused. Listening to Jessie, he looked at Scott.

"This is the door to the lab, but Jessie says she has no view inside. She doesn't know if there's anyone inside."

"Unlikely anyone in there would be armed, anyway," Scott said.

"True."

Jessie unlocked the door remotely. Talbot turned the handle slowly and carefully pushed the door open. Easing quietly into the room, Talbot looked around. The room was empty and dark except for the light from a computer screen on a desk across the room. Scott followed Talbot inside and softly closed the door behind her.

"Good work, Jessie," Talbot said. "We're in and the room is deserted."

Pulling a small, powerful flashlight out of his pocket, Talbot hooded the lens with his hand to limit the chance of light washing under the door into the corridor. Carefully he shone the light around the room. Except for the HazMat gear hanging on the wall and the computer on the desk, the room was empty.

A vacuum seal door was set in the wall beside the computer with a touchscreen keypad on the wall beside the door. Behind the computer was a large window. Expecting to see a deserted lab on the other side, Talbot shone his light through the window. The light gleamed off an impressive collection of lab equipment.

"Jessie says this door is off her grid. She can't open it."

Scott touched the keypad to life and the screen turned dark navy. In the center was a single white dot. A series of similar dots formed a circle around it, with another circle of more dots forming a second, outer ring. In the top left corner, a small digital clock counted the seconds. It was ten minutes to two in the morning.

"Both rings have twelve dots," Scott said puzzled.

"Maybe there's some clue on the computer," Talbot said as he jiggled the mouse to bring the screen to life.

The window that opened was a security camera screen view of the lab. A navigation bar down the side included and option to browse an activity log. Talbot glanced through the log file.

"One of the log files looks like it was from about four hours ago," Talbot said, clicking it open.

The silent screen came to life with four camera angles in high definition and color, one from each corner of the lab. As they watched, the door opened, and a tall man walked in. Despite the HazMat gear, it was obviously the man from the hotel.

He walked across the room to a safe with similar keypad. As he touched it, they could see the same two concentric circles of dots on the screen. The man touched the screen quickly and the safe door popped open. As he leaned forward to extract the contents, his name- badge showed up clearly on the screen. La Salle.

Reaching for his phone, Talbot rewound the recording, videotaped the keypad sequence, and texted it to Jessie.

"Jessie, check your text for a video. See if you can make sense of the code he types in."

Clicking play again, they watched as the man pulled a small, stainless steel case out of the safe, opened it, and pulled out seven of the nine vials inside.

"Eight delegates, seven vials," Talbot murmured. "We intercepted the DNA for the last one."

"And the ninth?" Scott asked.

"The stopper on the vial was a different color. I think it must be the antidote."

"Scribbler?"

"Right."

As they watched, La Salle added a label to the side of the vial and placed it in the agitator. Then he reached into a small refrigerator and pulled out a tray of vials. They looked like they would have been used by a phlebotomist to draw blood. Carefully La Salle inserted the syringe of a needle through the rubber top of one of the vials and withdrew a red, viscous fluid which he injected into the Orion vial in the agitator. With the needle still deep inside the Orion vial, La Salle doused a thick cotton swab with alcohol. He wrapped the soaked cotton around the needle and, as he slowly extracted the needle, pulled it through the alcohol before dropping the syringe into the incinerator.

One by one La Salle repeated the process. He closed the shatter proof lid and started the agitator to mix the vials up thoroughly. After a few minutes he turned the agitator off and opened the lid.

One by one he packaged them carefully into a small, stainless steel briefcase with a padded interior which had been customized to carry eight vials.

He walked over to the wall and pressed a red button. He stood for a minute, waiting for something, then hit the button again. Finally, he unzipped his suit and took a deep breath. He looked very pleased with himself. Reaching into his pocket, he pulled out his phone and sent a quick text. Then he picked up the case and let himself out of the door, disappearing from camera view.

"The red button?" Talbot asked.

"I would guess he was venting the air out of the lab through a scrubbing incinerator."

Talbot nodded.

"Any luck on that code, Jessie?" Talbot asked, speaking into the phone headset.

"I think so. He tapped the screen seven times. When I mapped them to the dots, it looked familiar... it's the stars of Orion laying sort of on his side. Two for the shoulders on the right side of the outer circle, two for the feet on the opposite end, and the belt is three vertically, with the center dot for the middle star."

"Can you reproduce the sequence?"

"I think so. The outer ring is twelve dots, so think of them like a clock. Press the hour markings of ten, then seven. Next use the inner circle and do a vertical line for the belt starting at the top. Last two are the number four and then the number one positions on the outer circle."

Talbot walked over to the door to test the code and keyed it in. The screen flashed red, then reset.

"Not working, Jessie."

"That's weird. It was very clear on the video. Let me take another look."

"Okay," Talbot agreed.

"Let's get suited up in case we can get into the lab," Scott said. "I think we need to get that Scribbler virus."

"Good idea."

Quickly they donned the bulky HazMat uniforms, checking each other for leaks and tears carefully while they waited for Jessie.

"I think I've got it."

"Tell me."

"There's a time stamp on the video you sent and that made me think. The Orion constellation rotates on an axis all through the night. So I checked and the orientation he typed in matched the real Orion's orientation for the time stamp on the video. Try rotating the whole image four hours counter clockwise."

Talbot retyped the sequence, this time with the four-hour offset Jessie had suggested. The touch screen turned green and the lock on the door clicked open.

"You never fail to impress, Jessie. Worked like a charm." Talbot started to push through the door, but Scott stopped him.

"Let me turn the lab cameras off before we go in. No need for them to know we were here."

"I should have thought of that," Talbot said.

"Well, if you weren't getting so old you probably would have," Scott teased as she accessed the camera controls on the computer screen and disabled them.

"I am a much-maligned man," Talbot said sadly, shaking his head. Pushing the door open he walked through with Scott following, the door locking behind them.

Quietly they walked across the cold floor, the night lights casting an eerie glow over the glossy white surfaces of the lab. Reaching the safe, Talbot repeated the Orion sequence of touches on the screen with the same layout of dots and clock. The screen turned green and the lock popped open with a hiss of cold vapor.

Carefully Talbot reached in and extracted the tray.

"See if you can find something to carry this in safely," Talbot said.

Scott rummaged through the cabinets above the lab counter against the wall and located an entIre section dedicatcd to more of the same stainless-steel cases La Salle had used. Pulling one down, she opened it and laid it on the counter as Talbot walked over, cautiously carrying the remaining two vials. Carefully he inserted both vials, Orion with the red rubber stopper and Scribbler with the blue, into two of the spaces in the case.

Closing the lid, they turned and headed for the door. Talbot keyed in the code sequence, but the screen turned red. Talbot tried again. Still red.

"I have an idea," Scott said. "Let me try."

Talbot stepped out of the way, letting Scott reach the screen.

"Maybe you key it one way to go inside, and key it in reverse to get out," she said as she keyed in the sequence.

The screen turned red and a phrase in Russian popped up at the bottom of the screen.

"Jessie, can you translate something from Russian for us, please?"

"Sure."

"Odna poptyka ostal'nyye."

"Spelling?"

Talbot spelled it out.

"It means 'one attempt remaining'," Jessie said after a moment. "What's going on?"

"There's a touch screen lock to get out of the lab as well, and it doesn't use the same code."

"Did you try it in reverse?"

"Yes, that's when it warned us about the one last attempt."

"Not good. Does it also have the two circles?"

"Yes," Talbot said, frowning. Suddenly he grinned and started keying in the code again.

The door clicked open.

"What did you do?" Scott asked, puzzled.

"It just passed two in the morning," Talbot said.

"So?"

"I offset the code counter clockwise one more hour."

"Well, maybe you're not as old as you look," Scott chuckled as she started to remove her HazMat suit.

"Always the comedienne," Talbot said, hanging his suit back up on the wall where he found it. "Turn the lab cameras back on so they have nothing to make them suspect."

"Right."

"Jessie, we're ready to leave the room. Is it clear outside?"

"Yes, you can go. About fifteen minutes ago six guys packed into a van out front and left. Place looks completely deserted."

"That's odd," Talbot puzzled. "Why would they leave?"

"Does it matter?" Scott asked. "Gives us a clear shot out of here."

"I know, but I don't like it. Something's fishy about it."

"Why? Maybe they patrol several locations?"

"Nothing about the people we've dealt with so far has struck me as leaving much to chance, so I don't buy that."

"What, then?"

"Smells like a trap. Jessie, can you see anyone anywhere at all?"

"No-one."

"Okay, can you scan the street out front of the building? Use the infra-red camera. See if you can see any heat signatures. We're about to come out."

"No, the place is completely deserted. So is the street."

"I've got a bad feeling about this," Talbot muttered as they slipped out of the door. He started to jog across the lawn towards the fence with Scott on his heels, worry driving him faster. Vaulting the fence, they jogged down the street through the misting rain.

At the corner, Talbot hesitated, peering carefully down the street to where they had left the rental car. There was no cover, and as best he could see, the street was deserted.

"Come on," Talbot said, slipping around the corner. Moving like ghosts they approached the car. It was completely deserted. Talbot unlocked and slid behind the driver's seat, Scott slipping into the seat beside him.

"Jessie, we're on our way. Make sure you disconnect from their servers and reset back the way it was, so they don't suspect, okay?"

"Already done and watching TV. How did it go?"

"No problems. We got what we were after."

259

"So we're leaving?"

"As soon as we can catch the next flight to Paris."

"Good, I..."

A crashing sound interrupted Jessie and she started screaming.

SUNDAY, February 1st, 2017, 01h45, Lear Jet, Chisinau Airport

"Surely they wouldn't be that careless?" La Salle thought to himself as he sipped a Gin and Tonic waiting for the plane to depart.

He picked up his phone and dialed the Hotel Chisinau.

"Good evening! This is Hotel Chisinau. Can I help you?" the desk clerk answered in Russian.

"I certainly hope so." La Salle's Russian was perfect.

"I am from the State Police Prefecture and I am confirming the arrival of three American guests joining the delegation. Have they checked in?"

"Yes, they checked in tonight."

"And are they still there?"

"I can call to check."

"No, did they stay checked in, or did they decide to go to another hotel?"

"They are still here."

"Very good, thank you."

La Salle hung up and sat thinking for a moment. Reaching a decision, he picked up his phone again and dialed a number on speed dial.

"Shevchenko."

"This is La Salle. We have a situation."

"What is it?"

"Three Americans checked into the Hotel Chisinau tonight. A man, a woman and a girl. They know too much and are starting to get in the way."

"How long have they been a problem?"

"Only a couple of days."

"And they have not talked? Why not?"

"They're on the run. Police think he's a cop-killer."

"Why do they think that?"

"We told them."

"I take it the story was a lie?"

"Of course."

"Why have you not killed them already?"

"He killed nearly a dozen of my agents already."

"These are the men who trained my men? I am not so sure your men are good enough to train mine, La Salle. Perhaps I should change the deal. Go to the Russians or the Chinese instead."

"We both know that's an empty threat, Shevchenko."

"Just yanking your chain, my friend. So, this guy, he must have some training too?"

"Yes, at least Special Forces, maybe other stuff, so don't under-estimate him."

"What do you need from me?"

"I just need you too look the other way and clean up any mess."

"I can do that. Tonight?"

"Yes."

La Salle hung up, and then dialed a third number.

"NeoDine."

"This is La Salle. How many on duty?"

"Good evening, sir. Standard six."

"I've got a job for you."

SUNDAY, February 1st, 2017, 02h15, Hotel Chisinau, Transnistria

There was the sound of a short struggle, then the phone went quiet. After a moment, a man's voice with an American accent took over the phone.

"We have the girl. I will text you an address. Turn yourself in and she lives. If you don't she dies, slowly. You have one hour."

The phone clicked as the call terminated.

The sound of the hissing tires whispered to the wet pavement, sharing the night silence with the car engine. Talbot's knuckles were white as his fists clenched tighter and tighter around the wheel. He could feel the anger crawling up from the dark places, the hidden places Talbot had avoided for years.

Suddenly his hands started pounding the steering wheel again and again as the rage coiled and writhed through his brain like a feral beast.

Scott watched from her side of the car, startled.

With a massive effort he struggled to cage it until only the throbbing vein in his forehead gave any sign of his anger. Taking a deep, shuddering breath, he relaxed into an icy calm.

"What happened?"

"They took Jessie. They want us to turn ourselves in, or they kill her."

"Where do we have to go?"

"They said they would text me an address."

"We can't just turn ourselves in, right?" Scott said carefully.

"Right, it's an obvious trap."

"How much time do we have?"

Talbot glanced at his watch.

"Forty-five minutes."

"Not much time for a plan."

"Better this way."

"How?"

"I know it's a trap. They probably suspect I know, which is why they made sure I had no time to plan. That gives us the advantage."

"How?"

"I have a plan."

"Of course you do. And how do you have a plan already?"

"Remember the cigarette burns?"

"Yes?"

"Same situation, same plan. Almost."

"Why almost?"

"My own rules of engagement."

Scott looked at the grim lines on his face and shivered. To her certain knowledge he had killed eleven men in the last week, and she was certain she had just heard a death sentence.

SUNDAY, February 1st, 2017, 03h00, Hotel Chisinau, Transnistria

For the third time in an hour, Talbot turned off the electricity main for the hotel. The first time had lasted just ten minutes and at a little after two in the morning none of the hotel's guests were awake to notice. On the other hand, it had given Talbot the chance to locate six heavily armed guards working in two-man teams. He suspected there were more in the hotel room, but he had no way of checking.

To Talbot's satisfaction, none of the three teams had line of sight to see each other. They were relying exclusively on their radios to keep in contact.

The first power outage Talbot had initiated had triggered high alert and a lot of radio chatter between the teams. The second outage lasted a little longer and the security team quickly decided it was just another power blip, common in a country with such limited resources and infrastructure.

With the power out again for the third time, Talbot slipped into the dark building, keeping to the deep shadows cast by the street lights into the windows in the front of the building. Gliding smoothly forward in sock feet he crept up on the glow of the cigarette being passed between the two guards stationed facing each other in the shadows beside the Grand Staircase leading upstairs.

Careful to avoid even the whisper of clothing in the dark, Talbot eased up on the first team carrying a heavy crowbar he had found in the tool chest in the breaker room. They were whispering quietly to each other and did not hear him coming.

Talbot lined up directly behind one of the guards, using his body to hide from the other guard.

Timing his move to coincide with the moment the further guard puffed on the cigarette, Talbot swung the crowbar hard into side of the closest guard's skull. The guard went rigid and, as he started to slowly collapse, Talbot thrust the sharp end of the crowbar like a sword over him. Angling the thrust from high to low, the tip speared through the other guard's eyeball, crunched through the occipital bone around his eye, and pierced the medulla oblongata.

Before either guard could collapse completely to the floor, Talbot grabbed them and then lowered both slowly and silently to the ground.

Holding himself still, Talbot waited to see if there was any reaction from the rest of the hotel, but it remained quiet.

Talbot searched through the gear the men carried and stripped them of two silenced machine pistols, two wickedly sharp daggers strapped in leather sheaths to their wrists, and one of the radios.

Easing quietly over to the front entrance, he opened the door slightly and gestured for Scott to join him. As she slipped inside, she lifted an eyebrow questioningly. Talbot held up two fingers and Scott nodded. Taking one of the silenced machine pistols from Talbot, Scott expertly flipped it to multi-shot and leaned in close.

"Where?" she barely breathed into his ear.

"Two more at the top of the stairs to the left, two more at the end of the hall to our room. Probably two more in the room with Jessie," Talbot answered, just as quietly.

Scott nodded.

Talbot strapped the daggers to his forearms, then took the lead, staying close to the stone balustrade as they crept silently up the wide staircase. Scott followed close behind. About half-way up, Talbot leaned in close to Scott's ear.

"I'm going to out flank them. When I reach the end, make some slight noises, just enough to get them moving your direction, okay?"

No longer bothering to question Talbot's methods, Scott nodded in the dark.

Talbot slipped over the side of the balustrade and started climbing the steps on the outside of the railing. When his head was level with the next floor, he slung the machine pistol over his shoulder and reached up. He grabbed the railing posts where they bolted to the floor and swung out over the empty space over the floor below.

Working quietly, he swung from post to post until he reached the corner at the end. The cross wall that extended from the floor behind the bar on the ground floor extended all the way up to the ceiling above the second floor.

Staying in tight to the corner, Talbot braced his feet against cross wall. The streetlights gleamed off his face, dripping with sweat from the exertion, as he nodded back at Scott.

Taking a coin from her pocket, she tossed it along the second-floor tile, rolling it away from the guards. Talbot could hear the guards between Scott and himself, whispering as they discussed the noise.

Scott tossed another coin slightly higher this time. It bounced along the tile before rolling down the hallway away from the guards.

A whisper of fabric in the dark let Talbot know that the guards were moving stealthily towards Scott to investigate. Using the counter-pressure of his feet against the cross wall, Talbot pulled himself up and over the railing in one fluid jump. The two guards were hyper-focused forward and did not hear Talbot just fifteen feet behind them.

The guards in front of Talbot were creeping up on Scott in staggered formation, one slightly behind the other. Pulling one of the daggers from a sheath strapped to his forearm, Talbot glided up behind the first guard.

Scott started walking up the stairs, muttering aloud in French, keeping the guard's attention.

Talbot drove the point of the dagger through the back of the closest guard's neck just below the skull, expertly severing the spinal cord.

Before Talbot could quietly lower the dead man to the tile the pistol he was carrying dropped to the tile.

The guard in front of Talbot spun around, his gun swinging around to line up on Talbot. Talbot flinched at the soft, clattering sound of the bolt sliding back and forth. He could almost feel bullets crashing into him. Instead the guard stumbled forward as the bullets from Scott's silenced machine pistol punched him hard in the bullet proof vest he was wearing. The impact made him stumble forward and into Talbot's reach. Talbot didn't hesitate, the second dagger flashing in and out in the dim light, stabbing repeatedly through the Kevlar vest and deep into the guard's chest.

As the blade punctured lungs and heart, the guard's knees crumpled, and Talbot eased him down to the floor. Scott came up beside Talbot in the dark as he straightened up.

"That was too close," Talbot whispered. "Thanks."

Scott nodded as Talbot retrieved the daggers and wiped them clean on the guard's clothing before tucking them away again.

"What next?" Scott asked quietly.

"The hallway. There's only one way in and they're at the other end, so they're going to see us as soon as we turn the corner. Any ideas?"

"Do you speak German?" Scott asked.

"Sure, but I don't see how that's going to help."

"That's because you have no imagination," Scott said. "Do you think we can get past the entrance to that hallway without them seeing us?"

"Probably."

"Good. We need to be seen and heard coming from rooms down one of the hallways on the other side."

"Where are you going with this?"

"This is a hotel, and the lights are out. Nothing more normal than for guests to be stumbling around looking for their room in the dark, especially if they're also a little drunk. The more obvious, the less suspicious."

"You're right," Talbot agreed, "I have no imagination. That's a great idea. But German?"

"Yes, German. We're going to have an argument in German about you getting me lost. They're waiting for someone speaking English to come up those stairs, and they'll pay no serious attention to a German couple where the guy is getting chewed out. Misdirection."

"Oh great, our first argument won't even be in English," Talbot muttered gloomily to himself.

Moving quietly, they followed the wall around, staying hidden in the deep shadows until they were halfway down the empty hallway on the far side.

"Ready?" Scott asked.

Talbot nodded.

As they started stumbling their way down the hallway back towards the center hall, Scott started nagging Talbot in German. Talbot kept his head down and pretended to test his key on each door they passed. Scott was starting to get a little louder, obviously more and more annoyed that he could not find their room. In fluent German she continued to harangue Talbot as they exited the passageway into the center hall.

Talbot responded, also in German, challenging Scott to pick the right hallway if she was so smart. Scott stalked away from him, angrily circling the center hall and peering down the hallways branching off. Talbot followed, pointing out that it wasn't so easy in the dark after all. Even though the volume stayed at a penetrating and not-so-quiet whisper, the sarcasm continued to escalate

Scott stopped in front of the center hallway and haughtily pointed into the dark, making it absolutely clear that she thought Talbot was an idiot, and of course this was the correct hallway.

Muttering under his breath in German, Talbot started down the hallway, pretending to test the key in each door as they went. Scott followed, her unsolicited opinion of Talbot's character, manhood and intelligence floating down the hallway ahead of them.

As they neared the end of the hallway, they could hear the guards chuckling at Talbot's misfortune. Talbot stumbled closer.

"Sprechen si Deutsch?" Talbot asked the closest guard, apparently too drunk to be in the least concerned with why two armed men were standing at the end of the hallway in front of a hotel room door.

Scott followed, still providing commentary, her subject matter now including both guards and men in general as she continued her acidic assessment of the general intelligence of the male of the species.

The radio crackled as the guards inside the hotel room with Jessie asked what the noise was about. The guard furthest from Talbot keyed the mike to answer.

"Just a drunk German couple looking for their room. She's a piece of work. Hilarious." he said in English.

The radio crackled again, and the guard looked at Talbot and laughed.

Scott pushed past Talbot who was hanging his head dejectedly, her body hiding his hands as she started to rebuke the guards for daring to comment about her man. Grinning in admiration they watched her as she described their questionable lineage in imaginative detail.

"Left," Talbot said quietly.

In mid-sentence, Scott stepped to her left as Talbot brought the silenced machine pistol up and fired twice into the brains of each guard. Dropping the pistol to the end of the sling over his shoulder, Talbot stepped forward to catch one of the guards as he started to fall.

Without pausing in her diatribe, Scott caught the other guard and slowly started lowering him to the ground.

Without warning the hallway lights came back on.

"Damn," Talbot said quietly, "I was hoping the night clerk would take longer to find the breaker."

"Smash and grab?"

"Smash and grab."

Snapping the folding stock on the machine pistols open they lifted them high and at the ready. They laid the butt across the top of their shoulders to shorten the barrel reach for close quarters.

Talbot positioned himself in front of the hotel room door, Scott in position behind him. He lifted his foot and kicked the door just under the lock as hard as he could. The door smashed open, swinging left as Scott pushed past Talbot and turned right into the room. Talbot followed fast, going to the opposite side.

Scott's gun fired twice, dropping a guard reaching for his gun against the far wall on the left. Talbot hesitated. The last guard was mostly hidden behind Jessie.

Jessie was tied to a chair. The guard was crouched behind her, his arm around her neck and a huge Bowie at her throat.

271

"Only one way this ends well for you, bud," Talbot said quietly. "You can't carry her out in that chair and if you move that knife to cut her free, you die."

The man eyed Talbot, weighing his chances.

"What are my options?"

Talbot looked at Jessie.

"Did this one hurt you at all?"

Carefully she shook her head.

"You have just one choice," Talbot said, watching the man carefully. "Put the knife down and step back. You get to walk away."

"Assurances?"

"One way or the other you die in the next sixty seconds if you don't. Kelly?"

"Yes."

"Can you check the bathroom and hall? I want no surprises if we can avoid it."

"Right."

Scott swept the bathroom.

"Clear."

"Okay."

She edged back to the smashed open door to check the hallway as Talbot waited for the man to decide.

Almost immediately there was a thud, and Scott staggered back into the room, a big, muscle-bound heavy hard on her heels. She tried to lift her gun, but without any effort he swatted it to one side and punched her in the head, driving her back into the wall where she collapsed, inert.

Talbot swung around to get a bearing on the man. He pulled the trigger and tattooed the bullet-proof chest plate with slugs.

The bullets slammed him back into the wall. Talbot kept squeezing the trigger, walking the line of slugs up his chest and over the vest until three bullets punched into his throat and head. He collapsed, and Talbot swung back to face the man with the knife.

The knife man had stood up smiling.

"One-on-one and you're out of rounds," he said.

Talbot pulled the trigger. The gun dry-fired. Talbot dropped the gun and pulled a dagger from the sleeve on his arm. Smiling broadly, the man saw the dagger in Talbot's hand and moved in.

Talbot's eyes narrowed as he watched how the man held his knife. He pulled the second dagger out. Stalking Talbot like a big cat, the man moved in closer, trying to crowd Talbot into the corner, but Talbot moved his hands fast, slashing back and forth to keep some distance.

Carefully they circled each other, sizing each other up. Talbot moved in closer, putting himself in front of Jessie but losing fighting room in the process. The man thrust hard and low, slicing through Talbot's shirt and tracing a thin line of blood across his belly. Talbot jumped back, nearly tripping over Jessie's chair.

As the man lunged forward with his blade again to take advantage, Talbot weaved to one side and flicked his blade out. The tip sliced deep into the man's forearm.

He grunted, stepping back to recover. Talbot followed in close, keeping him on the defensive. The deep cut made the heavy blade awkward and slow to use, and he started to back up. Talbot pushed forward, cutting and slashing at the man with short, fast movements, pushing him across the room.

Seeing the knifepoint dropping as his hand lost strength, Talbot parried with the blade in his right hand as he dropped to one knee. He plunged his left blade deeply into the man's thigh and the blade stuck tight. Talbot let go rising to his feet again to

273

re-center, but the man lunged for the machine pistol Scott had dropped.

He grabbed it up, swinging it to line up on Talbot. Talbot wasted no time. Flipping the blade over to grasp the tip between his fingers, he threw the knife. The blade buried itself to the hilt in the man's throat and he collapsed to his knees, clawing at the blade. Then he collapsed face-down on the floor.

Without even a glance at the body Talbot walked over to Jessie's chair, removed the gag and untied her. Throwing her arms around his neck, she clung tightly to him, shaking. He held her close for a moment.

"You okay?"

She nodded.

"Let me check on Kelly," he said.

Jessie let go and Talbot went over to where Scott lay, crumpled up against the wall. Gently he pressed two fingers against her throat to check for a pulse, then leaned in close to make sure she was breathing. Satisfied, he gathered her up in his arms and carried her over to the bed, carefully laying her down.

He dragged the two bodies into the bathroom, dumped them on top of each other in the tub, and pulled the shower curtain closed to hide them.

Then he walked back over to Scott where she lay on the bed.

"Jessie, bring me a cold wet cloth from the bathroom, please."

"Is she okay?"

"Yes, but she's going to have a splitting headache when she wakes up."

"Probably be mad as hell, too," Jessie added, fetching the cloth.

"No doubt. What happened before we got here?" Talbot asked as laid the cool cloth over Scott's forehead.

"These guys busted in and grabbed me, then tied me to the chair. One of them made a phone call and a little while later this big guy walked in wearing some kind of military uniform."

"Can you describe it?"

"Black riding boots, long gray overcoat with a red and yellow striped belt, furry gray hat with a red top."

"Did he have yellow stars on his shoulders? Red trim? Red and yellow patches on the front edges of the lapel?"

"Yes, how did you know?"

"Sounded like a Russian general's uniform. What did he do?"

"He walked around chain-smoking. The Americans knew him, but they didn't like him much. He got a phone call and left."

"And he was chain smoking?"

"Yes," she answered puzzled. "Why?"

"What did he do with his cigarette butts?"

"He stubbed them out in the ash tray on the desk. I didn't even know they still had ash trays."

"Still a lot of ash trays in eastern Europe," Talbot said as he walked over to the desk. "I don't think they pay much attention to the cancer memo."

Thoughtfully he studied the three cigarette butts in the ash tray, then walked over to his travel bag. Digging inside he extracted the envelope La Salle had dropped and pulled out the vial inside. Walking into the bathroom he dumped the contents and very carefully washed and dried it. Then he walked back

275

over to the desk and gingerly used a pencil to coax the three cigarette butts into the vial before sealing it.

"What are you doing?" Jessie asked.

"Just an idea, not sure yet."

As he tucked the vial away in his travel bag, Scott started to stir. Groaning, she rubbed the side of her head as her eyes started to focus on her surroundings again. Looking around, she saw Talbot and Jessie standing beside the bed, watching her.

"How you feel?" Talbot asked.

"Headache, blurred vision... you'd think I got knocked out or something."

"This should help a bit," Talbot said as he handed her a glass of water and a couple of Tylenol from his bag.

"Jessie, you okay?" Scott asked, struggling to sit up.

"I'm good."

"What's next?"

"Well," Talbot said, "the next flight out is in a couple of hours. We need to get out of here. We can rest on the plane. You good to go?"

"I'll manage. Just keep those Tylenol coming."

"Jessie, can you get our things together? I need to get hold of a guy."

She nodded. Talbot reached for his phone and dialed an international number. The phone rang on the other end for several minutes before redirecting the call to voicemail inbox with no message.

"Tango Echo Mike," Talbot said quietly into his phone. "Need a safe house in Paris."

After a few moments his phone beeped as a text came in.

"Okay, we've got an apartment in Paris." Checking the address on the text, he smiled. "You'll like this, Jessie. It's on the south bank of the Seine at Pont de l'Alma within walking distance of the Eiffel Tower."

"For real?" Jessie exclaimed. "That's so cool!"

"That really is pretty cool," Scott said. "How did you manage that?"

"Some guys and I pooled our resources. We buy properties we can rent out to tourists. If we need a safe house, it's equipped for that as well." Talbot replied as he grabbed up their bags.

"You should see what he means!" Jessie said to Scott.

"What do you mean?"

"The safe house thing? It's so cool!"

"And how do you keep track of it all?"

"One of the guys used to manage team logistics. Now he handles all the properties. He makes sure there's always at least one open property in each major city in case there is a need."

"Sounds like a good deal."

"It is."

Chapter Nine

The cab ride from Charles De Gaul International through Paris to the apartment on Quai D'Orsay would forever remain one of Talbot's signature memories as he watched Jessie's unbridled delight soaking up the sights and sounds of the City of Lights.

Beautiful old buildings, their impassive faces adorned with carved stonework and huge old doors, stood majestic guard over the many businesses and store fronts. The complex smells of exhaust fumes and French bakeries created a heady assortment of aromas uniquely Parisian, underpinned by the sounds of a city bustling about in French.

Their cab was a white Mercedes, typical in Paris. It came gliding to a smooth halt in front of the apartment. As they stepped out of the cab, Scott and Jessie looked around at their surroundings.

The building was one of many on the black, sandwiched together. The front at ground level was all glass, with a security door set in the middle. It looked out over the Seine across a busy thoroughfare. Almost immediately across from the apartment was the Pont de l'Alma, one of the bridges across the Seine. Looking left they could see the top of the Eiffel Tower just two blocks down stretching above the surrounding buildings.

Talbot waited in the cab. After a few minutes a lean man with swept-back black hair, eyes that were almost black, and a dark, deeply lugubrious face walked up to the apartment door. Despite the fact that he was an extremely energetic, happy man, his face exuded the impression that the apocalypse would be a welcome improvement to his gloomy perspective on life.

Seeing Talbot climb out of the cab, a smile transformed his face.

"Bonjour, mes ami! Ce' va?"

"Pretty good, Enzo. How about you?"

"As always, my friend."

Turning to greet Jessie and Scott, his smile widened even further. "This cannot be your daughter Jessie, my friend. She is too pretty to come from someone as ugly as you!"

"And this is Kelly Scott," Talbot grinned. "Jessie, Kelly, this is Enzo Dubois. We worked together a few times over the years."

"Welcome to Paris!"

"Thank you," Jessie said, smiling.

"You like what you see so far?"

"It's awesome!"

The corners of Enzo's eyes wrinkled deeper.

"Ah yes, the tourist view of Paris. It is so refreshing! I am compelled to be glad you like it!"

Jessie laughed.

"Make sure your dad buys you some crepes from the market on Rue Cler. It is just a few minutes' walk from the apartment."

Switching focus, he took Scott's hand in his, leaning forward gallantly to kiss the back of her hand.

"Mademoiselle, you are a vision."

"Careful, Kelly," Talbot said as he collected the bags from the cab driver. "Enzo is a notorious flirt."

"I am not a flirt," Dubois said, feigning hurt. "I just appreciate beauty. Something for which we already know you, my friend, lack the capacity."

Talbot grinned as he paid the cab driver and rejoined them at the glass entrance to the building. Dubois pulled a pass key from his pocket, waved it in front of the door lock, and the lock clicked open. He pushed the door open and led them into the foyer.

The wall on the left was covered in mail boxes and the wall at the back was a floor-to-ceiling mirror. There was a single door in the far corner of the right-hand wall next to a bank of elevators.

Once inside, he led them through the small door in the back right of the room, into a short hallway, down three steps and through another door.

It opened into a small inner courtyard surrounded by the six-story building. Balconied windows looked down over the courtyard, but the only doors were the one they had just walked through, and the door to the apartment to the left. Dubois unlocked it with the same key and ushered them in.

The door opened directly into a studio apartment. Immediately to the left of the door and under the only window was a tiny table and two chairs. A sofa barely large enough to seat three smaller adults was pushed against the left wall, and a small kitchen space was built against the wall on the right.

A counter-top separated the living area in the front of the space from what passed as the bedroom at the rear of the studio. Except for two feet of floor space on each side and at the foot, the entire bedroom space was consumed by a small Queen-size bed.

To the right of the bed was a pocket door that led into the bathroom area. The entire apartment was no more than twelve feet wide and perhaps twenty feet deep, and when Jessie looked into the bathroom she just started laughing.

"Dad, I don't think you can even fit in here!" she said. "This shower is barely wider than your shoulders! If you drop the soap you'll have to get out of the shower to pick it up!"

"Well, at least the apartment has its own bathroom," Talbot said. "I've stayed places where you share a bathroom that was on a different floor."

Talbot turned back to Dubois.

"Fully stocked?"

"Of course."

"Where's the screen hidden?"

"Top right corner of the bathroom mirror. You and Jessie still have same access as you did in the safe house in Washington. We just need to get the beautiful Ms. Scott added to the system and she will also have access."

"Can we do it now?"

"Of course."

Dubois pulled a tablet out of his small backpack and turned it on. After a moment he signed in to the hidden Wi-Fi in the apartment and pulled up a blank screen.

"Kelly, do you mind coming over here please?" Talbot asked.

Scott and Jessie walked back over to rejoin them from where they were laughing at the how tiny the bathroom was.

"Please put your right hand flat against the screen of my tablet," Dubois said to Scott.

She did so, a quizzical look raising one eyebrow. The tablet beeped once, and Dubois logged off.

"You are good to go," Dubois said.

"Good to go where?"

"You have security access to the rest of the place now."

"What rest of the place? There isn't any rest of the place!"

"You want to show her, Jessie? Top right corner of the mirror in the bathroom."

"Come see," Jessie grinned, leading Scott back into the bathroom. As they disappeared into the tiny room, Talbot and Dubois could hear Jessie instructing Scott to press her right hand flat against the mirror in the top right corner. There was a click and a hiss.

"Are you kidding me?!?" Scott said from the other room.

Talbot and Dubois chuckled.

"Anything else you need, my friend?"

"Just one thing I think. I'll need two official access passes that will let me into any door at the UNESCO offices day or night."

"How soon do you need them?"

"This afternoon."

"That is not much time, but I will see what I can do. Meet me at four o' clock at the Café du Marche in the market on Rue Cler," Dubois said as he let himself out.

The door clicked shut behind him and Talbot crossed the room and walked into the bathroom. The entire wall behind the vanity and mirror had swung away to reveal another room behind it. The room was laid out as a communications command center with high end electronics on one wall. The opposite wall was covered in shallow cabinets which Scott and Jessie had opened up to reveal an selection of firearms, ammunition and assorted gear.

"Unbelievable," Scott said, looking back at Talbot. "Are all the houses set up with a room like this?"

"Probably."

"I think there's more," Jessie said, putting her hand flat against the glass of a small, framed picture on the back wall. The wall swung away slightly, just enough to reveal a set of stairs leading down into the basement.

"What's down there?" Scott asked.

"Usually the second door is for a hidden exit that goes to a car of some kind."

"I'm going to look," Jessie said as she disappeared down the stairs.

"And just how is this normal?" Scott asked.

"It isn't, but some of the guys provide specialized international security services for hire and this is a good way for us all to benefit if we ever need it."

"How many of you are there?"

"It varies. The rentals without the security room are funded by a larger group of maybe a hundred people, but access to these rooms is by invitation only. That's a very short list."

"Is it legal?"

"Absolutely. That's why it's by invitation only."

"It's a black Audi in a parking garage," Jessie said as she walked back in. "The door is hidden behind a wall of storage bins."

"Was there anyone in the garage when you looked?"

"No, I checked the camera first."

"Good girl."

"So what's the plan?" Scott asked.

"Not sure yet, although I have a few ideas."

"Such as?"

"For all we know those coded vials of Orion have already been released. Even if they haven't, there's no way we can track down our guy by tomorrow. Right?"

"Right. So, we need to use Scribbler."

"Exactly. But we only have one vial. That makes it difficult to track down and infect all seven delegates with the antidote by tomorrow."

"Then we need to figure out a single location and time to release all of Scribbler so that all seven delegates are infected at the same time?"

"Bingo."

"UNESCO tomorrow. It's the only chance we have."

"I think so too. But that leaves the problem of how we infect them."

"I was thinking an atomizer."

"That should work, but the delivery system will have to target each delegate very accurately."

"Right. So these places always have them sitting at a table with microphones and headsets. What if we hide the nozzles in the brackets for the microphones?"

"Have you done this before?"

"Not exactly, but it shouldn't be hard to build. Just time-consuming to install."

"I can help with that."

"Good. There's a few things we'll need to build something like this. I'm going to pick those up. Can the two of you to hack into the UN servers?"

"You're talking to Jessie, right?" Scott said.

"What do you need?" Jessie asked.

"We will need a floor plan of the UNESCO building here in Paris and we need to find out where the vote will take place tomorrow."

"Easy. What else?"

"We'll need a roadmap to get in with the atomizer tonight. When I get back we will take a walk up the street to meet Enzo in the market."

"Okay," Jessie said. "Just as long as I get to see some of Paris."

SUNDAY, February 1st, 2017, 14h30, Quai d'Orsay, Paris

"Seriously? Again?" Jessie asked Talbot.

"You lose," Scott said to Jessie with a grin.

"Lose what?" Talbot asked as he dropped the large duffel bags he was carrying onto the table.

"We had a bet on whether you would come back in a different jacket," Jessie said. "I thought there's no way you'd find someone who needed a jacket in the middle of the day in Paris."

Talbot grinned.

"So what now?" Jessie asked.

"Meet Enzo and case out UNESCO," Talbot said.

Jessie looked disappointed.

"Which means stroll around Paris and enjoy the sights for a while, right?" Scott prompted.

"Right," Talbot agreed. "We're early to meet Enzo in the market, so we'll detour past the Eiffel Tower."

"Well come on then!" Jessie said, grabbing up her coat and waiting at the door.

Talbot laughed as he picked up the keys and ushered Jessie and Scott out. As they exited the building, Talbot steered them to the left, following Quai D'Orsay and Quai Branly along the Seine south west until they reached the Eiffel Tower looming massively over Pont d'Iena.

Turning south east, they joined the throngs of tourists staring up through the girders of the massive construction. Scott tucked her hand into Talbot's elbow as they strolled along, smiling up at him as he watched Jessie spinning under the tower.

Catching Scott looking up at him, Talbot stopped, slid his arm around her waist and gently pulled her against his body, leaning down to gently kiss her. He hesitated just over her mouth, waiting for a moment, then kissed her slightly parted lips in a warm kiss that deepened and blossomed. She looked into his smiling eyes as he pulled away.

"That was nice," she said, leaning against his shoulder as they walked over to a bench and sat down side by side.

"Very," he agreed. "I just wish we had more time to enjoy Paris the way it should be enjoyed."

"I know."

A comfortable silence warmed them with the moment shared, as warm as the tangle of their intertwined fingers.

After a few minutes Jessie rejoined them, the impatient teen inside her certain that, as good as the moment was, she was missing something even better somewhere else.

"What's down there?" she asked, pointing south east down the avenue.

Well, it's in the general direction of where we want to be, so let's go see," Talbot said, standing up.

As they strolled down the Avenue Anatole France, Scott's hand tucked into Talbot's elbow and Jessie took his free hand. Walking beside them, she chatted happily about everything she could see, asking Talbot one question after another, the teenage in her completely lost in excitement.

In front of the Ecole Militaire they turned left and followed the broad avenue north east, window-shopping their way until they reached Rue Cler. Talbot steered them up the cobbled road and into the famous open market. Easing their way between the selection of stalls and shops, Talbot guided them to a small table under the awning of the Café du Marche.

Giving lie to the popular notion of rude French wait staff, their waiter strolled over to take their order.

"Oui, monsieur?"

"Trois chocolats et crêpes, s'il vous plaît," Talbot replied, his French thick with an American accent.

"Of course, monsieur. And what flavor crêpes would you like?" the waiter said, switching to English.

"I'll have Nutella and strawberries, please," Jessie said.

"Same for me," Scott added.

"Grande Marnier, please," Talbot said.

"Certainly."

"I'm going to look at the shops while we wait," Jessie said, jumping up.

"Okay," Talbot said, "but stay close."

"So now what?" Scott asked as Jessie ambled off.

"So now we wait for Enzo," Talbot said. "He said he can get us passes into UNESCO. Tonight, we'll install the atomizer. That should change their DNA just enough to lock out Orion."

"And if you're wrong?"

"It's going to get very ugly in a hurry," Talbot said grimly.

"How can we stop these people doing things like this in the future?"

"Well, they won't stop just because we ask nicely. I think there's just one real, permanent solution."

"That's what I was afraid of," she said, somberly. "So how do we go about doing it?"

"I called a guy."

"Do you have any idea how often you have said that since we met?" Scott laughed. "You say it a lot!"

"I guess I do. That reminds me. One of them owes me an update."

Dialing an international number, he waited as it rang.

"Hello Matt."

Scott tried to listen to the call, but Jessie walked up as the waiter arrived and started placing their order on the table. Talbot stood up and walked off a short distance, the phone to his ear.

"Did you know they have stores in Paris with nothing but cheese?" Jessie said as she plopped into her seat. "And another one just for dried meats and another one just for truffles?"

"Truffles? You mean the chocolates or the mushrooms?"

"Mushrooms!"

"Well, that seems very specialized."

"I know, right?" Jessie said, eyeing the hot chocolate and crepe in front of her. "Should we wait for dad?"

"I think so, don't you?"

"Probably, but he better hurry. This looks amazing!"

Talbot returned to the table, slipping his phone into his pocket.

"And?" Scott asked.

"On track, but I won't know for sure until tomorrow," he said. "Ready to eat?"

"Starving!" Jessie said. "I was ready to start without you and then eat yours as well!"

Talbot grinned, taking an appreciative sip of the hot chocolate as he watched Jessie take a bite of her crepe, her eyes lighting up.

"That," Jessie said dramatically, "is the best thing I have ever eaten."

"She's not kidding," Scott agreed. "How's yours?"

"Remarkable. Would you like to taste?"

Scott reached over with her fork and broke off a piece of Talbot's Grande Marnier crepe, putting it into her mouth. A look of bliss crossed over her face.

"Okay, this is good, but I like mine better," she said.

Finishing their crepes, they leaned back comfortably in their seats, sipping their hot chocolate as they waited for Dubois.

After a few minutes he walked up and sat down at the table.

"Did you get it?" Talbot asked.

"Of course, my friend."

Reaching into the ever-present backpack, Dubois pulled out a small envelope and handed it to Talbot. Talbot opened it, glanced inside, and then tucked the envelope safely away in his zippered inner pocket.

Scott looked at Talbot.

"All your friends like this?"

"Pretty much," Talbot smiled.

"And he's not asking any questions?"

"If he needs to know, I would have told him. I didn't tell him, so he knows he doesn't need to know. So no questions. Simple."

"Must be nice not having to deal with a bureaucracy that asks you for an explanation in long-hand triplicate every time you try to get anything done," she muttered.

"So I see you ate already," Dubois said. "Let me guess… crepes."

"Of course," Talbot smiled.

"And hot chocolate?"

"It's awesome!" Jessie enthused.

"Of course, it is French!" Dubois chuckled.

"I spoke to Alexis a few days ago."

"He is well?"

"Going fishing. You been in touch with anyone?"

"Charlie Roberts. He moved back to America a few months ago. Said he needed a break from Morocco for a while."

"Where in America?"

"Maryland. You talk to anyone else?"

"Remember Jack Ingram?"

"Of course. Good guy."

"Yes. I just got off the phone with him. He's going to touch bases with you looking for me, probably tomorrow if everything goes well."

Dubois studied Talbot a moment.

"I know you know this, but if you need help tonight, call me. Not a problem."

"Thanks Enzo, but this should be pretty simple."

"Okay, if you say so. And now, my friend, I must go. I have a date, and she will not like it if I am late!"

With a quick wave, Dubois walked off into the crowd.

"Right," Talbot said, "We need to get back to the apartment. I've got some work to do."

SUNDAY, February 1st, 2017, 13h30, Beltway Loop, Washington D.C.

The only apparent difference a Sunday afternoon brought to the beltway in Washington D.C. was that traffic crawled steadily forward without all the stops, starts and painfully long waits.

Over the last decade Senator Whitfield had made a habit of getting a jump on the week by driving into the office every Sunday afternoon to squeeze in a couple of hours at his desk. Typically, he would close out the day meeting some of his equally ambitious political cronies for a late dinner and drinks. He had long ago become accustomed to the traffic and barely noticed the ambulance cruising behind him.

Another habit he had developed was to call in to his dictation service every Sunday, recording the initial outline of his autobiography. Every Monday afternoon he would receive an email containing the transcript typed up by one of the faceless drones at the service.   Then he would add the transcript to the rest of his book and massage it all into place, adding any edits he thought were necessary

The book was essentially a personal homage to his ego, with barely any resemblance to fact. The book devoted an entire chapter to landing an 1,100-pound marlin during a fishing trip off St. John in the US Virgin Islands, for example, despite the fact that the biggest fish he had managed to reel in personally had been an under-sized wahoo.

As he drove, his mind busily bending the facts around his most recent bear hunting trip to Alaska, he never noticed a slight hissing sound start under his seat. The odorless gas permeated the cabin and after a few minutes his heart started to race in his chest, and he started to breathe with difficulty. A feeling of panic overtook him just before his vision started to tunnel and he blacked out.

His Cadillac slowly drifted to the right before wedging itself into the guard rail and coming to a halt. The ambulance trailing him flipped on its emergency lights and pulled in behind him. Both medics hopped out. One immediately tossed out road flares to get the traffic to move around them, the other to check on the driver.

Quickly the medic smashed the driver side window, showering the unconscious Senator with glass fragments. He reached into the cab to turn off the ignition and unlocked the door. Carefully he eased the slumped figure back into his seat, then reached under the seat to extract a small gas canister. There was a radio receiver and remote-activated valve assembly bolted on to the end. He tucked it into his pocket.

His partner walked up beside him with a medical bag, and together they pretended to be busy working to revive the Senator while they waited for the effects of the gas to wear off.

As the fresh air cleared his head, the Senator started to stir, confused.

"What happened?"

"You started drifting in traffic and then crashed into the guard rail. How do you feel?"

"Woozy."

"Can you tell me what happened?"

"I'm not sure. I remember I was on the phone. My heart suddenly went into overdrive and I couldn't breathe. I guess I passed out?"

"That's what it looked like. And this has never happened before?"

"No. How long was I out?"

"Just a couple of minutes. We were actually right behind you when we saw it happen. Does anything hurt?"

"No, I feel fine. Even the wooziness is disappearing."

"I'd like to do a simple glucose test. If it's just a low glucose level I can give you a snack bar and be fine until you get checked out by your PCP."

"Okay," Whitfield agreed.

The medic rolled up Whitfield's sleeve, located a vein and quickly collected two small vials of blood. Using the first, he injected a reagent and shook the vial a moment. The blood quickly changed color.

"Yup, low blood sugar," he confirmed.

He nodded to the other Medic.

"Can you get him one of those snack bars?"

"Sure." The medic wandered off and came back with an assortment.

"I've got some nuts in the glove compartment as well," Whitfield said.

"That will be fine later, but you need one of these first. It's got some sugars in it that will boost your blood sugar right away."

Whitfield selected one of the snack bars, tore open the packet took a bite.

"Feeling better?" the first medic asked after a few minutes.

"Yes."

"You really need to get checked out at the ER. Besides, looks like you tore up your front end. I don't think your car is drivable. Can we take you to the ER?"

"No, I'm good."

Whitfield glanced around the cabin and located his phone in the pocket of the console.

"Seriously, you need to go to the ER as a precaution."

"I'm okay, dammit!"

"Do you have someone who can fetch you, then? You're not okay to drive."

"My assistant is just a few minutes away. He can fetch me."

"Make sure you get checked out, okay?"

"Yeah, yeah, yeah," Whitfield said irritably as he dialed.

Whitfield dialed the number for his assistant. After telling him where to fetch him, Whitfield pushed the medic out of his way. He climbed out of the car, still a little shakier than he cared to admit. After he shook the broken glass off his clothes, he walked around to the front of his car and sat on the hood, holding his laptop. He completely ignored the medics behind him as he waited for his ride.

After watching him for a moment the medics walked back to the ambulance and disappeared inside, waiting.

Twenty minutes later a small sedan passed the wreck and pulled onto the side of the road in front of the Cadillac. It backed up and stopped just in front of Whitfield. Without a backward glance he slid off the hood of his car, stalked over to the sedan, pulled open the passenger door and disappeared inside. The sedan pulled away and merged into traffic.

"Piece of cake," Jack Ingram said to Charlie Roberts sitting in the driver's seat beside him.

While not related, the two men had almost an identical look about them. Both were fair-skinned men in their late forties with close-cropped, light brown hair and blue eyes, both stood just under six foot tall, and both were in excellent physical condition.

Roberts eased the ambulance into traffic and took the next exit as Ingram prepared the blood sample for its journey through airport security.

"Can't believe he bought that bogus glucose test," Roberts said.

"Nobody asks a medic much."

"No kidding. So how much time have we got?" Roberts asked.

"Plenty. We can take the ambulance back to that maintenance lot and make it to Dulles for our flight with plenty of time."

"Good. I want to eat American before we get on the plane."

"American? Like what... Sushi? Pasta? Pho?"

"BBQ," Roberts said with a grin.

Ingram finished packaging the sample.

"Matt will be surprised to see us both."

"Probably, but he may need help."

"Doubt it."

"Probably not. You got anything better to do?"

"Touche`."

Chapter Ten

After reviewing the tools and toys in the Safe Room back at their apartment, Talbot had decided to use a large quadcopter carrying a military-grade, miniaturized sonar and infra-red imaging system to limit interaction with UNESCO staff.

Even though he had no expectation that the Security passes Dubois had provided would raise any eyebrows, the odd assortment of tubing, nozzles and other gear was likely to be an issue.

The quadcopter was designed to hover two hundred feet above a primary portable locating transmitter and track up to five additional transmitters. The coolest part about it, as Jessie had pointed out, was that it used a combination of sonar and infrared data to link back to a command center where the data was translated into a 3D map of the area.

Sitting in the Safe Room in front of a bank of monitors, Jessie was able to move anywhere on the 3D map like a ghost gliding through the space. She could choose to wander around any floor in the building, pivot and turn, and easily see her surroundings.

At that moment the quadcopter was hovering directly above the locating transmitter Talbot was carrying in his pocket. It was also tracking the secondary transmitter Scott was carrying. As she watched, Jessie fed Talbot directions and information about the movements of other relevant heat signatures in the building.

As expected, the Security ID Cards Dubois had provided had made access to the building laughably simple. Talbot and Scott had experienced no difficulty pushing the wheeled media cart, covered in a drape cloth, unnoticed through the unmanned side entrance and into the building.

The fact that Jessie had infected the UNESCO security system with a virus which had temporarily frozen the camera images on the security monitors had made it even easier to gain access without being seen.

Now Talbot and Scott were standing just inside the door to the conference room allocated to the morning meeting.

"Are we sure this is the right place?" Scott asked.

"Well, this is the room they're scheduled to use," Talbot replied. "Why?"

"Just seems too easy."

"Wait until we start installing this thing."

Quickly they surveyed the layout. The building had been built in the late fifties and the visual look and feel of the meeting room had not been updated. It was a wedge-shaped auditorium-style presentation room with the lectern at the narrow end. The back wall was curved. In fact, the room looked exactly like a slice of pizza with the tip cut off. The entrance was in the side wall of the room alongside the lectern.

Each curved row of seats, one built higher than the next, followed the same arc-radius as the back wall. The chairs, comfortable and padded, were arranged behind curved desks, one per level, which extended from the aisleway on one side of the room to the other.

Built into the desk in front of each chair was a small, old-school voting panel attached to the table. A small microphone on a flexible arm was built into the corner. Each panel had a "For" and "Against" voting button. The panels were only activated when a voting member was seated in front of the panel. Since there was no predefined seating chart and the boxes collected the votes randomly, the voting was intended to be completely anonymous.

"I wish there was a seating chart," Talbot muttered as he started to unload the trolley. "Then we would only have to rig up for seven, instead of all of them."

"True, assuming Orion is supposed to only target seven," Scott agreed, slipping a one-inch bit into the cordless drill.

"What do you mean?"

"Well, what if we only know about seven of the targets?"

"I never thought about that. Just as well we're going to rig something for all of them, then."

Working quickly and taking care not to damage any wiring inside, Scott drilled a one-inch hole in the faceplate of each panel, and another into the panel from underneath the table. Talbot followed, threading a short, clear pipe through the top hole and out of the bottom. A small, button-shaped screen masking a spray nozzle was already attached to the end and sticking out the top. Scott pushed the screen down into the hole until the mounting clips clicked, holding in in place.

Talbot had just finished connecting all the dangling ends to the master tube for each row which he had taped hidden beneath the tables.

"Dad," Jessie said into Talbot earpiece.

"Yes?"

"Someone outside the door."

"Okay."

Talbot stood up and started to fiddle with the microphone in front of him.

Talbot turned his back to the door as it pushed open, talking to Scott.

"Have you figured out what they were complaining about yet?"

Scott looked up to see Talbot pointing at the microphone as the door swung open. Behind Talbot stood a security guard in the doorway.

"No idea," she said. "I've checked most of the microphones this end already. They all seem okay to me."

"Well, this one had some loose wiring, but I don't think it would have caused the problem."

"What are you doing in here?" the guard asked. He looked very bored.

"Maintenance," Talbot answered.

"Why are you doing maintenance in here at night?"

"This room is used almost all every day, all day, so we have to take care of the complaints at night."

"Why is an American doing maintenance?"

"Same reason a German is doing Security. It pays well."

"Please, not German. All they know is beer and bratwurst. I am Swiss. From the border with Germany. What is the problem?"

"Someone complained his microphone was not working, so we are checking."

"Ah."

The guard wandered over to the push cart and picked up the atomizer with the compressed air cylinder.

"And this?"

"More complaining. They say it gets too hot in here," Talbot said, thinking fast.

"Hot? It is winter."

"Yes, I know, but the heater in this part of the building is mostly used for much bigger rooms and hallways. This room is too small, so it gets too hot."

"Why don't they turn down the thermostat?"

"The system is old. It does not have a zone just for this room."

"And how will this make them cooler?"

"Come see," Talbot said, taking a chance.

The guard walked up the stairs to where Talbot was standing.

"See here?" he said, pointing at one of the caps he was still installing.

"What is it?"

"It's a tiny nozzle. We install it like this and connect them all to that tank you were holding. Every few minutes, we turn it on and it forces a gentle breeze over their face to cool them off."

"Why not fix the air conditioner?"

"Good question, but I just do what I'm told."

"That air tank... how long will it last?"

"We have to change it out every two hours."

"Not very efficient. Why not put in a bigger tank?"

"I think they're just testing the idea for now."

The guard studied the tubes, then turned the atomizer over in his hands a few times. On the one side was an aerosol access port, the kind usually found on the nozzle of a butane burner in a kitchen. It was used to attach the butane tank before they fired it up to caramelize the sugar on a Crème Brule.

"This looks like you are going to add something to the air."

"Sure," Scott said as she joined them. "Once a week we have to disinfect the lines. We just screw in a compressed can of

301

Lysol, run the system for a minute, disconnect, flush with air, and bingo... clean."

The guard studied them for a minute, then the atomizer, turning it over in his hands. Talbot could feel the tension building up inside his body.

"Why do I suddenly smell coffee brewing? I thought the coffee shop across the hall was closed." Scott asked, interrupting his train of thought.

The guard grinned.

"Yes, it is closed," the guard said smiling.

"But you have a key, don't you?" Scott asked with a sly grin.

The guard grinned back at them.

"Yes, I have a key. Nothing better than espresso at two in the morning."

"I would kill for some about now," Scott said.

"Same here," Talbot added.

"No problem, I just started to make some. When you finish here, come across the hallway and I give you some."

"Sounds great," Talbot said. "Sooner we get busy again, the sooner we can get that coffee!"

"Okay, I leave you to it."

The guard ambled down the stairs and dropped the atomizer on the push cart as he walked out.

"Pretty quick thinking," Scott said.

"Not too shabby yourself," Talbot said.

He connected the master tube from each row to a single manifold already attached to the atomizer attached to the compressed air. Then he connected the remote control to the master valve.

"Ready to test?" he asked.

"Yes."

Using a remote he extracted from his pocket, Talbot triggered the valve and released the compressed air through the tubing. Working together they made sure that whoever was sitting in every chair would feel the cool breath of air pushing through the nozzles hidden in plain sight on the voting boxes.

Satisfied, Talbot turned off the master valve and checked the compressed air cylinder. Only ten percent of the pressure had been used in the test.

Carefully, he screwed the container containing Scribbler into the supply dispenser access port between the compressed air and master valve of the atomizer. Then he carefully tucked the equipment away inside the electronics box recessed into the end of the front table.

Meanwhile, Scott installed a small, Wi-Fi-enabled camera in the corner at the back of the room.

With a final glance around to make sure everything was tidy, Talbot and Scott loaded up their cart.

"Okay Jessie, we're out. You can call the drone back. It should drop straight back down into the courtyard outside the apartment door. We'll be there in a little while."

"Okay," Jessie replied.

"Coffee?" Scott asked as she held the door open for Talbot to push the cart out.

"Don't mind if I do."

MONDAY, February 2nd, 2017, 05h30, Hotel Room, Paris

Some hotel owner a few decades earlier had made a dispirited effort to make the hotel room feel upscale, but the inevitability of time had faded the opulence to the point of sadness. Everything about the room was depressing. Even the air smelled of dust and disappointment.

La Salle didn't notice.

Earlier in the morning he had mixed a cocktail of the Orion viruses coded for the UNESCO delegates and carefully poured the contents into a small squeeze bottle. Ironically enough, the label on the bottle was for an alcohol disinfectant hand rub.

Tring to kill time, he was going through his usual morning exercise routine. Over and over, faster and faster, he repeated the same complicated rhythm of moves and exercises with his preferred dagger. Dressed only in black sweatpants, his toned physique gleamed with sweat in the early morning light washing weakly into the room through the dusty window.

His cell phone rang.

He picked up his phone, checked the Caller ID and answered.

"Good morning Senator."

"Did you talk to Shevchenko yet?"

"Last conversation I had with him his team had caught the girl and he was waiting for word on the others. He never called. I called him, but he didn't answer."

"I spoke to him."

"And?"

"Talbot and Scott found Scribbler and took it with them. Shevchenko's goons are dead, and the girl is gone. Customs says they flew out of Transnistria for Paris last night."

"Nothing about Talbot has been easy. Now what?"

"They were spotted on camera close to the Eiffel Tower. I have a team on the street looking for them. In the meantime, get to UNESCO early, and get Orion out."

"Easy enough."

"Not so fast. Talk to Shevchenko. You're going to have to adjust your plan slightly."

"Why?"

"I had Shevchenko make some changes."

"Okay," La Salle shrugged.

"One more thing."

"Yes?"

"Wait for Talbot and Scott to show up and kill them. Don't get fancy."

La Salle smiled as he hung up. Dropping the phone on the bed, he picked up his routine where he left off, his controlled breathing and the whisper of his feet in the carpet the only sound in the room.

MONDAY, February 2nd, 2017, 08h45, Apartment on Quai D'Orsay

"That auditorium is still empty," Jessie said, walking out of the safe room with a pastry in one hand and a glass of orange juice in the other.

"What do you mean?" Talbot asked.

"Isn't the meeting supposed to start at nine?"

"That's what their schedule said last night. They wouldn't have had time to change it this quickly."

"Well, the meeting starts in fifteen minutes and there's no-one in the room. I would have expected them to start coming in already, even if it was just to save their favorite seat," Jessie said.

"You're right," Scott said thoughtfully. "That's odd."

"Do you think they changed the time?" Jessie asked.

"Can you check?" Talbot asked.

"Sure. Take me a minute to hack in, though," Jessie said over her shoulder as she walked back into the safe room.

Talbot poured a fresh cup of coffee for Scott and himself before they followed Jessie into the safe room. The keyboard clattered as Jessie hacked into the UNESCO network and started looking around their website for the itinerary. After a few minutes she pulled up the schedule for the day.

"That doesn't look like the same meeting room name," Jessie said, pointing at the schedule.

Quickly she pulled up a building map of the meeting rooms and located the room listed for the vote.

"It's not the same," Talbot confirmed.

"Why would it have changed?" Scott puzzled.

"Some guy named Shevchenko requested the change," Jessie said, pointing at the meeting room notes. "He's going to be speaking to the delegates before the vote."

"Wasn't that the guy on that recorded phone call you got from Alexis? The one with the accent talking to Whitfield?" Scott asked.

"That's right," Talbot said. "He'll be the de facto President of Transnistria if the vote passes."

"It's the same guy," Jessie said. She had pulled up a picture of the scheduled speaker. "It's the guy in the hotel when they caught me, the one in the uniform."

"The chain smoker?" Talbot asked sharply.

"Yes. I couldn't remember why his voice was familiar, but it was the same voice as the guy on that recording."

"The atomizer is in the wrong place!" Scott said.

"We need to get over there," Talbot agreed with sudden decision.

"What can I do?" Jessie called after them as they pushed through the second concealed door leading to the garage.

"Stall the meeting somehow."

"How?"

"You'll figure it out, just hurry!"

Jessie turned back to the computer as they disappeared, thinking for a moment. Then, working quickly, she started scanning the building's security software, looking for ideas.

Grinning suddenly, she pulled up the door access control module and hijacked control of all the electronic locks to every doorway in the building. Then she locked them all at the same time.

After a couple of minutes, she re-activated the doors for a minute, then locked them again. She repeated the process, over and over again, to give the impression of an intermittent failure.

"That will keep them guessing," she chuckled.

Downstairs, Talbot started the engine of the powerful Audi, opened the garage doors with the remote, and threaded the vehicle through the pedestrians crossing in front of them on the sidewalk, Then he merged into the one-way traffic headed east on the access road on Quai D'Orsay.

"What's the plan?" Scott asked as Talbot pushed the Audi through traffic.

"We need to disconnect the atomizer and get it into the new meeting room as fast as possible. If anyone starts having symptoms, we need to mist them with Scribbler, preferably directly into their airway."

"Then what?"

"Hope for the best."

As Scott glanced back at Talbot, she saw the black-clad biker in the traffic next to him pull a gun and aim it at him.

"Watch out!" she shouted. Quickly she grabbed the wheel and forced the Audi over towards the motorbike, making him swerve away just as he pulled the trigger. The bullet shattered the driver window and buried itself in the console between them.

Looking around quickly, his head on a swivel, Talbot saw five motorbikes with armed riders converging quickly on them from all around.

"How did they find us so fast?!" Scott asked, pulling her gun out and rolling down the window.

"Probably caught us on camera near the apartment yesterday and posted these guys all over the area waiting for us to show up somewhere," Talbot said, gunning the big engine and weaving through traffic.

The motor bikes, fast and powerful, had no trouble catching up. His head still on a swivel, Talbot checked his rear-view mirror again. Two large black sedans were bullying their way through the traffic behind them to join the chase.

Keeping a lane of traffic between them as a buffer, two of the bikes raced up parallel to the audi on Talbot's side and opened fire. Talbot ducked low as the wild rounds ricocheted through the traffic. Quickly Scott leaned backwards into the gap between the two front seats, aimed through the rear window behind Talbot, and carefully fired six fast rounds. The 9mm slugs smeared both gunmen off their bikes.

"Nice shooting," Talbot said.

Accelerating hard as he aimed for a narrow cross street, he drifted the big car expertly around the corner and straightened it out, trying to lose their tails. The bikers quickly adjusted, but the first sedan behind them couldn't make the turn in time and clipped a power pole. The sedan spun out of control and into the corner of a building. The impact ruptured the fuel tank and crumpled the driver's door, trapping him in his seat.

Scott looked back to see who was still on their tail just as the power pole toppled over in a spray of sparks. The spilled fuel ignited. The shock-wave and fireball consumed the third biker as he passed by, slamming him bodily into the wall of the building on the other side of the street.

A bare heartbeat later the smoke billowed open as the remaining pursuers gunned their way through the acrid, sooty smoke.

" Two bikes and a sedan left," she said, reloading quickly.

Talbot raced headlong down the empty street until he ran up on a slow-moving van carrying fresh produce in from the farms. He timed it perfectly. Jamming his hand down on the horn, he ripped the car up onto the sidewalk and around the van. Customers in the weak sunshine enjoying coffee around small outdoor tables fled in panic. Horn blaring, Talbot whipped through the tables, scattering them in front of him like chunks of ice tossed out over a frozen pond.

As they came up on a smooth, straight stretch of road Scott watched the motorbike sweep easily around the van. The rider accelerated up behind them and quickly stood upright, gripping the gas tank with his knees for stability. He reached into his jacket and pulled out a small machine pistol. Then he flipped the collapsible stock out and lifted the gun to his shoulder. He leaned into the stock for maximum stability and opened fire in short, expert bursts. The bullets tattooed a pattern into the back window and slammed into the armor plate custom-built into the driver seat.

"Hold on!" Talbot shouted, standing on the brakes. The Audi's ABS juddered hard as the big car came to an abrupt halt. The bike behind them slammed into the car, but the rider saw it coming. He adjusted, leaping high off the bike to land on the roof.

Talbot accelerated hard, swerving from side-to-side trying to shake him off, but he hung on grimly. Scott lifted her gun to shoot through the roof.

"Don't shoot!" Talbot said urgently. "It may be bulletproof!"

The road ahead narrowed, forcing Talbot into a straight line. The man on the roof let go with one hand and tried to aim his pistol in through the window.

Talbot saw his chance and braked hard again. The man slid off the hood and onto his feet. Talbot accelerated. Springing onto his feet immediately, the biker was already raising his pistol. Talbot swerved directly at him, forcing him to jump to the side. As the Audi swept past, Scott threw her door open, swinging it like an oversized bat to smear the biker into the pavement. The impact slammed the door shut again.

"The sedan is back, and he's got another buddy," Talbot said, looking through the rear-view mirror.

Scott looked back.

"Another biker?"

"Yes."

"I see him."

"We're running out of time! We need to get rid of them fast!"

Talbot braked hard to avoid hitting a pedestrian, ripping the wheel over to turn down a narrow alley as the pursuit gained ground. The sedan behind them skidded around the corner and into view. Talbot whipped the car into another alley and hit the brakes hard, coming to a sudden stop about 20 yards from the corner. The car was still rocking on its suspension when Talbot stepped out of the car and sprinted back to the corner, gun in hand.

As he reached the corner, the pursuing vehicle drifted around the corner within feet of Talbot. Talbot triggered his 9mm rapidly three times into the near window and killed the driver. The car lost control and slammed into the corner of the building. Talbot followed fast. Standing just behind the rear-window post, Talbot took deliberate aim and shot the stunned passenger in the head before sprinting back toward his car.

"Down!" Scott shouted.

Talbot looked up. Scott was leaning out of her window and aiming her gun at him. He dived for the ground as Scott opened fire. A the storm of bullets zipped and buzzed over his head like angry hornets as he hit the ground rolling. Looking back, Talbot saw the last biker knocked backwards off his bike as the bullets slammed into his chest. The bike kept rolling directly at Talbot, defenseless on his back in the street.

Desperately he kicked a trash bag off the sidewalk and into the path of the bike. The front wheel hit the trash, losing traction. The handle bars turned the wheel hard at right-angles to the bike. As the wheel slipped over the bag and gripped the street again, the bike somersaulted over Talbot.

Talbot rolled to his feet and sprinted for the car where he threw himself behind the wheel and slammed it into gear. Driving quickly, he worked his way through the streets back towards UNESCO.

"Did you know that bike would somersault?"

'Nope."

"What made you think of it?"

"Saw it in a movie once."

You bet your life on a movie?"

"All I could think of! Anybody else following?" he asked.

"I don't see anybody."

"Okay. I'm going to get us close, then we'll have to ditch the car. If we show up there in a car that looks like this we will never be allowed past security."

"Good thinking," Scott agreed. "When we get there, we only need the atomizer, right? No need for the hoses?"

"Right."

UNESCO, Public Hallways

The wide hallways of the UNESCO building were lined with art from around the world. It looked like people of every possible ethnicity and language were wandering through the hallways, including delegates, staff, and even some tourists. Easily blending into the mix, La Salle stationed himself outside the meeting room. He was holding a pump bottle labelled as hand sanitizer. A group of delegates approached the door, chatting amongst themselves.

"Hand Sanitizer?" La Salle offered as they approached. "There is a bug going around and we want to make sure no-one gets it."

One by one La Salle pumped a small amount of liquid into the delegates' outstretched hands, their conversation barely pausing as they took their turn before passing through the door and into the meeting room.

After thirty minutes La Salle had used up the entire contents of the pump bottle and managed to directly infect well over half the delegates with Orion. Confident that the inevitable greetings and handshakes inside the conference room would infect the remaining members, he walked away, dropping the pump bottle into the nearest trash can.

Walking quickly, he worked his way through the hallways to the meeting room originally scheduled for the vote. It was located on the far side of the building. Just a short distance past the meeting room and tucked away under a discrete sign was a small coffee shop. It was the same coffee shop where the security guard had made Talbot and Scott coffee the night before. A heady blend of aromas from a variety of exotic roasts from around the world wafted out through the doors and into the hallway. In the back corner of the shop was a small prep station set up for crepes. The combined smells diverted a steady

313

stream of people out of the hallway and through their double doors.

La Salle stationed himself just inside the coffee shop doors, keeping a careful watch on the hallway stretching in either direction. Large concrete statues, some abstract, some geometric, were scattered on either side of the long hallway in both directions. Their random placement through the hallway forced the foot traffic to ebb and flow around them like the ocean around a rock outcropping in the beach sand.

Despite the silenced 9mm concealed in the folded newspaper in his hand, La Salle was just another speck in a sea of humanity moving through the building, too self-absorbed to notice.

La Salle glanced casually down the hallways, carefully searching through the faces in the crowd for either Talbot or Scott. The thick crowds in the hallways made the task difficult and he nearly missed them until he saw the only the door to the conference room swinging open.

He had no time to react as they disappeared inside, the door swinging shut behind them under the pressure of the concealed, spring-loaded hinges.

The automatic lights flipped on as Talbot and Scott entered the room, lighting up the empty conference room with the cold, artificial neon light. It was the kind of light that reminded Talbot of public schools and old government offices.

He scanned the room to check for unexpected surprises before hurrying over to where the atomizer was hidden. He checked the equipment to confirm that it had not been disturbed, then disconnected it from the set of tubes run through the tables.

While he collected the atomizer, Scott quickly disconnected a nozzle and short tube from one of the voting boxes and brought it to Talbot. He quickly attached it to the set of canisters. The he disconnected the small canister containing Scribbler and triggered the compressed air to test it. The air flowed cleanly through the piping and out of the nozzle. Test successful, he reattached the Scribbler virus to ready the atomizer.

"Let's go," he said urgently.

As he pushed open the door he felt three hard punches to the chest, knocking him backwards into Scott. They staggered back into the room where he collapsed to the floor. The spring-loaded doors closed behind him.

Stunned for a moment he lay there, gasping desperately for air that would not come. His chest felt paralyzed. Ripping open his shirt, he checked the vest for punctures. Nothing. He picked the slugs out of the vest, sucking at air as the feeling of paralysis faded from his lungs.

"You okay?" Scott asked, her gun already in her hand and trained on the closed doorway.

"Just about," Talbot croaked with the little air he could get as he struggled to his feet. "May have a cracked rib." He gingerly prodded on his ribs to check. "No, I think I'm good. Did you see anything? Hear anything?"

"Just you falling back into me. Any idea how many?"

"Not for sure," Talbot said, regaining control of his breathing. "No more than two or they would have waited for a clean shot on us both."

"Now what?"

"You need to get Scribbler to the other conference room. I'll cover you."

"How you want to do this?"

Talbot studied the door a moment.

"That's a fire-proof door, so it should stop bullets at least as good as my vest. Pull the door open and stay behind it. I'll go through and draw fire, so we can see where they are. If the shooting is from one side only, break the opposite way. If it's from both sides, wait 'til I tell you which way to go. Then move fast."

"Okay." Scott wrapped the small device in her jacket and tucked it under her left arm like a running back with the football. She kept her 9mm tucked up under the bundle and out of sight to leave her right hand free. "Ready when you are."

Talbot positioned himself tight against the wall next to the door on the side opposite to the hinges. He took three deep breaths, wincing at the stabbing pain in his chest, then nodded.

Scott yanked the door open and propped it open with a chair, careful to use the door as a shield. The crowd continued to drift past the door, completely oblivious. Talbot quickly stepped into doorway. He tried not to focus his eyes on any one thing so that his peripheral vision would take a mental snapshot of the hallway. Then he ducked quickly back behind the wall to give his brain time to process the image.

As he disappeared behind the doorframe, the edge of the desk behind him splintered and chipped twice as two bullets chased the swinging door open.

A large man walking past the doorway staggered and collapsed as a third bullet lodged itself in his chest. Recent terror attacks in the city had made the crowd ever wary. Already jumpy, they panicked, screaming and running in every direction.

Overloaded with adrenaline, Talbot's brain sorted through the image of the hallway in his head. He could see in his mind's eye a tall man in a shooter stance with the blaze of white in his dark hair framed in the doorway of the coffee shop.

Talbot immediately stepped into the doorway, his left foot stamping into the corner where the door frame met the floor. And pushed hard and fast to his right and out of the doorway again.

The scattering crowd had already cleared the hallway immediately outside the doorway. Without the crowd Talbot was painfully exposed. He kept moving fast across the fifteen feet to the closest statue, sliding feet first on his left side across the smooth tile floor as if he was stealing home. As he slid, he triggered his gun three times in the direction of the shooter. The suppressive fire made La Salle instinctively flinch back behind the door frame.

"One shooter, go left now!" Talbot shouted to Scott from behind the statue. As Scott broke through the doorway, Talbot leaned out past the statue again. He triggered his 9mm fast to push La Salle even further back into the small coffee shop.

La Salle cursed, leaning out quickly to shoot after her, but his snap shots were too hurried. The slugs whipped past her, knocking down two of the crowd in the hallway ahead of her.

Scott checked the wounded as she went past. The wounds were not critical so she sprinted on down the hallway, quickly putting one of the statues between her and the shooter before disappearing into the frantic crowd.

Talbot watched her disappear from his scant cover behind the statue as he quickly reloaded his 9mm. Then he removed the sunglasses from the top of his head. Holding them in his left hand, he carefully extended them past the statue just above the floor, using the dark lens as a mirror to locate La Salle. At the same time, he held the 9mm above his head just below the edge of the statue, turning it to roughly track where the lenses where pointing.

As the lenses lined up on La Salle, Talbot caught a glimpse of him before the lenses shattered under a hail of bullets. Even as

La Salle pulled the trigger, Talbot raised his pistol slightly and fired three times fast in La Salle's direction. The bullets made La Salle jump back again. As the third bullet left the muzzle, Talbot pulled the gun down again. La Salle lined up his pistol to shoot across the top of the statue, but Talbot dived out sideways from behind the statue.

As he landed, Talbot paused a moment to make sure of his aim. He lined his sights up center mass on La Salle's chest and fired three times, the slugs knocking La Salle back into the café.

Immediately realizing La Salle was wearing a vest, Talbot sprang to his feet again to chase him down. He kept his gun lined up on the door of the coffee shop.

Suddenly La Salle erupted from the café, pistol blazing from one hand while the other dangled loosely at his side. A bright blot of blood had started to seep through his shirt at the bicep. Talbot was still running forward when one of La Salle's wild shots clipped the outside of his thigh. His leg buckled under him and he went down hard.

La Salle started sprinting down the hall after Scott. Some of the terrified crowd was still crouched down in the hallway around him. Talbot steadied himself, carefully lining the sights of the 9mm up on La Salle's back. La Salle ducked left down another hallway and out of sight before Talbot could take the shot.

UNESCO Hallway, Outside South Meeting Rooms

The size and design of the UNESCO building meant that news of the shooting had not made it across the building yet. The attitude and body language of the people she passed reflected no more than mild confusion by the time Scott reached the far corner of the building. The crush of panicked bystanders she had had to push through had all ducked through the many exit points on the way, so she was the first from the gun fight to reach this end of the building.

As Scott approached the meeting room the doors burst open doors and a translator in the UNESCO uniform burst out.

"Nous avons besoin d'un medecin rapidement!" she shouted, running down the hallway calling for a doctor.

Scott pushed through the doors and into the conference room. Small clusters of people were scattered throughout the room trying to help the delegates who had collapsed writhing to the ground. Others had gathered off to one side to stay out of the way.

Scanning the room, Scott quickly isolated and counted the groups gathered around the sick. She slipped her pistol unobtrusively into her hidden holster. Then she unwrapped the atomizer and walked up to the first group, pushing her way through the crowd of people trying to help or rubberneck.

A security guard was bent over the man convulsing on the floor, desperately trying to help. Scott came up behind the security guard and aimed the atomizer over his shoulder and right into the patients face. She triggered the compressed air and a fine mist hissed softly out of the spray nozzle and directly into the agonized, gasping face.

Without waiting to see the result she turned away to help the next patient. The startled security guard sprang to his feet and grabbed her from behind, wrapping her up in a huge bear hug and lifting her off her feet. Scott twisted and struggled, but he had the advantage of size and leverage and just gripped her tighter. Scott slammed her head back, trying to break his nose, but he kept his head tucked low. The reverse head-butt had no effect.

"Let me go! I'm trying to help them! It's an antidote!"

She tried without success to stamp down on his foot, but he had her lifted too high off the ground to be able to reach. Hating to hurt someone doing their best to protect and serve, she bent her leg up at the waist and swung her heel hard and high backwards into his knee. He grunted as his leg buckled, but he resolutely held on as he fell, taking Scott down to the floor with him. The impact with the floor knocked his grip loose and Scott slammed her elbow hard into his sternum.

"Aidez moi!" he gasped, calling for help as he struggled to hold on.

Before she could break free or reach her weapon, two more security guards came in fast, piling on top of Scott and holding her down.

UNESCO Hallway, Outside North Meeting Rooms

Working as quickly as he could under the circumstances, Talbot pulled his belt free and strapped it around his leg to slow the bleeding. The belt was too long and had very little effect so he ripped off his shirt sleeve and tied it around his leg instead. It was better, but still not ideal.

Then he hobbled over to the first gunshot victim crumpled in a pile at the door to the meeting room. Talbot rolled him onto his back. He was barely conscious, but his breathing wheezed and bubbled through the bullet hole in his chest.

"Help me," he pleaded, his eyes desperate. Bright red arterial blood frothed at the corner of his mouth.

"Hold on, bud, I got you."

Talbot gently rolled him onto his side to check his back for an exit wound. Seeing none, he laid him carefully on his back again.

"I'll be right back," Talbot said. "You're going to be just fine."

Talbot hobbled into the café and rummaged around quickly until he found a roll of packing tape and a broom. Snapping off a short segment of the broom, he pushed it into the loop of the sleeve tied around his leg and twisted it to add pressure until the blood slowed and stopped. He taped the broom in place and continued to search for what he could in the coffee shop. Until he found a rack of Visa gift cards. He grabbed one up and headed back out of the coffee shop to help the fallen man.

As he left he made a mental note of a smear of blood on the doorway that had caught his eye as he hobbled in.

Kneeling painfully beside the wounded man, Talbot ripped his shirt away from the bullet hole in his chest. Then he securely taped the Visa gift card flat against the bullet hole with the tape, leaving one edge of the card open.

"Okay bud," Talbot said. "Every time you take a breath, you're sucking air into your chest wall through that hole. Without this card in place like this that air is going to fill your chest and collapse your lungs. That's why it feels like you can't breathe right now. But this card will work like a one-way valve. It's going to let the air in your chest out a little at a time and stop any air going back in. You'll start feeling better in a minute or two, okay?"

The man, pale with shock, took a breath, and the card bubbled as it eased some of the pressure in his lung. After a couple of breaths, he nodded.

"I have to go get help," Talbot said. "You're going to be fine, okay?"

"Okay," he whispered.

Standing up, Talbot hobbled back over to the coffee shop. He pealed a length of tape free and dabbed it into the blood smear, then folded the tape back over itself. He had effectively sealed a small smear of the blood inside.

Tucking the piece of folded tape carefully into his pocket, he headed down the hallway after Scott, reloading his 9mm. The two gunshot victims further down the hallway had managed to get out of the building under their own steam.

Hurrying along the deserted hallways as quickly as his injured leg would allow, Talbot could hear a commotion as he got closer to the south meeting rooms. Scott's voice was angry and desperate. At the door he ducked his head around the corner to assess the situation. All eyes were on Scott struggling desperately against the three security guards who had her pinned to the floor.

Stepping into the room, Talbot wasted no time. He pulled the trigger on his Glock, the 9mm shell burying itself in the wooden floor. Every head turned, eyes wide in shock and fear, to find Talbot's gun covering the room. He focused especially carefully on the group around Scott.

"Let her go! Now!"

The guards stared blankly at him, their eyes wide.

"Laissez-la partir!" Talbot said, switching to French.

Warily the guards let her go. Scott moved away, picking up the atomizer?

"Okay?"

"Yes, you?"

"I'll make it. How'd it go?"

"I only got to one so far."

"Hurry, I've got this."

"Okay."

"Everybody except the guards can leave," Talbot said as he moved away from the door.

The crowd eased out, careful to avoid getting between Talbot's gun and the guards. Meanwhile Scott moved quickly from one writhing delegate to the next, carefully misting the Scribbler virus directly into the gasping faces.

Finally, she hurried back to the first victim she had sprayed. He had stopped writhing around and was laying quietly. His breathing was still stertorious but was already improving. Kneeling beside him, she checked his pulse.

"How's he doing?" Talbot asked, keeping a close watch on the guards and a wary eye on the rest of the people in the room.

"I don't know what's going on inside his body, but at least his breathing and pulse are settling down. He's probably going to need hospitalization, but I think he's going to make it."

"Good. Do you think you got to the others soon enough?"

"I hope so. They weren't as bad off when I came in, so maybe they were infected later."

'Monsieur," one of the guards said carefully, "I think we made a mistake. The spray is medicine?"

"Medicine? Yes, kinda."

"Then there is no need for your weapon, monsieur. But I think perhaps we can help them? We are also trained medics."

"Go ahead," Talbot said, lowering his gun watchfully. "There's a gunshot victim in front of the North meeting rooms as well."

"We will send someone immediately, monsieur."

Pulling out his two-way radio, the guard started talking urgently in French as Scott walked over to Talbot.

"I guess you got the shooter?"

"Winged him, but he got away. Same guy with the blaze."

"Pity. He's trouble, that one."

"I have a plan."

"I guess I shouldn't be surprised. You get shot again?"

"Yeah. Burns like fire, too."

"No doubt. Take a seat and call Jessie to tell her we made it while I take a look at it."

Chapter Eleven

The Pont Neuf was the oldest bridge still standing across the Seine and Talbot, Jessie and Scott had opted to leave the cab on the north bank and walk across. Jessie was walking in front of them and Scott's hand was tucked deeply into the corner of Talbot's arm, ostensibly to help him walk. She looked up at him, smiling.

"Doing okay?"

"So far so good, just very tender."

Ahead of them Jessie stopped and leaned over the edge of the bridge to watch one of the well-lit dinner-cruise boats pass below. The ceilings were glass and they were so clean she could even see the food selection on the plates.

Halfway across on Île de la Cité, the island on which the Parisians had built Notre Dame, they paused to sit on a bench. It was one of a line of benches surrounding the statue mounted at the western tip of the island of King Henri IV. Talbot gingerly stretched his injured leg out in front of him to give it some relief. Scott leaned comfortably into his shoulder, content and happy in the moment as they watched Jessie bounce from one vantage point to the next.

A thin man walked around the statue towards them, his skin as black as ebony and his teeth gleaming in the lights of the bridge.

" English?" he asked.

"American," Talbot answered.

"Ah, John Wayne, bang-bang!" the man said, his accent a powerful mix of Nigeria and Paris. "You like the cowboy movies?"

"Sure," Talbot said, smiling. "Let me guess... you're selling padlocks?"

"You a clever man, mister! Just 20 Franks!"

"Okay, sure," Talbot agreed.

Talbot reached into his pocket and pulled out some cash. He peeled off a single bill and handed it over in exchange for a small brass padlock and a set of keys. Reaching into his pocket, the man handed Talbot a back permanent marker.

"You know, we only met seven days ago."

"You're thinking this might be too soon?"

"Well?" she asked.

"After what we've been through?" he said, smiling. "Hell no. Besides, those seven days aged me twenty years. That's plenty long enough."

Scott's delighted laugh bubbled over as Talbot grinned at her.

"I must say, you aged well over the last twenty years, then."

"And you look much more beautiful than the day we met!"

Pulling the cap off the pen, he wrote their names on the padlock and handed the pen back. The man wandered off.

"Hey Jessie!" Talbot called. "Can you do us a favor?"

"Sure!" She said, walking over. "What do you need?"

"Would you lock this padlock to the fence with the others overlooking the river over there?"

"Sure," Jessie said delighted, "but the fence is covered with them. There must be thousands!"

Talbot watched Jessie walk off, then looked thoughtfully down at Scott. She was studying his face carefully. His eyes wrinkled in the ghost of a smile, then he leaned down and kissed her gently. She reached up with her hand, her palm cupping his bristly chin as she kissed him back, the slow kiss deepening.

"We're going to be late!" Jessie said, interrupting them.

"Do you mind?" Talbot objected. "We're having a moment here!"

"I could see that, old man, but you walk so slow we're going to be late!"

"Mock a man when he's crippled, why don't you?" Talbot sighed. "Help me up."

Scott laughed as Jessie reached out a hand and pulled him up.

"I'll go ahead and make sure they don't sail without us," Scott said.

"Okay, we'll see you there."

She kissed him quickly on the chin and walked off.

"So you really like her, don't you?" Jessie asked.

"I really, really like her."

"Good. I like her too."

Walking slowly, they crossed over the second span of the bridge and turned right to follow the river along the road. About two hundred yards along they came across a set of old stone steps that led down from the upper road level to the embankment level where the tourist barges tied up. Talbot worked his way down one step at a time, finally reaching the bottom with Jessie.

There was a flicker of movement in the shadows against the stone wall. Looking carefully, Talbot could see an older couple sitting on the cobbles, their back to the wall. The woman was huddled against the man to keep warm in the cold night air, and he had his arms wrapped around her shoulders. Despite shivering in the cold air, they were sound asleep.

Talbot reached into his jacket pocket, pulled out his billfold, and emptied the cash into one of the pockets before slipping his billfold back into his jean pocket. Then he slipped his jacket off, hobbled over to the couple and gently spread his jacket over them without waking them.

As he straightened, Jessie's arm came past him, her jacket in her hand as she wordlessly handed it to him. Talbot glanced at Jessie, then spread her jacket over them as well.

"That's my girl," he said quietly.

Together they walked slowly along the pier until they reached the ramp onto the Caliphe, a quaint barge set up with a high-end kitchen in the back and lines of dining tables inside a glass dining room running the length of the upper deck. Scott was waiting for them at the top of the ramp.

"Just in time," she said. "They weren't going to wait much longer."

Talbot and Jessie walked up the ramp and into the bright lights at the top.

"Wait a minute," Scott said as she realized they were both missing their jackets. "Him I knew about, but you too?"

"Afraid so," Jessie said.

"Are you kidding? I'm so proud of you!" Scott said, giving Jessie a hug.

Leading them inside, Scott showed them to one of the small tables lining the glass wall on the port side. As they settled into their seats, the barge started to pull away from its moorings and joined the boat traffic on the Seine. The up-lighting on the old buildings and bridges along the river served as a stunning backdrop for their five-star meal as the barge sedately pushed its way upstream.

The thrumming murmur of the engines underscored the soft background music as the dinner crowd enjoyed their menu, from Fois Gras to Duc l'Orange. The food was so spectacular that even the view of Notre Dame on the east end of the island could barely distract the diners from their meal as they eased by. Just before the Marne flowed into the Seine, the boat used the current to sweep around and head back down stream, gliding down the historic river past Notre Dame again and slowing as it passed under Pont de l'Alma.

"Look," Talbot said, interrupting Jessie and Scott as they discussed the desserts.

Timing it perfectly, the barge cleared the bridge just as the flashing lights on the Eiffel Tower began their spectacular light show. The iconic Tower glittered and flashed like cascading streams of diamonds.

"Oh wow!" Jessie exclaimed. "That's awesome!"

Talbot and Scott watched, smiling, as Jessie crowded against the glass for the show. The barge turned back upstream as it drifted slowly past the Tower. As the short display ended, Jessie sat back down.

"That was so cool!"

"Between the company, the food and the light show, this has been an amazing evening," Scott agreed.

"Good," Talbot said as he took her hand. "I can't think of anybody else I would rather share this with."

"And what about me?" Jessie interjected, teasing.

"Well, of course! I can't think of anybody else I would rather share this with rather than the two of you!"

"That's what I thought," Jessie said sternly.

Scott laughed.

"So now what?" Jessie asked.

"That's a very open-ended question," Talbot said.

"Well, for one thing, can we go back home or not?"

"Not anytime soon," Talbot said. "I'm going to have to pull some strings to get all this cleaned up."

"Awesome!" Jessie said with a grin.

"What about Senator Whitfield and that lot?" Scott asked.

"You remember Alexis?"

"Yes, your Russian friend."

"I asked him to hack into Whitfield's email. He sent out a meeting request to La Salle and Shevchenko. My sources tell me they're in their meeting now."

"And?"

Talbot pulled out his phone and sent a quick text.

Scott reached over and took the phone from him to read it.

"'It's a go'? What's a go?"

"Let's just say I arranged for a taste of their own medicine."

WEDNESDAY, February 4th, 2017, 14h20 Local Time, Washington, D.C.

"Why are you here?" Whitfield asked irritably from behind his desk.

"You asked me to meet you," Shevchenko said, ignoring the view of the city as he poured himself a brandy from the wet bar in the corner of Whitfield's sumptuous fifth floor office. "You said you had a plan."

"I didn't ask for a meeting, you idiot. And even if I did, I wouldn't bring you to my office!"

"So if you didn't ask for a meeting, what the hell is going on?" Shevchenko asked, turning his back to the window.

There was a knock on the door.

"Come!" Whitfield called out.

The door opened to let La Salle in, his arm in a sling.

"What are you doing here?" Whitfield asked.

"You sent for me."

"I didn't. I didn't send for him either," Whitfield said, jerking his head at Shevchenko.

"This is a set up then," La Salle said.

"Of course it is, Sparky!" Whitfield snapped. "What we don't know is what for."

"Obviously someone wants us all together," La Salle said. "Question is why."

There was another knock on the door.

La Salle reached into his jacket and pulled out his 9mm and a noise suppressor, carefully screwing it onto the end of the barrel. Moving against the wall a few feet from the door hinge, he nodded to Whitfield.

Whitfield had opened the top drawer of his desk and slipped his hand inside as Shevchenko moved into the corner out of the way.

"Who is it?" Whitfield asked.

"Just me," a woman's voice said. "An "Eyes Only" envelope for you from the White House."

"Come in."

The door opened. Whitfield's AA walked in, dropped the White House envelope on his desk, and walked out. Whitfield reached over and picked it up. Slipping an old-school horn-handled letter opener into the envelope, he slit it open and a stack of black-and-white photos cascaded out and over his desk top.

Puzzled, he picked them up and started to flip through them.

"What the hell...?"

"What is it?" La Salle asked as he tucked the gun away and walked over to the desk. Whitfield handed him some of the photos off the top of the stack.

"Shevchenko," Whitfield asked, puzzled, "why is the White House sending me pictures of you getting into a limo at Dulles International?"

"What are you talking about?" Shevchenko asked, joining them at the desk.

La Salle handed him some of the pictures as Whitfield flipped through the rest of the stack.

"There's pictures of all of us," Whitfield said, puzzled.

"Spread them out so we can see," La Salle said.

Carefully Whitfield laid them out, grouping his in one set, La Salle's in another, and Shevchenko's in a third. There were four seemingly random images left.

The images of Whitfield were all of him driving recently, showing the dent still in the front of his car where he had rammed the guardrail a couple of days earlier. La Salle was walking out of the hospital, the white arm sling in stark contrast to the dark suit he was wearing. And every picture of Shevchenko showed him sucking deeply on yet another cigarette.

"This makes no sense," Shevchenko muttered.

"Let me see the other four pictures," La Salle said.

Whitfield handed them over. Studying them carefully, La Salle pulled out the picture of a dirty ashtray and dropped it on top of Shevchenko's pictures. The picture of the French Bistro doorway, a dark smear on the door frame, he dropped on the pictures of himself. The last image was a close-up of an arm with a syringe in it attached to an ampule collecting a blood sample.

"Anybody take your blood recently?" La Salle asked, holding the picture up for Whitfield to see.

"Some ambulance medics took a sample to test my glucose after a fender bender a couple of days ago."

"Anything else?"

"No."

La Salle took a deep breath.

"Anything else in the envelope?"

"No," Whitfield said after checking. "Why? What's going on?"

"Those weren't medics. That's your blood in that vial and my blood on the door frame of the Bistro in Paris."

"No blood of mine," Shevchenko pointed out.

"No need. Saliva from cigarette butts. They got our DNA."

There was a long silence as that settled in.

"What's the last picture? Whitfield asked, the tremor in his fingers betraying his fear.

La Salle tossed it onto the desk. The picture was a beautiful long exposure of the night sky, the stars arcing lines of light against the inky black of deep space as the universe wheeled around its distant axis. Instantly recognizable in the center of the picture was the constellation Orion.

"What's it mean?" Shevchenko asked.

"We knew there was a break-in at Neo-Dine in Chisinau while you were gloating over catching the girl," La Salle said. "The lab there had vials of un-coded Orion stored in it. They sent this picture to prove they knew the security code to get into the lab."

"So?"

"Are you really that stupid?" Whitfield asked, acidly. "They have Orion and they have our DNA. All they have to do is mix the two, let it go, and we die an ugly, painful death bleeding from our eyeballs."

La Salle leaned closer, looking intently at one of the pictures on the desk. It was a picture of himself walking out of the hospital front entrance. Beside him on the wall next to the doorway was a small sign, easily missed. Looking closely La Salle could see that the sign had been digitally altered.

Wordlessly he pointed to the sign.

Seeing the look on his face, Whitfield looked closer as La Salle walked across the room to the wet bar, picked up a bottle of Scotch and sat down in a deep chair facing the window.

Suddenly it clicked, and Whitfield slumped back into his plush leather office chair.

"What is it?" Shevchenko asked.

"They changed the sign."

Shevchenko looked closely. "Orion is loose? They coded this thing and set it loose already?"

"Yes," La Salle said, wiping his mouth after a long pull from the bottle. "Just a matter of time."

Whitfield bolted upright.

"Get Scribbler! We can rewrite our genetics Orion can never find us!" Whitfield said, hope blossoming in his voice.

La Salle ignored him as he took another long drink from the bottle.

"He's right!" Shevchenko said, striding up to La Salle and knocking the bottle from his hand. "If you value your life, move!"

La Salle reached into his jacket and pulled out his 9mm, gesturing with it in Shevchenko's direction.

"I would say that if you ever do that to me again, I would kill you, but what's the point. You're a dead man already."

"No, there's still time!" Shevchenko insisted.

"Don't you get it?" La Salle asked wearily. "Scribbler is more than an hour across town. We'll be dead by then."

"Rubbish!" Whitfield said. "It can't travel that fast from France. We have plenty of time!"

"No, my friend," Shevchenko said calmly. "La Salle is right. We are out of time."

"What do you mean?"

"Orion was all over those pictures we've been passing around," La Salle said, taking another swig from. Then he calmly put the barrel of the 9mm deep into his mouth and, before either Whitfield or Shevchenko could react, pulled the trigger. His head snapped back as the slug destroyed the medulla oblongata, the exit wound a bloody mess behind him.

"I wonder," Shevchenko mused, "if La Salle did not choose the best answer. Mostly I would say it is coward's way out, but this time..."

Frozen in fear, Whitfield stared horrified as Shevchenko walked over to La Salle's chair, stooped over, and picked up the 9mm from the floor where it lay beside the body. Casually he turned and fired six rounds through the glass of the picture window closest to Whitfield's desk, the gunfire crashing and echoing through the building. Then he stood leaning nonchalantly against the fragile glass, drawing deeply on yet another cigarette as he waited.

Without warning the office door crashed open and a flood of armed security rushed through the door, assault rifles ready. Spotting the gun in Shevchenko's hand they fanned out and trained their weapons on him.

"Drop the gun! Drop it now!"

"A warrior death," Shevchenko smiled in satisfaction. "Much better."

Jerking up the 9mm, he lined it up on Whitfield and pulled the trigger as fast as he could before a hail of bullets from the security SWAT team slammed him back against the window. The glass shattered under the impact of Shevchenko's body as he disappeared backwards through the window, still smiling.

One of the security detail rushed over to Whitfield.

"He's alive," he said. "Call an ambulance!" Working quickly, he pulled field dressings from his emergency pack on his vest. He ripped open a gauze pack and tried to apply pressure to control the bleeding from Whitfield's chest. Whitfield was still conscious, blood bubbling from his mouth with every breath, but he was unable to speak.

Without warning, his body convulsed violently, his jaw clenching so tightly that the sound of his dentures fracturing could be heard across the room. His eyes rolled back into his head as the convulsions strengthened. The Medic could not hold him still in the chair and he bucked off the chair and onto the ground. Within minutes blood started to seep from his nose, ears and eyes. Finally, the convulsions faded until nothing of Whitfield was left but the bloody huddle of flesh on the floor of his office.

EPILOGUE

Thirteen years earlier... DNC Think Tank, DNC Headquarters, Washington, D.C.

"Have you heard about that new social networking site on the web?" Baxter asked.

Hired specifically to lead strategic planning, Brent Baxter was a bald, immensely fat man. Almost unknown outside a select group of people, he was considered by those in the know to be one of the most brilliant political strategists of his day. He was also widely recognized as vastly domineering, contemptuous of others, and completely amoral.

His gluttony was legendary, and he had the body frame to prove it. His eyes were small and deeply embedded behind fat jowls that wobbled whenever his mouth opened. And his mouth opened constantly, either to talk or chew. His rolls of fat had their own rolls of fat, and no normal clothes would fit. As a result, his entire wardrobe consisted of loose, floor-length robes. He claimed he had given Pavarotti the idea for his choice of clothing.

The select group of elite DNC leadership in the room nodded in answer to his question but made no effort to speak. They already knew that Baxter had no intention of giving them the floor.

"And I'm guessing none of you see the potential? Of course not." He sighed in mock frustration, delighted at the chance to prove once again how brilliant he was and how stupid they were.

"How do you win wars?" he asked. He waited for one of the others in the room to take the bait. "Well?"

"Superior weapons and tactics," someone suggested from the back of the room.

"No, that's what stupid people think. War by conflict means you have an adversarial relationship. It sets up resistance. No. You win by popularity. You win because you get the population majority to agree with you. Now do you see the potential?"

"No, we don't. As usual, you're taking the long way around."

"History provides the precedence. Pharaoh understood that, which is why he enslaved the Israelites when their population exploded. Hitler convinced the majority that the Jews were a scourge to be eradicated. English nobles in Scotland would own the first honeymoon night with any Scottish woman so that they never knew if the firstborn's father was English or Scottish. Get it?"

"Just get to the point."

"The point is, you win by breeding the population with mindset that you want. You breed a majority voting population."

"Don't be ridiculous."

"Don't be ridiculous!" Baxter mocked. "Obviously we can't enforce breeding programs on our esteemed voting population. But we can certainly manipulate the breeding program, and thanks to social networking we now have the means to do it."

The room studied him for a moment.

"Okay," someone said, "I'll bite. Tell us what you're thinking."

Three months later... DNC Think Tank, DNC Headquarters, Washington, D.C.

"In theory, can you do it?" Baxter asked.

It had taken Baxter three months to find someone with the necessary skill set and potentially fluid moral and ethical compass. Simmons was a non-descript young man wearing thick glasses and a dirty T-shirt. A winking, digitized happy face was printed on the front of the shirt. Underneath it the caption read 'Coders do it bit by bit'.

"Theoretically, yes."

"Tell me how."

"I would hijack voter rolls, blog submissions, social network comments, pretty much anything online that hints at how people think. Next, I would build thousands of current state demographic groups based on what they think and believe. Finally, I would build a custom, influence-modeling protocol for each demographic that would manipulate the web content they see. By manipulating what they see, I can influence the direction their opinions take to herd them into target-state demographic groups."

"And why would you do that?"

"The protocols would be like mental candy trails. They see their own, personalized candy trail. They follow the trail into herds of thought, and they all end up with the same very narrow point of view we manipulate them to adopt."

"Outcome?"

"Based on what you were telling me, those that herd together, get together. And enough getting together will quite literally breed your own customized voting population."

"Exactly."

There was a pause.

"You know, for the right price, I can double down," Simmons added with a crafty grin.

"What do you mean?"

"How long do you think your idea will take before you reach critical mass on your voter counts?"

"Thirty years seems reasonable."

"I can cut that down by more than fifteen years."

Baxter gave him a hard, calculating look.

"You have my attention."

"Your model is designed to breed Democrats, right?"

Baxter nodded, waiting.

"How about a concurrent model that converts Republicans to vote Democratic?"

Baxter studied him for a moment.

"Explain."

"Just spit-balling here, of course. Let's assume Republicans are full of themselves and want to know more about where they come from. So they get an exclusive offer for an inexpensive DNA test that tells them all about their heritage."

"How does that help?"

"Well, now we have their DNA. With the right tests, we can identify and manipulate troublesome genetic markers combinations."

"Meaning?"

"It means we influence who Republicans breed with by herding them into demographic groups based on their gene pool instead of how they think. Put the right combinations together, and you can exponentially increase the odds that their

341

babies will be born with a lifetime need for very expensive medical treatment."

"How do I benefit from that?"

"You start now by manipulating the health care message. Crowd Republican policies ever further away from supporting government-subsidized healthcare. With the right messaging, by the time these babies reach critical mass by volume it will look like only the Democratic platform is willing to legislate a solution that will make medical treatment available for these Republican babies."

"So design an environment where a Republican will vote Democratic no matter what the other DNC policies are just to get the medical help they need for these kids."

"Exactly."

Baxter closed his eyes with a sigh.

"Theoretically, of course," Simmons added with a sly smile.

The silence stretched out between them.

"And how would you make all this happen? Theoretically, of course."

"I would need to get a job at the right social networking company, get access to their coding protocols, and insert the code piece by piece."

"Why do you need to work there? Can't you just hack them and insert it?"

"A hack insert has a very high risk of being identified and kicked out over the length of time this would need to be in place. But if I build it from the inside it becomes embedded native code."

"Fair enough. How would you get hired?"

"Oh, that's the easy part. I send them a sample of my coding that makes their computer guys look like amateurs. Usually at this point they just invite me to join the team. I do it all the time. Usually as a consultant, though."

"How much do you want? Again, theoretically."

"Fifty million, non-negotiable."

Baxter studied him for a moment.

"Okay. But you get paid at the end."

"No deal. But have you ever heard of sprint development?"

"No."

"I'll lay out blocks of work in ten monthly increments. At the end of each month I'll demo the completed work for the month. After each demo you pay five million into a Swiss bank account. Last installment for the finished work."

"One condition."

"What?"

"You get no access to the account until we pay for the last installment."

"Done. There's just one more thing."

"What?"

"I'll need someone inside the FBI."

"What for?"

"Let's just say a subpoena from the FBI makes data collection much easier."

"How well-masked will your requests be?"

"Meaning do I need someone that can be bought?"

"Yes."

"Ideally, I need someone who will ask no questions, so I need him hooked three ways."

"Meaning?"

"Meaning bribed, threatened, and blackmailed."

"I'm sure it can be arranged."

"He needs to be high-ranking."

"How about the highest?"

"Sounds like you already have someone in mind."

"Not just in mind, in hand."

www.ingramcontent.com/pod-product-compliance
Lightning Source LLC
Chambersburg PA
CBHW060355260626
47160CB00006B/2320